BEAR OF A HALLOWEEN

WHITE BEAR SERIES
BOOK 3

TERRY SPEAR

PUBLISHED BY:

Wilde Ink Publishing

Bear of a Halloween

Copyright © 2023 by Terry Spear

Cover Copyright by Terry Spear

Discover more about Terry Spear at:

http://www.terryspear.com/

Print ISBN: 978-1-63311-095-3

Ebook ISBN: 978-1-63311-094-6

Shawn Swartwood, thanks for following all my series and loving my books as much as you do. Love your creative soapwork and it's so cool that you created a wolf howling at the moon that I inspired! Your lavender soap sounds divine. Thanks for your army service too. I salute you as a fellow veteran!

SYNOPSIS

Margot Anderson goes with her girlfriend to White Bear, Alaska, from their home in North, Alaska, to enjoy all the Halloween activities the town has to offer. What she doesn't expect is to get a rescue from a seaplane pilot who happens to be from White Bear and a polar bear just like them.

Craig MacMathan had a delivery to make when his cousin sees a vision of a couple of polar bears needing Craig's help. Not only are the ladies single, but they're coming to his town to have fun. And he's more than ready to help them have a great time.

But Margot is having nightmares related to something that has to do with White Bear, her mother doesn't want her to go there, and they have a mystery to solve as Craig gets deeper into his relationship with Margot. Until she solves it, she doesn't want to drag another bear into her world of nightmares, but Craig isn't just any other bear.

1

Polar bear shifter, Margot Anderson settled down in bed in her home in North, Alaska, hoping the nightmare wouldn't return tonight, but that was only wishful thinking. As night winked out and she fell into a deep sleep, she was thrown back into the reoccurring nightmare.

She fought with a drunk, but in her mind, the figure morphed into two people—her brother and her father. She was fighting over the car keys, furious with whoever she was trying to get the keys from. And then the car was in motion. She was driving it, or was someone else? The hazy details put her in the back seat, and then in the front— driving or as a passenger in the back, but never a passenger in the front seat.

It didn't make any sense. She felt bruised from the encounter with her...her father, she thought. But his face kept turning into her brother's. She didn't have a brother. And then the real nightmare began. The one where she was seeing the accident before it happened. The headlights shining in her eyes. Her car swerving to miss the other vehicle. The pummeling she was getting as the car rolled and she felt she was going in slow motion, up, down, up, down, up, down...and then everything was pitch black.

She woke with a start and stared at her dark bedroom. It was just the dream. The nightmare that had been visiting her frequently for a year now. Tired, she rubbed her eyes and sat up in bed. She needed to open her shop. She never could understand why so many shops didn't open until ten. So many people were out running errands earlier that she often caught sales at nine in the morning.

She sighed and got up, had a bagel with cream cheese and a cup of black tea, then pulled on a Halloween sweater of a cat dressed as a wizard reading a spell book, and a pair of wool slacks, boots, and coat, made herself a thermos of tea, and headed to the shop. It was nearly Halloween, her favorite time of year, and there was snow on the ground. She loved how quaint her shop, Dreamy Designs Boutique, was and it did quite well, at least well enough to support her. Her pumpkins sitting outside of the shop were wearing a fresh coating of snow and she unlocked her door and put her purse, coat, and thermos behind the counter. As soon as she put out her "Open" sign, her first customer arrived. See? It helped to open early.

"I'm so excited to see my wedding gown." Tricia was human and a great customer. She often shopped here, and she was so thrilled to be able to buy a Medieval wedding gown from Margot's shop.

"Oh, I was too when it came in. And I'm so happy for you." Margot's own wedding had been a disaster, but she was always glad to help the bride look her best in her own gown. She unveiled the gown to show her and Tricia smiled.

"That's it. That's the perfect one for me."

Wearing a fall sweater featuring a polar bear reading a book —another one of Margot's new sweaters from her artist sweater collections—Stephanie Stone hurried into Margot's dress shop carrying a brochure, waving it at her as Margot was ringing up her customer. She gave her a look to cool it until after Tricia left with her white winter, Medieval-style wedding gown. Steph had been Margot's best friend since Margot had moved to North eleven years ago when she was fifteen, both of them polar bear shifters. Steph was known to be super exuberant about lots of things, which was one of the reasons Margot cherished their friendship.

"Thanks so much, Margot. The gown will be perfect for my wedding. It's just beautiful," Tricia said.

"You're so welcome. Congratulations and best wishes." Margot was glad for Tricia that she was getting married soon.

Margot was also so glad her own fiancé had stood her up at the altar after she'd learned he had been seeing someone else in the weeks before their wedding day. But her parents were still mad at Margot over it, claiming she had to have been the one to make her fiancé wander! Sure, she could understand they were angry because they had paid the expenses for the wedding, but she'd shown up for it! He was the one who hadn't! Not to mention she wasn't responsible for her ex-fiancé seeing another woman.

When Tricia left, Margot said to Steph, "Okay, so what do you have to show me?"

"This. Look. Halloween is your favorite time of year and look at this place! Most of the town is decorated for the holiday. They even have two standing, hand-carved wood polar bears guarding the entrance to this rustic-looking tavern. We could go to White Bear for a week and just have fun. We could take a tour into the wilderness where they go to see wild polar bears feeding off whale carcasses. We've never seen anything like that before." Steph pointed out the tours given by the MacMathan brothers and Casey McIntosh. "They have special Halloween-themed ones. The White Bear Lodge has an indoor swimming pool even."

"What about my dress shop?" Margot couldn't close it up for a week.

"Faye can manage it while you're gone. You were going to be off on your honeymoon after your wedding and that all fell through. She already planned to run the shop for you while you were away." Steph always had a ready solution for everything, which Margot found admirable.

"That was three weeks ago."

"I know. But Faye can always use the extra money. She's always asking for more hours to work."

"That's because she's saving up to get married. I hope she knows what she's doing."

Steph clucked. "Just because Howie wasn't a good match for *you*, doesn't mean *her* fiancé isn't good for her. Just like Tricia's will work out just fine."

"True." Like Margot and Steph, Faye was a polar bear.

Margot looked over the brochure and smiled. She loved the pictures of the White Bear businesses decorated in a pirate theme. She even had several costumes that she'd ordered for her dress shop—and ended up taking them home because she'd wanted to wear them at the store on special occasions. But she also sold several different styles of pirate hats, corsets, skirts, and blouses that could be worn for any number of costumes— pirates, vampires, witches, steampunk, whatever the customer had in mind. And accessories—belts, sashes, jewelry to go with them that Steph could get if she wanted some too.

"It's pirate-themed this year." Steph winked. "Your favorite."

"Right." Margot sighed. Steph could practically talk her into anything, though she hadn't paid attention to her friend when she told Margot that Howie was not a good match for her. She should have listened to her.

"So?" Steph asked, looking eager to see what Margot decided about the impromptu trip.

"I'll have to call Faye first to see if she can do this." Margot wouldn't leave it to chance that Faye really wanted to work at the shop all week and Steph hadn't bamboozled her into saying yes.

"I called her already—for you. She's thrilled."

"Steph." Margot wasn't annoyed with her friend, more amused than anything. She wondered how Faye had taken it.

"I knew you would want to go," Steph said, looking through the pirate costumes on the rack Margot still had in stock. "But of course she'll wait for confirmation from you first."

Margot's boutique had regular dresses and gowns, slacks, and skirts too, but she got a lot of calls for her fancy and fun gowns that women loved to purchase for weddings, cocktail parties, and New Year's Eve parties and other events that women needed gowns for.

"Which one of these pirate costumes are you going to wear so I can pick out the one I want?" Steph pulled out a purple corset and held it against her body as she peered at the mirror.

"What about Ames?" That was Steph's on-again, off-again boyfriend of the year, but Margot guessed he was out of the picture for the week or Steph wouldn't want to go on a trip like this.

"You know him, he's off on another business trip and I don't think he's ever going to want to settle down. So let's go have some fun, shall we?" Steph held up a black corset and looked at herself in the mirror.

Margot flipped through the brochure and saw one event that looked like it would be a hoot. "Ohmigod, zombie paintball?"

"Yeah, see! It would be just the thing you would love. The haunted house, you know, all that stuff."

"My parents told me never to go to White Bear, you know." Margot didn't know why. If she'd been more curious about it, she might have checked it out already. But if she and Steph were going to be there for a week, why not?

"Right? They don't like that you didn't marry Howie even though he was the one at fault for that and it's your good fortune. They don't like that you opened this shop instead of becoming a lawyer like the two of them are. They don't like that your favorite 'holiday' is Halloween. I mean, so come on. You're twenty-six and you can live your own life. I've never been to White Bear either, but it looks like a really fun place to go. And if you look at the crime statistics, they're low compared to other places in Alaska. I don't know why they are so against you going there."

"Another family secret? Like my biological dad leaving us instead of dying when I was in the car accident? I couldn't believe my mother had kept that from me for so many years. Who knows." And yet, something wasn't right with that scenario. But try as Margot might, she couldn't remember what was wrong with it. Something told her it wasn't like that exactly in her nightmares, but once she was awake, they faded like mist on a hot day and she couldn't recall them at all.

"Maybe you could discover what the secret is—if it has anything to do with your family and White Bear. Maybe that's where your dad went and that's why your mom didn't want you to go there."

"Now that's a possibility." If her dad had ended up in White Bear, Margot wanted to see him if she could, just to learn if he had abandoned them and why.

"Then you'll want to check into it, right?"

"Yeah. When we have time, I do." Margot hoped if she could find him, it wouldn't ruin their trip there. Her priority really was to have fun, not search for her father. She wanted to do everything listed in the brochure because they might not ever have the opportunity to do this again. Especially if Ames and Steph ended up marrying.

"So which outfit are you going to wear?" Steph asked.

"Let me talk to Faye first." Margot wanted to make sure Faye was really all right with this. She got on her phone and called Faye. "Hey, so Steph dropped in to tell me—"

"You're going, aren't you? I'm all set to work. You'll have a blast. Steph said you would be leaving Friday."

Margot glanced in Steph's direction, but she was already in one of the dressing rooms, trying on one of the pirate costumes. She sighed. "Uh, yes, we'll be leaving Friday. You've got keys to the place. I'll leave it in your hands." She knew she could rely on Faye to take care of the shop like it was her own.

"Yes! Thanks, Margot. You won't have any problems while you're gone."

"Okay, thanks so much, Faye. I guess she told you why we're doing this impromptu trip, right?"

"Yep. You love Halloween and she just found the perfect place for you to live out your fantasies. I was so looking forward to some extra income, so I'm happy to do this for you. And I adore working in your shop."

"Great! Then we're all set."

"Happy haunting!" Faye said.

Margot laughed and thanked her, then they ended the call and Margot looked for her favorite pirate costume on the costume racks and breathed a sigh of relief. She was afraid Steph might have gotten it and Margot wouldn't have the heart to tell her that she wanted that one.

Steph called out from the dressing room, "I left the one you adore on the rack. I know you."

"Thanks. You're right. And it's a good thing or we might have had a jolly good fight over it." Margot wanted to wear white like a winter pirate because it was already feeling like winter with half a foot of snow on the ground. Not to mention as a polar bear shifter, she loved white. Though she had costumes in other colors she would wear too. One of her favorites was a burgundy and beige outfit that made her feel sexy. She often wore it for work and other activities, so it was going to be nice wearing it someplace new where no one knew her.

"Argh," Steph said, getting into character. "But I havena my cutlass."

Margot laughed. She knew that going with her friend would make their trip the best ever. Forget Margot's unfaithful fiancé or Steph's boyfriend who couldn't make up his mind about wanting to mate her.

"Oh, I should have asked, are you free to do this? I guess you are or you would have told me already." Steph came out of the dressing room and put her costume—black skirt, purple corset, white blouse, and black pirate, three-corner hat on the counter.

"Yeah, you were right. Faye was delighted that she could earn some extra money." Margot gave Steph the usual friend deep-discount rate, just like she did Faye.

"We're going to have a ball," Steph said.

"We sure are." Though Margot hoped she wouldn't learn that her parents' warning to stay away from White Bear had some merit and she should have left well enough alone.

POLAR BEAR SHIFTERS Craig MacMathan and his parents, brothers, and cousins, along with their mates, were even more excited about decorating the White Bear Tavern for Halloween this year. The businesses in town were all decking out for the bewitching hour even more than usual. But this year, his cousin Edward and his mate, Robyn, had six-year-old twin boys, and so that made it even more fun. Right now, the boys were helping to hang up a couple of parrots wearing pirate hats. The tavern with its darkly stained, distressed wood paneling on the walls and ceiling, the scarred wood tables and chairs and the long bar all already exuded old world charm. Smoky mirrors were hanging behind the long bar, which made it appear that the tavern was really a pirates' den when they weren't out on the Seven Seas terrorizing merchant ships.

White Bear Deli was the popular pastry and sandwich shop down the street, also polar bear run, and they went all out to create Halloween-themed treats for the month. They made the best berry pies that everyone loved, especially the bears in White Bear and those who visited the town.

Frosty Dreams, a new ice cream and cookie shop, was all done up in pink by two foxy sisters. The White Bear Lodge, owned by bear shifters, though they were grizzlies, Meghan and Thomas Bearsteau, was also decorated for the affair.

White Bear was getting to have the reputation of being the most entertaining place to go for Halloween fun. It helped with their tourism as snow was falling and made Halloween appear like it was being held in winter instead of autumn. Even Andy's cousins, Edward and Rob, and their partner Casey MacIntosh, who took tourists on guided wilderness tours, marketed their tours during the month as special Halloween tours because everyone could see the town filled with businesses that were decorated for the occasion. They also did some fun Halloween activities on their trips.

The town usually had a theme for Halloween, though only a few businesses in the past had decorated for it, so this year it was truly special. Craig's regular job was serving as a seaplane pilot and he took tourists for sightseeing tours all over the Alaska wilderness, delivered supplies to outlying areas, and helped with emergency rescues. But right now, he was having fun setting up the trunk of gold coins—chocolate—for the kids and adults alike, on top of an old oak table in his parents' tavern. Everyone knew their cousin Edward was prone to eat more than his share, loving chocolate better than berries like the rest of their kind.

Edward would normally be helping out, but he and his mate had two-month-old twin boys, in addition to the six-year-old twins, so he and Robyn were home taking care of the babies right now.

Craig's brother Andy, the trooper, came in to have lunch before he returned to work. He saw Craig filling up the pirate's chest with gold and silver wrapped chocolates. "Okay, so that's for Edward. What do *we* get to snack on?"

Craig laughed.

"I already called an order into Dad that I want a bowl of chili and crackers," Andy said, headed for an empty bar seat. "Something quick."

"Do you have any hot cases that you're working on today?" Craig asked, going behind the bar to get his brother a bottle of water.

"Nah."

Their dad set a bowl of chili on the counter for Andy. "Don't be asking your brother lots of questions now, Craig. Andy has to get back to work to protect us."

Andy laughed. He also needed to eat, and as long as he didn't have an emergency call, he could tell him some interesting cases, if he was working on any. But as soon as Andy spooned up some of his chili, he got a call.

"See? What did I tell you?" Their dad went into the back to grill up some more hamburgers for an order.

"Yeah, thanks, I'll be there in a few minutes," Andy said to the person on the phone, then once he was finished with the call, he started to eat his chili in a hurry.

"So now you have a case."

"Yeah, vehicle theft, but I'll tell you all about it later." Andy finished his chili and hurried off the barstool. "See you later, brother."

Things always seemed to get crazier as Halloween approached. Hopefully, Andy wouldn't find an injured mummy this year. Last year, the guy was so drunk, he nearly hung himself with his mummy wrappings at a wild, home party. Andy put in leave for Halloween because he always helped his brothers and cousins and parents at the tavern for one of their busiest nights of the year. They figured since the town had been going all out to decorate for the month of October this year, they would be even busier. But his fellow state troopers knew if they needed his help, Andy would be there.

Just like Craig would be on his way if he was needed to drop off supplies via his seaplane to outlying areas to someone in need or if he had to make an emergency pickup.

Their brother Ben actually worked at the tavern full-time and had brought Edward and Robyn's boys over to help with decorations to give them something to do. With the new babies in the house, the boys needed some more attention since the babies were getting a lot of it. The boys were having a ball decorating the tavern.

Then Craig's phone growled, telling him someone was calling. He pulled it out of his pocket.

"Hey, Craig, another seaplane pilot was supposed to deliver some much-needed medicine but his plane is in the hangar for repairs. Can you deliver them instead?"

"Yeah. I'm on it. Be there in an hour." Then Craig ended the call and said to his dad, "Hey, I got a call that someone needs some supplies. I'll see you when I return, Dad."

"Stay safe," his dad said.

"Thanks. I will." But before Craig headed out the door, his cousin Rob called him on his cell phone with a warning.

"Keep an eye out for polar bear shifters in trouble on the way to your drop off or on your return trip," Rob said, and Craig wondered if he'd had a premonition like he was known to have on occasion.

"Where?"

"I don't know. You know how it is with these things and me. But I see they need some help and you're going to be in the area. Just keep a hawk eye's look out."

That's all Craig would be thinking of now.

2

Margot was driving Steph's car to White Bear, but Steph had planned the whole trip out, including a detour to go to the scenic Seward that would take them past the Portage ghost town. Steph liked to navigate, not drive as much which worked well for Margot. She loved to take road trips. They were perfect together, stopping when they wanted to, exploring new places that they might find. No rush, no hurry to get to where they were going.

"After the 1964 earthquake, the town sank from six to ten feet and the people had to abandon their homes and move. What's really cool is that the animals are returning to the area," Steph said.

Margot wholeheartedly agreed. "That's what's always amazing to me. The vegetation takes hold and the buildings all but disappear."

"Right. There's one building the bears now frequent even."

"How cool is that?"

"Pretty cool. Though I wouldn't want to check it out as a bear even, since the bears there are grizzlies. And not of the shifter variety."

"I agree with you there."

They saw cabins that had sunken and only their roofs and part of the cabins were still exposed. It looked eerie, like something out of an apocalypse, perfect for a Halloween trip.

"Saltwater filled the area and killed the original trees and preserved them. They call it a ghost forest." Steph motioned to the trees.

"It does look ghostly," Margot admitted. "I would have thought the trees would have just decomposed after a while and vanished."

"I thought the same. It has been fun going this way as long as we don't see any ghosts, right?" Steph asked.

"You say that after having us drive by a ghost town?"

Steph laughed. "It's the week of Halloween. There isn't a better time to see a ghost town than that."

Smiling, Margot shook her head. "You are the perfect friend to go a haunting with during Halloween week."

Steph laughed. "I love Halloween, although not the real scary stuff like you enjoy."

"Yeah, I don't know of anybody in my family who is into it so I don't know where I get that from. Okay, so which place are we staying at in White Bear? You said it was a secret, but now that we're on the road, I want to know."

"A bed and breakfast. I tried to make reservations at the hotel that has the indoor swimming pool, but it was booked. The bed and breakfast had a cancellation, or we wouldn't have gotten in there either. I would say that was a sign that we should be there."

Margot laughed. Everything to Steph was a sign.

"We'll have breakfast there and then eat lunch and dinner elsewhere. There are lots of places to eat in town and every place I checked on is decorated for Halloween."

"That will make it really special. That's why you insisted we take three pirate costumes apiece." Margot hoped other visitors to the area or locals would be wearing costumes as they were out and about, and she and Steph wouldn't feel too out of place, though they were dressing up no matter what.

"Well, not three whole costumes. I brought just a change of skirt and jewelry or blouse. That way we won't look like we are wearing the same costume every day."

"As if anyone is going to notice us in White Bear," Margot said.

"True. We have one more stop to make before we go into the town," Steph said.

"Oh?" So far, Margot had loved all the things they were doing, so she was certain she would love this too.

"Yeah. Beautiful waterfalls are nearby. Neither of us have been there before and we can even go off the beaten path so that no one will see us."

"As polar bears?" Margot wasn't sure about that. It was broad daylight for one thing.

"Black bears and grizzlies are in the area. I would feel better being in our fur coats."

"Oh." That made more sense then. "As long as no one sees us." As in human types. Polar bears wouldn't live in this area.

"Right. That's why we'll be in forested terrain. If anyone sees us by the waterfall, we only have to slip back into the forest and shift, dress, and no one will be the wiser. I mean, they could report there were polar bears, search for us even, but they won't ever find us, and the authorities will think whoever saw us was mistaken."

As long as Margot and Steph didn't shift and run into grizzly bears!

After they parked the car at the trailhead, they grabbed their backpacks filled with emergency gear, bear noisemakers, bear spray, and headed out on the trail. For trips like this, in case they had car trouble along the way, they were always prepared for any emergency.

They hiked for a couple of miles off-trail where humans couldn't see them.

"This should be a good place to shift. We're under the cover of the forest, so no one will see us shift. There are no human trails, no scents of anyone in the vicinity, and we can still see the falls just up the way," Steph said.

"That sounds good." Margot hadn't envisioned seeing waterfalls on this trip, but she was so glad they were doing this too.

They stripped off their clothes and tucked them in their backpacks. Then they shifted into their polar bear forms, leaving their backpacks hidden in the woods, and walked toward the waterfall. They could smell the water, heard the roar of the falls, and were excited to reach them.

This had been such a special trip already. Margot was glad Steph had planned these extra excursions. When they finally saw the falls, the beautiful blue water cascading over the moss-covered rocks, Margot just sighed. She could sit here all day and just soak this in.

That's when she and Steph heard a grizzly sow growl and saw her and her two cubs nearby. Crap!

Margot hadn't thought they would run into any bears here. She hadn't smelled any sign of them. Boy, were they mistaken. And to see the cubs, that was bad news. They didn't want to hurt the mother, but they had to defend themselves. Even though they were a couple of polar bears, an angry grizzly mother could still be dangerous.

She rose up on her hind legs and roared.

Steph and Margot headed out of there, but the sow came after them. They didn't want to fight her. She had to protect her little ones and they didn't want to injure her unnecessarily. But she was persistent and hit Steph with her powerful paw. Margot bit the grizzly in the shoulder, hard enough to get her to quit attacking them, trying to get her to leave them alone and go back to her cubs, but not hard enough to cause her any real injury.

The bear took a swipe at Margot's chest and Steph roared at Margot to just leave. To get as far away from the grizzly and her cubs as they could. Margot agreed that was the best course of action.

The bear kept after them, and they ran as fast as they could through the trees. Margot watched Steph in the lead, running on three legs. She'd been injured. Margot stayed in the rear and would steer the bear away from Steph if she didn't quit chasing them. They were headed for their clothes, but they couldn't shift and change, not while they had to deal with the grizzly if she was still out for their blood. They were finally getting some distance from her. Margot hoped that Steph's injury wasn't too bad. They might have to call off their trip to White Bear after all.

Then they noticed the bear was getting farther away from them, slowing down, then returning to her cubs.

Thank God for small miracles. But Margot worried about Steph's injury now, and where they could go to take care of it. When she saw a doctor, that was going to take some storytelling finesse.

BEFORE LONG, Craig was on his way to deliver medical supplies to an isolated clinic, the warning Rob had made to him about watching out for polar bear shifters in trouble on this trip on his mind the whole flight. Wild polar bears wouldn't be on this route normally. He flew over the snowy ground, landed in the bay, and then offloaded the medical supplies to the clinic staff who needed them. He saw no sign of any polar bears on the trip there, but he would be watchful on the way back to White Bear. The thing of it was, Rob's visions could be of something that would occur a few weeks from now, so it didn't mean it would actually happen on this trip.

The people at the clinic were thankful that Craig had brought them their supplies and he always loved how appreciative everyone was. But he still couldn't shake free of the thought he might be needed to rescue a couple of polar bears once he was in the air.

On the return trip, Craig was really watching for any sign of the bears when he saw a grizzly bear and her two cubs. Some distance from them, he saw a polar bear running on three legs. Polar bear—that had to have been the vision that Rob had seen. The polar bear had to be a shifter. As close as she'd been to the sow and her cubs, Craig figured she had to have fought with the grizzly and been injured. Then he saw another polar bear. The polar bears disappeared under the cover of the forest again. That's what Rob had said. He would need to help out a couple of polar bears—not just one.

He found a lake to set down his plane that was about a twenty-minute hike from where the two polar bears were. He anchored the seaplane, then packed a sled with emergency equipment, put his cold weather gear on, grabbed the sled, and headed across the snow-covered ground to reach the two polar bears.

He finally reached the women, both now dressed in parkas and snow boots, sitting on the ground, the one favoring her left arm. The pretty brown-eyed, auburn-haired woman, who was wearing some blood on her cheek, called out to him, "I think my friend might have broken her wrist." A tangle of long curls framed her face and reached down past her waist. "I'm Margot Anderson, and this is my good friend Stephanie Stone."

"But everyone calls me Steph." The blond-haired woman

laid down on the snow and closed her eyes, and he hoped she wasn't injured severely somewhere else, but he would fly them out of here and get them help.

"I'll take you to White Bear," he called out. They had a regular medical clinic there for humans, but also one that only handled shifters. They required referrals so they knew the person was a shifter who came to the clinic run by a gray wolf doctor and his staff.

"Oh, White Bear is where we were going before we had our unfortunate accident," Margot said.

The two women were wearing heavy parkas, but even so, he smelled they were polar bears, and he was certain they were the ones he had seen when he was flying above the treetops.

"Oh, oh, you're one too." Margot sounded thrilled then to meet him.

"Yeah, through and through like the two of you are." He smiled, but then he noticed Margot had blood on her glove. "Are you injured also? Besides the cut to your face?"

"My hand's cut. A grizzly bear attacked us. We...we were wearing our fur coats, enjoying the waterfall when we saw the sow coming. We tried not to fight her, except to defend ourselves, and just retreated until she figured the two of us were not going to bother her cubs. Then she took off with them. We were lucky because we sure didn't want to hurt her when she was just protecting her cubs."

"Hell, that's good that she took off." Even though the women matched the grizzly bear in size, two of them could be a match for an aggressive grizzly, but a female protecting her cubs? He wasn't sure. "She wasn't a shifter then or she would have realized that you were also, or you wouldn't have been there." He started checking out Steph's wrist. "No compound fracture, so that's good news. But you'll need to have it x-rayed. I'm Craig MacMathan, by the way, seaplane pilot." He secured Steph's arm to immobilize her wrist. He used his sat phone to call this in to the doctor at White Bear. "Hey, Doc, this is Craig. I'm bringing in a couple of injured women. It'll take me about an hour to get there. Uh, possible broken wrist, cut hand—wild grizzly bear fight with the two female polar bear shifters."

The doctor said, "Bring them in. We'll be ready for them."

"Okay. Thanks."

"We have our own vehicle about two miles from here," Margot said. "We'll just drive to White Bear like we had planned."

He checked Margot's hand and bandaged it. "We have a shifter clinic. Several of our businesses are shifter run." He cleaned the cut on her cheek. He gave them the address.

"Oh, that's great. Thanks so much for helping us," Margot said.

"Yeah, thanks," Steph said.

"Are you sure you're not injured elsewhere?" Craig wondered why Steph was lying down in the snow.

"I think my ribs are bruised. It feels better to lie down for a moment."

"Okay." He just hoped she didn't have any broken ribs. He helped Steph stand and she groaned. "Would you feel better lying down on the sled?" he asked.

"No, I can walk," Steph said.

"All right." He loaded up their backpacks on the sled. "Let's go. I'll take you to your vehicle." He didn't want the women to have to deal with another grizzly bear on their own if one decided to tear into them. As humans, they wouldn't do well. Steph couldn't fight, but he could match a grizzly's strength and between him and Margot, they could make a stand of their own. But he preferred getting the women out of here. That was when he saw a couple of muskoxen, which could be dangerous if provoked.

"Muskoxen," Margot said under her breath, sounding worried. "One killed a state trooper in North. They're dangerous."

"Yeah, they are. Let's just keep moving. They're watching us but they're not advancing." He continued to help Steph move across the snow. She was in pain, moaning a little.

Margot was behind them, trying to keep up.

"Are you all right?" Craig was afraid Margot was more injured than she thought she was.

"Yeah, just achy from all the fighting, so moving a little slower than I normally would be, but I'm keeping up. I'm sure after a good night's rest, I'll be fine."

"Okay." He slowed down so he wouldn't lose her, while he continued to cast glances over his shoulder at the muskoxen. He saw Margot looking that way a few times and he figured that was also slowing her down. "Where are you from?"

"North. Steph saw the brochure on White Bear and that the town was decked out in Halloween decorations, so we decided to go there for a week. We've had a great time on our way there so far, but this was kind of a disaster," Margot said.

"An adventure," Steph said.

"That we couldn't share about with anyone else," Margot said. "But I'm really worried about your wrist."

"It'll be fine. We're going to have a good time."

"If you are sure." Then Margot said to Craig, "We're glad you came to rescue us. We had no idea one of our own kind would be doing the rescue."

"I've done rescues all over the state where I'm needed the most. I'm glad I could help the two of you out, especially since you're shifters too. Have you ever been to White Bear before?" Craig didn't want to tell them he had been on the lookout for them once his cousin had told him he had a premonition about it. Not everyone was receptive to the notion that some could have psychic abilities. And he thought it best if Rob wanted to share his abilities with others, that was his duty, not Craig's anyway. "You'll enjoy the fact that shifters own several of the businesses."

"We've never been to White Bear. Margot's favorite 'holiday' is Halloween so when I saw the brochure, I had to convince her that we had to come out here for the week and check it all out. We had no idea it has a number of shifter-run businesses also which is really great," Steph finally said. "Oh, would you happen to know if the Primrose Bed and Breakfast is run by shifters? That's where we're staying."

"It sure is. A polar bear couple. You'll really like them, and they'll be thrilled to learn you are also."

"Oh, how fun," Steph said.

"I hope you brought costumes. Everyone will be wearing them in most of the establishments," Craig said.

"And you?" Margot motioned to the way he was dressed because he wasn't outfitted as a pirate for this venture.

"Yeah, I will be too. For rescue missions or dropping off supplies—which I was doing before I saw the two of you running as polar bears, well, Steph was limping pretty badly— no. But for working at the tavern, I'll be dressed up for sure. I figured the two of you had to be shifters since polar bears don't come to that area ever."

"We thought no one would witness us in the forest," Margot said.

"Sometimes it happens. But if anyone went looking for you because of the unusual sighting, you would have been gone long before they could reach you and they wouldn't have found you, no worries. If someone calls me up to do a tour in this area because they heard rumors polar bears had been sighted, I'll know they were you and I won't be trying to learn who the bears were."

"That's the fun part of being what we are," Margot said.

"Yeah, it's like trick or treat," Steph added. "We're the tricksters."

Craig smiled.

They finally reached Steph's car, and Craig helped Steph in. After that, he loaded their backpacks in the vehicle. "Are you sure you'll be all right?"

"Yeah, I'll be doing the driving," Margot said.

Craig wanted to see more of Margot and quickly came up with a plan. "My parents, Ned and Genevieve, own the White Bear Tavern and you can have a free dinner on us." His parents would be thrilled to serve the ladies a free meal when they'd had a dangerous encounter with a grizzly bear.

"Wow, does that come with the rescue service?" Margot asked.

"Only for single she-bears of the polar bear variety," Steph guessed.

Craig laughed. He didn't even know they were single, which he wanted to learn pronto, but yeah, that would be a good reason.

"She's more single than I am," Steph said. "I have a boyfriend who's out of town more than he's in town. But Margot isn't dating anyone."

"The offer of dinner is wonderful. Thanks so much," Margot quickly said.

Craig got the impression she didn't want to talk to him about her love life.

"If we need your further rescue services, do you have a way for us to get in touch with you?" Margot asked.

Craig knew she was teasing him, but he promptly pulled out a business card. "Just call me." Then he frowned, thinking something about Margot seemed familiar, but he couldn't place why he felt that way. "You look familiar to me. Are you sure you've never been to White Bear?" Her scent was totally unfamiliar to him to though. He knew he'd never smelled her before. So how would he have known her? He was probably mistaken about having seen her before. He would have remembered her better than that. She was drop-dead gorgeous and all he wanted to do was run his hands through her long curls and kiss her kissable mouth in the worst way.

Still...he just had the eerie feeling that he had seen her and if he had, then he wondered why she would deny that she'd ever been to White Bear.

3

—————

Margot and Steph shared conspiratorial looks when Craig had mentioned thinking Margot seemed familiar somehow. He really wondered what that was all about. He thought the two women shared some secret before he waved goodbye to them, told him he would see them in White Bear at the tavern most likely, and reminded them to call him if they needed his help.

He was curious about Margot not dating anyone right now. Had she recently broken up with someone? He wondered if Steph was also really more available to date than not. He thought one of his brothers might be interested in her. It sounded a bit like the guy Steph was seeing wasn't a real steady guy in her life. A lot of bachelor polar bears in White Bear would be interested in the women—a couple of new polar bear shifters in town—him especially. Not that anything would come of it since the women lived in North, but what if one of the polar bears from White Bear wanted to relocate to North to be with one of the ladies?

They were both beautiful, adventuresome, and especially Margot piqued his interest. He thought it was cute that they'd never been to White Bear but wanted to come to see the Halloween decorations. He was glad Edward's mate was such a genius at marketing. Robyn was the one who had proposed to the White Bear Council to really make Halloween a special event for the month and coordinated with other shifters in the community who had businesses. Likewise, human-run businesses also got involved in decorating for the occasion and paid her to help advertise for them too.

Then Robyn made up the brochure that was sent to every community in Alaska to advertise it. She'd also shared the happenings for the month on her website to help push sales to places outside of Alaska. Normally, she worked with individual businesses to help them market their goods and services. But in this case, everyone who benefited from her marketing services paid her for going the extra mile to put this together.

They'd had a ton more people coming for the MacMathan brothers and the McIntosh tours and all of the businesses in White Bear had shown a large increase in sales. All of the hotels and bed and breakfasts had been booked to capacity.

He guessed that one of the places must have had a room cancellation so that it had been available for Margot and Steph, unless the ladies had actually reserved the room much earlier. But it sounded to him like they had done this on the spur of the moment. He would have offered one of his spare bedrooms to the ladies if they had needed a place to stay. Some of the local residents would rent out rooms when other shifters came into the area and couldn't get any accommodations.

He called his dad to tell him about Margot and her friend Steph and helping them out, but mostly he had to mention that he had offered them a free dinner at the tavern.

His dad laughed. "Sounds like one of them has got her hooks in you already."

The auburn-haired lass who loved Halloween did for sure.

"They're from North, so they live too far away from here for me to date either of them seriously. And one of them, I believe, has a boyfriend. I'm not going there. Edward's the one who got into trouble like that before he was mated." Despite that Margot was from North, Craig had every intention of showing her a good time here in White Bear as long as he didn't impose on the ladies' trip plans too much.

His dad laughed. "That's because your brother Ben convinced Edward to go out with the woman. You know how Ben is, always trying to matchmake but I wonder when he'll find a mate of his own."

"We'll have to do some matchmaking for *him*," Craig said. "I'll be at the tavern in a little bit." Then he let his dad get back to work.

Craig was glad that he had been in the area when the women had had the trouble with the grizzly and was able to provide some assistance. He smiled. Unless he got called up for an emergency, he was serving the ladies dinner at the tavern. And he would be regally dressed as a gentleman pirate.

He called up Rob and said, "Your premonition was spot on. Thanks for the heads-up. But I thought you didn't get premonitions about family any longer."

"That's what I thought, but now it seems that because Alicia and I have connected, our psychic abilities have collided, and things are changing for us."

"I hope only for the better. Oh, and does Alicia see anything about Margot Anderson's past? I swear she seems familiar somehow, but I don't know her scent at all."

"Margot Anderson?" Rob asked, sounding like he'd turned his head and was talking to Alicia.

"Nope, no visions of her in the past," Alicia called out.

Craig kept wracking his brain for the elusive memory of seeing her before...or someone who looked similar to her, but in a...well, different way. He just couldn't recall and it was driving him crazy.

"Well, if Craig is anything like the other bachelor bears in the sleuth, we're going to have some fun," Steph said.

Margot raised her brows at Steph's comment. "Okay, so are you giving up on Ames?" She was surprised that Steph would date anyone in White Bear if she thought there was a chance to make it work with Ames when he returned to North after this latest business trip he was on.

"Hell, yeah, if I find someone who I really, really like and he really, really likes me, you never know. I mean, what if we were hooked on each other and we knew just what we wanted with each other? We do, you know. Well, not in your case with Howie, and maybe not in my case with Ames. I think sometimes it's just because we're...I don't know, comfortable with each other? And he's fine with the status quo. But once I have a hotel management job, I want to settle down and have a home, kids, dog, or cat, and well, the mate too. I don't know if I'll ever get that with Ames. Oh, sure, I could see having the home, kids, dog, or cat, but then Ames would never be there for any of us because of all his travelling. And truly, I'm not sure if he really wants all of that. He always says we'll talk about it when I have my job. I think it's a way for him to avoid the issue.

"His parents are divorced, you know. So I think marrying and having kids scares him. Anyway, for now, we're on vacation and we can just have some fun, right? That's all I'm thinking about," Steph said.

"Certainly. That's what it's all about." But Margot was surprised to hear this coming from Steph. She thought there was major trouble in their relationship unless Ames changed his tune. She wasn't getting involved in it though. Steph knew him better than Margot did and she would have to live with or without him. It was her decision, just like Margot agreeing to marry Howie had been.

"What about you? What if you met some guy you really like in White Bear? Like the hot pilot that came to rescue us? You don't have to worry about the fact you're seeing anyone, because you haven't been after the fiasco with Howie. Craig really likes you, I could tell."

"Oh, he liked both of us. He didn't show one of us any favoritism." Which wasn't true, but Margot didn't want Steph to think Craig only liked her.

Steph smiled. "When I mentioned Halloween was your favorite time of year, he smiled like he got the biggest kick out of it. And though he took care of my wrist first because it was the worst injury, he kept smiling at you, his dark brown eyes following your every move and he was definitely trying to get your attention."

"You have a great imagination." But Margot had caught his eye a couple of times and had smiled back. How could she not? He had a beautiful smile, and his eyes were the darkest chocolate and truly magnetic, capturing her gaze and holding on in an interested way. Plus, he had the most beautiful black eyelashes.

"I'm serious. He is cute though. And heroic. I mean he could have been in the middle of a bear fight, when he came to our aid."

"Not to mention he was ready to protect us from the muskoxen." Margot was totally impressed with his chivalry.

"He was."

He had even gotten in between them and the muskoxen in the event they had charged their party, proving just how protective he could be, even in his human form.

"I guess after we go to see the doctor at the shifter clinic to have your wrist and your ribs x-rayed, we'll check in at the bed and breakfast. We can drop off our bags, and then go over to the tavern and have an early dinner," Margot said.

"Lunch first. We haven't had any. But we have to change into our pirate costumes and check out some of the shops also. Then we can have dinner at the tavern. Unless you're too eager to see Craig again and want to go early."

Margot laughed as she turned onto another road. "I look forward to seeing him again." And truly, she hadn't thought she would feel that way again about a guy so soon after she and Howie had broken up. "Your plan sounds like a great idea. How are your wrist and your ribs feeling?"

"They're throbbing."

"We'll have to get you something for the pain."

"Hmm, I guess that means having a drink at the tavern is out then."

"Not if you're taking pain medicine," Margot said.

"I'll just take some over-the-counter medicine then," Steph said.

That's usually all they took as shifters because they healed so quickly.

When they finally arrived at the clinic, Margot was glad that Craig had called ahead so that the staff knew they were coming and took them both right in. A nurse saw to Steph to get x-rays, and another nurse checked out Margot's scratches. They had to make sure they wouldn't become infected. The nurses and other staff members were a mixture of gray and Arctic wolves, the doctor being a gray wolf. Everyone was so friendly, and Margot felt truly welcome there, which was nice. It felt great to be around other shifters who could understand what they'd done when they came upon the grizzly bear. They would have to have made up some story about being humans and being attacked and none of it would have made any sense to humans otherwise.

Not when they came away from the attack without life-threatening wounds.

"It's a good thing you two didn't have more injuries than that," the nurse said. Phyllis was an older woman with graying hair and golden eyes, and a gray wolf.

"Yes, we were lucky. We didn't see any sign of the mother bear before she suddenly appeared. We had to have startled her as much as she startled us. I was glad we didn't have to really hurt her since she had to take care of a couple of cubs."

"I agree," Phyllis said. "You were lucky Craig saw you."

"I hope no one else did."

Phyllis smiled. "Right."

Then Phyllis finished bandaging Margot and she went to see Steph to learn how she had fared.

"Torn ligaments and a wrist bone fracture," Steph said. "It will take about three weeks to heal. It would have been six weeks if we didn't have our enhanced shifter genetics, so it won't be too bad. My ribs are just bruised. No broken bones, thank goodness."

"Good." Margot hoped Steph would feel okay during their week of adventure. She was concerned about that. They had put an easily removable splint on Steph's wrist, and Margot might have to help her dress. Margot was glad she loved to drive so Steph didn't have to.

They paid their medical bills and thanked the staff, then left the clinic. "Now to check in at the bed and breakfast," Margot said.

"I'm starving. Those granola bars we had on our hike have long since worn off."

"Yeah, I agree. My stomach has been rumbling."

"Mine too." But then Steph frowned at Margot. "Why did Craig think you looked familiar to him when you've never been to White Bear?"

argot wondered the same thing as Steph. Why did Craig think he had seen her before when she'd never been to White Bear that she could recall? "I don't know. I don't remember ever having been here." And that had her wondering again just why her mother hadn't wanted her to go to White Bear, ever.

Before Margot and Steph arrived at the Primrose Bed and Breakfast, they saw a few pirate women and men walking into shops and restaurants so Margot felt more comfortable about dressing up to wander through the area.

Then they parked at the blue, two-story bed and breakfast, all trimmed in white, the sign hanging in front wearing hand-painted purple primroses. On the second floor was a balcony for guests furnished with two primrose fabric covered couches and a wrought iron table and chairs.

Purple, orange, and white lights decorated the roof and bannisters. A sign out front said, "Come in for a spell" and had a hand-carved raven sitting on top of it with a cauldron of bubbling purple liquid and bubbles. Another sign said, "Well-behaved children welcome—the rest will be made into pies."

The ladies laughed. This establishment had tons of decorations of black cats wearing pirate hats for its pirate theme. So cute. The lobby was filled with carved pumpkins and several that were in their natural state still and seating for guests, though everyone seemed to be out enjoying the town. A treasure chest filled with chocolate money sat on the checkout counter and a black cat was guarding it.

A black-bearded man quickly greeted them, tall, broad shouldered, nearly black eyes and smelling like he was a polar bear. "I'm John Snow, the owner, manager, anything you need me to be. And you must be our guests from North showing up at our fair port."

"Yes, Margot Anderson and Steph Stone. We're so glad you had a room for us at the last minute." She was glad it was shifter run and that he was in costume.

John was dressed in a brown faux suede jacket, large, collared shirt, feathered tricorn hat, antique brass buckle, knee-high, leather buccaneer boots, and a wide red waist sash. He was definitely playing the part of a black-bearded pirate. She was thinking if she had a shop here instead of North, she might even do more business.

Coming to White Bear had already been so much fun.

"You're on the second floor, room eight, and we serve breakfast in the dining room from seven until ten, so no rush to get up in the morning. I hope you ladies enjoy your week here." John helped take their bags to their rooms.

Margot thought that was so sweet of him, though she guessed Steph really had needed his help.

"I heard you tangled with a momma grizzly," he said.

Margot was surprised he would know. Had the medical staff alerted him? She would have thought that was privileged information. Or had Craig mentioned it to him? She wouldn't think he would have.

John said, "Word gets around. At the White Bear Tavern, Craig told his father and brothers what had happened. My wife was in there getting us some take-out dinner and overheard it. She called me before you got here to tell me to give you extra special treatment."

Margot smiled. "That's nice of her." She was glad that was all there was to it. She had never thought anyone would even notice them in White Bear. Now it seemed they could be the center of attention.

"We're just glad the two of you are fine." He glanced at Steph's wrist. "For the most part."

"Yeah, well that's not so bad compared to how it could have turned out," Steph said.

"So true." Then he deposited their bags in the room and left them alone.

Margot unpacked their suitcases and then pulled out one of Steph's pirate costumes to wear and got hers out too.

"I really like that white one on you. You look like a winter pirate for sure," Steph said, as Margot dressed.

"Yeah, it makes me feel like a polar bear pirate."

Steph laughed and Margot helped her remove her boots, jeans, and sweater. Then she assisted in dressing her in a black peasant blousy shirt, red corset, black skirt, boots, and a black pirate's jacket, otherwise that could be used for the Renaissance Era or steampunk festivities, and a red sash.

"I can't believe I need to have all this help to get dressed."

"I'm happy to be there for you. I would have needed your assistance if I'd been injured like you had been." Margot wore a white skirt, brown boots, a white embroidered corset, a white pirate's jacket and a brown sash. Steph's hat was black, Margot's brown as they headed out to get some lunch.

White Bear was also laid out really well. The bed and break-fast was on the street behind main street where many of the restaurants and shops were located so they could just walk there.

"I'm so glad that the weather is just perfect for this. Cool enough to dress up, but not so cold—or hot—that we would be uncomfortable," Steph said.

"Yeah, it's perfect. When we drove in, I thought that deli would be fun to eat at. I'd also looked up their menu online before we came here and knew they offered the kinds of food we both like. Aww, look at all the pumpkins in the window." Margot loved how owls, black cats, wolves, and polar bears had been painted on them. Someone was a real artist.

"I love how artistically the pumpkins were painted. Me? I can't paint even stick figures." Steph pulled the door open, and they smelled pastrami, garlic pickles, corned beef, German sausages, and onion soup.

"I know what you mean." Margot followed her inside. It all smelled so delicious. As hungry as she was, she felt like she could eat one of everything they had to offer.

A woman wearing a brown skirt, gold corset, an orange and gold scarf around her head, and an ivory peasant's blouse greeted them with a big smile. She was a polar bear also, to their surprise and delight. Craig was serious when he said that they had a lot of shifters in town.

"Oooh, new bears." The server guided them to a booth and once they sat down, she straightened and looked very serious. "Sorry. Avast, ye, maties. Here are your menus. I'm Cpt. Jenna at your service."

They laughed and tipped their pirate hats to her, then Jenna smiled and bounced off to give them some time to look at their menus.

"I want a Reuben sandwich." Margot closed up her menu. "As soon as we walked in and I smelled them, I knew I had to have one."

"Oh, I want a hot pastrami sandwich." Steph leaned against her seat back, looking a little worse for wear.

"Are you going to really be all right? You look tired after our ordeal."

"Yeah. I'll get a good night's sleep and I'll be fine in the morning. I'm not giving up on having a blast while we're here on vacation."

"Okay, but you let me know if you need to take a break and just rest." Margot was serious, but she would have felt the same way if she'd been injured like Steph had but that they had so many fun activities ahead of them to do.

Jenna returned to take their orders, bringing them glasses of water. They both ordered pirate mate chai tea and chips with their sandwiches. "I'll be right back with your tea for a couple of fellow pirates."

"Thanks!" Margot sat back on her bench seat and pulled off her pirate's hat, setting it on the bench beside her.

Steph did the same with her hat, then pulled her phone out and texted someone.

"Did you text your boyfriend?" Margot asked, figuring Steph was finally going to let him know where she was if Ames even wondered.

"No way. Ames has been gone for a week to God knows where and he hasn't contacted me once. He won't even realize I've left town."

"Who then?"

"Faye. I took a photo of us when you weren't looking after we dressed as pirates and sent it to her to show her what our costumes looked like." Steph got a text back. She smiled. "She said she'll post it on our website to help advertise your costumes in case someone hasn't bought one for Halloween yet." She showed Margot the picture.

"Aww, that's cute." Margot had often taken pictures of Faye

and Steph dressed in the clothes from her shop, but never any of herself. She should do some of the three of them together for fun sometime.

Jenna brought their tea. "Your sandwiches will be out shortly."

Margot and Steph glanced around the deli at the other people dressed in costume. Not everyone was, but the women and men who were had worn fun pirate costumes too. The women were wearing fancy corsets, long skirts, pirate jackets with flouncy sleeves, and boots. The guys were wearing pirate-styled jackets, embroidered vests, pants, and boots.

"I wonder how many shifters are in here," Steph said low for Margot's ears only.

"I smell snow leopards, foxes, brown bears, black bears, polar bears, wolves, but they could have come in at any time and be gone now." Except for Jenna of course.

Then Jenna brought the lunches to their table and Margot asked, "So how many shifters are here in the deli now?"

Jenna smiled. "The couple in the pirate costumes in the booth nearest us are gray wolves—Wolfrun and Erin, not mated yet, but everyone's figuring it will happen soon. In the booth behind them, they're Arctic wolves. Across the deli over there, that rowdy group of three are snow leopard brothers, Simon, Jasper, and William, and we have a grizzly sitting alone over there. The rest are humans."

"Wow, that is so cool," Margot said.

"It is. My family moved here a decade ago and my parents started this deli. It's so neat that so many of the businesses are shifter run. Once the word gets out, we get more and more shifters from all over coming to check out the town, some even staying here after all also."

"I can see why they would," Margot said.

"It's good for business for all of us." Jenna glanced at the door of the deli as another group of people came inside. Then she frowned as she considered Margot's bandaged cuts and Steph's wrist In a splint. "Ye didn't have any troubles with the locals, did ye? If so, I'll put in a word with the pirate council to take care of the blighters."

Margot smiled, loving that Jenna was trying to be in character. "A run in with a grizzly defending her cubs."

Jenna's jaw dropped. Then she scowled. "Near White Bear?"

"Nay, farther north of here near some falls," Steph said. "But we got out of there before we had too much more trouble."

"Then Craig MacMathan came to the rescue," Margot said.

Jenna smiled. "Aye, he's a right good one to help out in a crisis. Some of me pirate mates were snowed in, and he dropped supplies for them next to their cabin. A jolly good sort he is. He has even helped me out a time or two when my car, uhm, ship got stuck in the snow, uhm, ice floes, and he towed me out. For a polar bear shifter, he's not bad on the eyes either." She winked at them. "Enjoy your meal, maties." Then she hurried off to seat the new patrons. "Ahoy, maties."

"Wow, it's nice to get to know a guy who has a good reputation in town. I love it here. What if you relocated your dress store to White Bear?" Steph asked, then took a bite of her pastrami sandwich.

"Then I would be leaving you behind." Margot ate some of her Reuben. "Wow this is good."

"Yeah, mine is too. But no way. I would move right here with you. You would probably get along better with your parents if you didn't live close by."

Margot laughed. "You're probably right. I don't see them much anyway. They're both too busy with the cases they're defending. I didn't even bother telling them I was leaving for the week because they wouldn't have liked hearing the reason we were coming out here—I mean to enjoy Halloween activities."

"If you had, you would have had to tell them where you were going and that wouldn't have gone over very well with them either."

Margot agreed. "What about Ames? Could you convince him to move here?"

"Why? If we're not going to be in a permanent relationship, it won't matter. I might just find what I need in a man here." Steph took another bite of her sandwich.

"Well, before I could even consider such a move, we would need to learn why my mother didn't want me to ever go to White Bear. So far, it has been great." Then Margot smiled. "Though I'm not really moving away from North, but it's just fun to think about."

"Not unless you hook up with a hot polar bear." Margot raised her brows and smiled.

Then yeah, that would be a whole different story.

Once they finished their meals, Jenna took their payment and said, "Ye've taken our booty, come back, me hearties, soon. Oh, and dinna mess with the wildlife any longer."

They laughed.

"Aye-aye, Cpt. Jenna," Margot said, saluting her.

Then she and Steph left the deli to explore some of the shops.

"Now that was good food," Steph said. "I wouldn't mind living here and eating there from time to time."

"It sure was. I hope their food is just as good at the White Bear Tavern since we're getting a free meal there and I would hate to fib about it to Craig if it isn't," Margot said.

"I know what you mean. Especially after Craig came to rescue us." Steph opened the door to a gift shop all decorated in orange lights and crows wearing pirate hats. "This is so cute. We would have so much fun decorating your place for the holidays if it was the same as here."

"I agree." Margot had done some fall decorating in her shop, but not so much Halloween stuff. None of the other shops near her did either. They went inside and browsed a bit and saw the advertisement for taking a tour with the MacMathan brothers and their partner, MacIntosh. She picked up the brochure and read it. "They have two- and three-day tours."

"I would love to go on one of them."

"Yeah, me too."

A pretty blonde with clear blue eyes, wearing a gypsy skirt of gaily colored layers of fabric in golds and greens and blues—something Margot would love to have—greeted them. She wore a gold scarf on her head and a peasant blouse, boots, and a ton of gold necklaces—the one standing out to Margot—a hand-carved stone polar bear. Her wrists were likewise adorned with gold bracelets and she wore rings on nearly all her fingers. Not only that, but she smelled like a polar bear. "You're one of us." She smiled broadly. "I love your costumes. They're beautiful."

"Thanks. They're from my shop in North," Margot said, smiling. "I love your costume too. Your skirt is to die for."

"You like it?" She beamed. "I'm Amy. I actually made this one."

"Oh, I would love one like that," Margot said.

"Me too, though different colors," Steph said. "Maybe we could commission you to make some for us and for Margot's dress shop."

"Oh, wow, let me think on that. I don't know how much it would cost to make one to sell, but I'll get back to you on it."

Margot handed her one of her business cards.

"Thanks." Amy stuck the card in her pocket and then pointed to the brochure. "You will love their tour if you go on it, particularly the third one that is listed. It's a shifter tour," she said softly because she had other people in the shop perusing the shelves for gifts.

"Oh, wow, how neat. We're only going to be here for a week though," Margot said.

"You could make the two-day trip. All three of the guides are polar bears. Casey MacIntosh is a bachelor." Amy smiled at them.

"We'll, uhm, check into it. Thanks," Margot said, her cheeks heating a bit. That was one thing she didn't think she would be doing. Looking for guys to date in White Bear. Who would have known they had such a large polar bear shifter community here?

"Okay, well, I'll let you look at what we have to offer and if you need any help, just ask."

"Thanks, Amy." Margot hadn't planned to buy anything in particular, but shifters supported other shifters so she felt she had to buy something. She hoped Amy could come up with a good price on the skirt she was wearing, and Margot would definitely buy them for her to keep in her shop. Or if they were too highly priced, just buy one for herself. She loved having handmade items in her shop so that she had some unique clothes or gifts for customers to purchase. Her regular customers would check with her, or she would send out a newsletter blast telling everyone she had some new items in the store. That would be a problem with moving to a new location. She would have to build up her clientele all over again.

"Hey, why don't we get something for Craig for coming to our rescue and then for giving us a free dinner at his family's tavern," Steph said.

"Yes, that's a perfect idea." Margot was glad Steph had thought of it, though she suspected Craig didn't often get a gift for helping others out. She looked through the items on the shelves, but she didn't have a clue as to what he would want. She didn't want to just get him something to get him something. She wanted it to be useful. "What would a seaplane pilot need or want?"

Steph opened her mouth to speak but just then Amy returned to their aisle. "Sorry for overhearing—shifter hearing, you know. Are you talking about Craig MacMathan?"

"Yes, he came to our rescue," Margot said.

Amy glanced at Steph's injured wrist.

"It was a grizzly bear attack," Margot said, not thinking they would be telling everyone they met what had happened to them. "We fended her off, she had cubs, but Craig came to help us out. We were really grateful for that."

"I was there at lunchtime—at his family's tavern, I mean— and I overheard him talking to his parents about the two female polar bears that had tangled with a wild grizzly momma bear. I hadn't realized it was you two though. I have a special item that might be just the thing. It's a small handy survival gear kit with a durable case. It's portable, waterproof, shockproof, and features tactical tools. It includes a para cord bracelet with compass, army steel knife, tactical pen that can be used for writing, self-defense, and breaking glass if he had to rescue someone from a car, an emergency knife, emergency blanket, whistle, small flashlight, and a fire starter." Amy showed it to them.

"I hope he doesn't have anything like it." Margot figured it was the thought that counted.

"It's lightweight and compact and can be carried anywhere, anytime, even when he's not planning to rescue anyone. I think he would really like it," Amy said.

"I'll get it." Margot figured, since they really didn't know him all that well, this was as good a choice as they could make. She paid for the gift and thanked Amy and then she and Steph left the store. "Okay, what do you think about the shifter tour? They'll probably give us the opportunity to explore the area in our fur coats. And it would be fun to do that in someplace different. Plus, we've never been on a shifter tour period."

"Yeah, sure. I'm all for it. I want to do everything we can while we're here."

Margot got on her phone and pulled up their web page and made the online reservation. "I'm glad we could get in this late."

"Yeah, me too."

"Okay, we're booked. We go tomorrow morning." Margot got a call from a Robyn MacMathan. Margot's heart instantly sank. Did Craig have a mate already? "Hello?"

"Hi, I'm Robyn MacMathan, Edward's mate. His brother, Rob, is one of the tour guides who will be taking you out tomorrow. Edward and Rob are Craig's cousins."

Oh, wow, Margot couldn't believe how relieved she was that Robyn wasn't Craig's mate. Margot put the call on speakerphone so Steph could hear the conversation too.

"Craig told us you might be signing up for a tour and we're thrilled to have you. You'll have a blast. Edward wanted me to tell you that he, Rob, and Casey will be meeting with everyone to have a hearty breakfast at six in the morning at the White Bear Tavern and then you'll be leaving in a couple of vans. You'll be staying overnight at cabins near where they will take you to a place where wild polar bears feast on whale carcasses the fishermen leave for them. You'll see a ton of eagles feasting there also. Be sure to bring your cameras and have some warm weather gear in case it gets cold. We never know about the weather at this time of year. All food, snacks, and sodas and water will be provided. We'll send you an email with all the details."

"Will you be going also, Robyn?" Margot asked.

"No. Not this time. I do all the advertising for the business, including businesses all over the region and we have two-month-old twins and six-and-a-half-year-old twins, so Edward and I are staying in the area for the time being."

"Oh, I don't blame you. Okay, we'll see Rob and Casey in the morning then?" Margot asked.

"Yeah. They'll both be there. Edward will be there also. Hope you enjoy the trip."

"I'm sure we will," Margot said. Then they ended the call, and she realized there might be a problem. "Steph, I forgot all about your wrist and your ribs."

"The doctor said I could shift because the splint can easily be removed. It should be okay, and I'll just run on three paws like I was doing when we were trying to get away from the grizzly mother and her cubs. As to the bruised ribs, those should fade fast. A couple of weeks and I'll be back to normal."

"Are you sure? I'm certain they will refund our trip if I call them back." Margot felt guilty that she hadn't thought about it.

"Don't you dare. We'll have a ball."

"All right." Margot was glad Steph still wanted to go, but if they did shift on the tour, she could just sit it out with Steph if her wrist or her bruised ribs couldn't take the shift. "I wonder what kind of shifters will be there. I should have asked."

"That would be fun to know." Steph pointed to an ice cream shop. "We have to go in there."

"That's exactly what was calling my name too." Margot could never give up trying out an ice cream shop in a new area and this one was just too cute to pass up. She felt the same way about cute little antiquey tea shops.

They walked into the Frosty Dream Ice Cream Parlor, their sign featuring a hand-carved, Arctic fox. It was all done up in pink and black. For Halloween, white pumpkins were painted with pink foxes wearing pirate hats.

All dressed up in a pink and black pirate's costume, a woman was serving up a hot fudge sundae for a customer behind the counter, a witch of green mint ice cream with a witch's hat, and for another customer, an orange sherbet with bat ears. At once, Margot realized she was an Arctic fox.

The other customers left the shop with their to-go sundaes.

All the treats they had on display were so cute. It was hard to choose which one to get.

Another woman came out of a back room, and she was also wearing a pink and black pirate's costume. She was an Arctic fox too. "How can I..." She smiled, instantly smelling they were polar bears. "Welcome, maties, to the Frosty Dream where we fill your sugary needs from the tip of your pirate's tricorn hat to the pointed toes of your boots."

Margot and Steph smiled at her. Everyone was giving them such a warm welcome, especially because they were shifters too. And maybe because they were dressed in costume.

"Ooh, two more polar bears have sailed to our fair isle," the woman said, the other smiling and shaking her head. "I'm Eliza MacGraw and this is my sister, Barbara."

Margot and Steph introduced themselves to the ladies.

"Oh, you're the two that fought a grizzly bear," Eliza said. "Argh, if you'd stayed on the High Seas, no trouble like that would have befallen you."

"Before ye know it, the bears will take over the whole of White Bear and then where will we be?" Barbara said.

Margot and Steph laughed.

"Well, we'll take off fifteen percent on your orders to make up for all the trouble you had in getting here," Eliza said.

"Thanks so much!" Margot couldn't believe how generous everyone was. "We're just here for the week but when we saw your shop, we had to come in for dessert. We love how it's decorated for Halloween."

Steph agreed. "Though who knows? Maybe we've found a place to move down to from North."

"See? What did I tell you?" Barbara said.

Everyone laughed.

The sign on the wall behind the counter listed all the different ice cream flavors and Margot finally decided on the dish she was going to order. "I'm going to get the Pirate's Bounty hot fudge sundae with maple ice cream and the gold candy sprinkles."

"Hmm, that looks yummy. I'll have that too but make it chocolate chip ice cream," Steph said.

"We're glad you came to visit us," Barbara said, tipping her tricorn hat to Steph and Margot.

"We are too," Margot said.

Once they had their hot fudge sundaes in hand, Steph and Margot sat down at one of the little round tables that had seating for four.

"I love how everything is decorated so cutely. Not just scary Halloween themes but suiting each of the shops." Margot ate a spoonful of her ice cream.

"I agree. And the shifters are fun. This is delicious."

"Yeah. It's great."

"You know, so far several of the businesses we've learned about are shifter run. You really ought to add yours to the number." Steph ate some more of her ice cream.

"It's tempting." Margot swore Steph was already sold on the idea. "So what's next on the agenda?" Margot loved to plan trips out too, but Steph seemed to really be enjoying figuring out what they were going to do this time.

Steph smiled. "Check out the rest of the shops and then go to dinner at the inn and give Craig his gift. We should turn in a little early after we pack up our things for the trip for tomorrow."

Normally, Steph didn't go to bed that early, but Margot figured she was feeling some pain or soreness from her injuries and needed to lie down and rest, if she could sleep okay. "That sounds like the perfect plan."

"You know"—Steph frowned—"I keep thinking about Craig saying he thought you looked familiar though you've never been in White Bear before. Maybe you have been, when you lost your memory, and you don't recall having seen him."

Margot wondered then if she was right. "Unless he saw me at some other location when he was dropping of supplies and then didn't remember where he'd seen me."

"But you've never seen him before?"

"No." And Margot thought she would have surely remembered the hunky pilot if she had laid eyes on him before.

5
———

Craig swore both his brothers were as excited to meet the two she-bears from North as much as he wanted to see them again, especially Margot. He hoped she was enjoying all the Halloween decorations in town. His brother Andy was off from work and Craig saw him watching the door around suppertime. Ben, likewise, kept taking customers' orders who were at the tables located closer to the door. Craig figured Ben would pounce on the ladies as soon as they walked into the tavern.

Craig was hoping the ladies would come in as soon as Andy and Ben were serving other tables and didn't see them arrive. But as luck would have it, Craig was serving a table across the tavern when he heard the door open, and he glanced in that direction. Two beautiful pirate women walked into the tavern, Margot and Steph, and he waved his hand at them. They smiled back at him and tipped their hats. Steph was wearing a splint, but he didn't know if it was for a sprain or a broken wrist. But Robyn, Edward's mate, had told Craig that the ladies had signed up for the shifter tour and he was glad Steph must be feeling well enough for that.

Standing much closer to the door, Ben also saw the ladies, and he hurried to get them a table and offered them a couple of menus. He was being his jovial self, but Craig suspected he would be making a play for one of the women, if either of them seemed to be interested in him. He was talking away to them, but Margot kept looking over in Craig's direction and smiling.

Craig was glad for that and then he finished delivering meals to a table and headed across the tavern to reach Margot and Steph's table. "Hi, lasses. It's so good to see you again."

"We love the tavern," Margot said and reached into a large purse and handed him a case. "It's a gift to you from us for coming to our aid."

He smiled. "You didn't need to do anything for me. But thanks so much. I really appreciate it."

"I hope you can get some use out of it," Margot said.

He opened it up and found it was a miniature survival kit. "Oh, man, this is perfect." The ladies looked immensely pleased that they had gotten him a gift he was really grateful for. It could really come in handy on some of his excursions.

Ben was still standing there, looking a little surprised that the women had gotten something for Craig when that normally never happened when he helped someone in need out. "Did you get their orders?" Craig asked Ben.

"I was going to let them have some time to figure out what they wanted."

So why was Ben still hovering over the ladies? Craig suspected he was trying to figure out if one of the ladies and Craig had more of an interest in each other.

"I'll be right back with your waters and some bread and butter," Ben said, sounding as though he better get on the ball if he was going to serve the ladies their dinner.

"Thanks," Steph said.

"Do you like the town so far?" Craig asked them, realizing

after he did, they wouldn't have time to look at their menus because of *him* now.

"Yeah, we loved all the decorations inside and outside of the shops," Margot said. "Most of the businesses where my shop is located don't do anything for Halloween. This has been a lot of fun."

"I'm glad you're enjoying everything. When it gets really dark out, it's like Christmas, only with a Halloween feel. Some have orange and purple lights, others have just purple lights decorating their eaves. We went with white and gold for more of a vintage pirate theme."

"I can't wait to see that. What about the cute ice cream shop?" Margot asked. "Do they have lights?"

"White, pink, and purple. Eliza and Barbara love pink. So for Christmas, the sisters are all set with pink, green, and white, and for Valentine's—pink, red, and white."

"Do they have mates?" Margot asked.

"Not yet. I imagine that if they both end up with one, their mates will have to like their shop the way it is. The sisters jointly own it," Craig said. "I heard you are going on the two-day shifter tour tomorrow."

"We are," Steph said. "We look forward to it."

"But no wearing costumes, I guess," Margot said.

"Absolutely you can wear them and then your fur coats too." Craig glanced at Steph's wrist. "Oh, how are you going to manage it?"

"I'll manage. I did before I had a splint on it by just limping on three legs, and the doctor said that I can just remove it before I shift as long as I don't walk on my paw."

"That's good."

Margot was looking at her menu and pointed to an entree. "Hmm, I'll take the Pirate Captain's Lobster dish—baked potato, and asparagus. Sounds like good pirate fare."

"Oh, the menu." Steph quickly glanced through hers. "I'll take the Bos'n Mate's Deluxe dish with crab, lobster, shrimp, and halibut, baked potato, and butternut squash."

"Would you like champagne to go with it?" Craig asked. "On the house, of course."

They smiled. "Yeah, sure," Steph said. "I'm not on any pain medication."

"Yeah, that's perfect for our first night here." Margot smiled at him.

Yeah, champagne, dessert, whatever they wanted. His brothers would give him a hard time after the ladies left for the night—in a good-humored way.

"Okay, I'll put these orders in for you right away," Craig said.

"Will your brother Ben be mad that you took over?" Margot asked, sounding a little concerned.

Craig laughed. "He'll get over it. See? He's smiling and shaking his head at me at the take-out counter."

Margot chuckled. "Okay, good."

Craig went to turn in their orders and knew he was in for a ribbing from both his brothers. Sure enough, before Ben could say anything to him, Andy came over to place a couple of orders.

"Hey, I've never known anyone you went to assist actually thanking you with a gift," Andy said.

"Yeah, that probably means one of us is out of the running," Ben told Andy.

"I thought you were always into matchmaking," Craig said to Ben.

His brothers both laughed.

Ben said, "I'm going to have to find a match for me one of these days."

"Mom and Dad will insist on it," Craig said.

Their dad arched a brow at them. "Aren't you supposed to be serving the customers?"

The brothers laughed again and began taking plated dinners to serve to other patrons' tables. Craig brought the bread and drinks over to the ladies' table and before long, he was taking the tray of dinners to Margot and Steph. "Lasses, here's your loot from the Seven Seas."

They smiled and he knew they were enjoying themselves here. Maybe enough to relocate to White Bear? He didn't even know what they did in real life. Maybe moving wasn't an option.

"If you weren't so busy, I would ask you to join us," Margot said.

"He has to eat a meal too sometime, right? And since your parents own the place, surely if your customers want to eat something with you, they would be fine with it," Steph said.

"If you're sure?" Craig didn't want to interrupt the ladies' dinner when they were here on vacation together.

"Aye, lad, make it happen or you'll join the others in Davy's Locker," Margot said.

Craig laughed. "Aye-aye, Captain." He saluted her, then he returned to the counter to tell his dad he wanted a cheeseburger, and he was having his dinner with two of the pirate women at yonder table.

His dad glanced at Margot and Steph. They were drinking their champagne and waved their glasses at Craig's father.

"You might have to escort a couple of tipsy pirate wenches to their bed and breakfast after dinner."

Craig smiled. "I am honor bound to do so." He grabbed a soda while his dad made him a cheeseburger. Then he thanked him and carried it to the rowdy pirates' table. "Dad said I'm to join me two beautiful lasses to make sure ye don't get too rowdy."

They laughed.

"We were telling each other how much fun we're having here," Margot said.

"I'm glad that you are." Then Craig asked what he should have earlier, "So what kind of work do you do? I guess you said you have a shop, Margot. But maybe you're independently wealthy also."

"No such luck. But yes, I own a dress shop in North," Margot said. "I'm the purveyor of fine ladies' garments, including costumes, such as these for scallywags who want to be seadogs."

Craig chuckled. He loved that the ladies were wearing such beautiful pirate creations and playing the game.

"I'm finishing up inn management training online and then hopefully I'll become a manager one of these days," Steph said. "I've worked in every position in hotels already."

"Both of your jobs sound great." He was thinking that both women could end up working here then, if they were in the least bit interested. They could always use another shifter-run shop, and one of the hotels might be in need of an assistant manager until Steph could work her way up to a management position. Though they might have families that wouldn't want them to leave North either.

"Oh, wow, the food here is so fresh and cooked to perfection," Margot said. "My compliments to the chef."

"Dad is a perfectionist when it comes to preparing meals. That's why I stay out of the kitchen."

They laughed.

"Not that I don't know how to cook, mind you. Growing up, all of us, my brothers, my cousins, and I learned to cook under his tutelage. But we all prefer to wait tables and let him do the cooking. We have staff who help him. I think it's because we're so close to Dad that it makes it harder to work for him. Ben does from time to time when it gets really busy, and Dad needs another pair of hands to grill. I do too if I'm really needed to."

Once they finished dinner, Craig said, "So are you planning on plundering anything more tonight?"

Margot smiled. "We might sound like a couple of tired old pirates, but we're going to set sail for the nearest port, grab a bunk, and sail out first thing in the morning."

"Did you come by ship? If not, I'll walk ye lasses home." He suspected their ordeal with the bear was the reason they were ready to call it a night after dinner.

"Are you sure you're not needed?" Margot asked, sounding surprised.

"It was the captain's orders, and when he gives them, we obey, or he'll make us walk the plank into the briny sea."

The ladies laughed.

"We wouldn't want that to happen," Steph said.

"No, I agree," Margot said.

"How about dessert?" Craig asked.

"Oh, we've eaten enough of your food for free already." Margot patted her tummy.

"Nay, we have plenty for our fellow pirates." Craig wasn't going to force it on them, but he wanted to offer it to them.

"All right, you talked me into it. I'll have the Triple Berry pie," Steph said.

"Make that two. I want one also," Margot said.

Then Craig hopped up from his chair and went to the pie counter and served three pieces up himself, then topped them with whipped cream. He brought them to the table and retook his seat.

"Wow, these look delicious," Steph said.

"Yeah, perfect for hungry bears," Craig said.

Margot shook her head. "Two little piggy bears. The dinners we had were perfectly filling and delicious."

"These well help you have the most pleasant of dreams."

Once Margot took a bite, she agreed. "Aye, ye are so right."

Then they finished their pies and Craig had the pleasure of walking them to their bed and breakfast while the full moon shown down on them and the snowy streets and sidewalks. All the shops' festive lights reflecting off the snow were on that really added to the beauty and Halloween atmosphere on the chilly night.

"I'm glad we had that hike to the falls and walked around the town to see the shops since we've eaten so much." Margot was glad they had brought their gloves and were wearing thermal underwear because it was a wee bit chilly when they returned to their bed and breakfast.

"You'll get some hiking on the tour and running in your fur coats," Craig said.

Margot really wished he was coming with them.

Once they arrived back at their bed and breakfast, they thanked Craig for everything, and he thanked them for their fine gift. Steph quickly left Margot alone as if she thought Craig should kiss Margot or something! It made for an awkward moment, but oh, what the heck. She wanted to do it and she took hold of his shoulders and kissed him lightly on the mouth, hoping he wouldn't be too shocked. *There.* She did it.

He wrapped his arms around her waist, telling her he was just as desirous of kissing her. She was glad she hadn't been reading him wrong. He kissed her lips like he wanted a whole lot more of this than she thought he would, since she didn't even live here, and long-distance relationships could be difficult to maintain. He ended the lip-sealing kiss with a brief soft one to say goodnight.

Then he smiled such a devilish smile like he was appreciative that she had initiated the kiss. She was glad they had kissed, and yeah, she was ready for more!

"I'll see you in the morning when you have breakfast at the tavern before you head out of town on your tour."

"I look forward to it. See you then."

To *her* surprise this time, he gave her one last kiss. "For the road."

She laughed and went inside and saw John Snow watching her. He winked and went back behind the counter. Oh, no. If he had seen her kissing Craig, she was afraid the whole bear sleuth would find out about it. She didn't want everyone speculating about where this might go between Craig and her. "Steph and I are going on the Halloween wilderness tour, so we won't be here for breakfast tomorrow or the next morning."

"You'll have a grand time. We'll fix you up for breakfast on the other mornings you're here."

"Thanks. We look forward to it." She said goodnight to John. "Night, Pirate Captain Snow."

He smiled. "Night, Pirate Captain Anderson."

She laughed and headed up the stairs. She reached the room and unlocked the door. "Just me." But she heard the shower running.

Steph called out from the shower, "Did he kiss you?"

"I don't kiss and tell."

"He *did*." Steph sounded like she knew that he would.

"All right, so this one time I'll kiss and tell. I kissed him first, if you must know." Margot didn't want Steph to think that she wouldn't take the first step.

The shower shut off and Steph laughed. "You are ready for a new bear in your life."

Margot smiled. She really hadn't thought she would be interested in anyone anytime soon, but Craig sure made her think differently about that scenario.

Then Steph came out of the bathroom wearing a bath towel, her hair still damp. "The bathroom's all yours."

"Thanks." Margot headed into the bathroom. "I'll be out in a jif, and we can go to sleep. You need to really rest up from your ordeal."

"Yeah, I'm feeling it. I really need to sleep. If I don't wake on time in the morning, wake me, won't you?" Steph started using a hair dryer to dry her hair.

"I will." Though Margot really wanted Steph to rest if she needed to. Still, they had a schedule to meet if they were going to be on the tour.

Then Margot took her shower, thinking about the kisses she and Craig had shared. She really wished he was going on the tour tomorrow!

6

After Craig returned to the tavern to work, Andy told him about the stolen car case. "The guy whose car was stolen was named Kyle Rider and he's a polar bear. He's new to town and it was an awful beginning for him."

"Did you catch the car thieves and return his car?"

"Yeah. The car thieves are in jail and Kyle was appreciative. He was glad to have gotten his car back in one piece. So I take it Margot is the lady you're really interested in," Andy said.

"Yeah, but she lives in North, and you know how that goes."

"Yep, you just have to work a hell of a lot harder to prove to her that you're the bear she wants in her life and maybe she'll consider moving to White Bear. Night, Craig. See you later."

"Night, Andy." Craig knew his brother was right and he did feel that way about Margot already. There was something about her that lit up his life.

He didn't believe he would get any sleep that night when he returned home, thinking about Margot and the kisses they had shared—and he was so glad she had initiated the kiss showing she was as interested in him as he was in her. But he didn't have that long to really get to know her while she was here. Which made him want to go with her on the tour group tomorrow, conscious of the fact she was with Steph and not here to date a guy. At least he could see her at breakfast in the morning.

He couldn't quit wondering why Margot seemed familiar to him somehow. He hadn't had time to mention it to his family, so he called Rob before he went to sleep to see if he or Alicia had any premonitions about Margot. "Hey, I know you're probably getting ready to go to bed, but I swear Margot looks familiar to me, but I'd never met her before. I would have remembered her scent. Yet she appeared different from my memory of her. She might have been much younger."

"We haven't gotten any premonitions lately or we would have told you if it had anything to do with the ladies. I hear you really hit it off with them."

Craig smiled. "I'm all for the family's help in convincing the ladies they need to move to our friendly shifter town."

"We'll do whatever we can to help...uh, yeah, okay. Got to run. I'll tell Alicia what our mission is. She needs me to change one of the toddler's diapers. You're having breakfast with the tour group in the morning, aren't you?" Rob asked.

"Yeah." Craig knew the family would be speculating all over the place about that. He rarely had breakfast with the tour group. But because Margot was going to be there, he had every intention of having breakfast with her. "Night, Rob."

"Night, Craig."

Then Craig called Andy because he knew he would still be up. "Hey, about Margot Anderson. I feel like I've seen her before. Maybe when she was younger. Can you check and learn if she has ever been here before, like lived here? Though I'm sure we all would have run into her or her family members at some point."

Andy said, "Yeah, sure. Did you ask her if she had ever been here before?"

"Yeah. She said no, but I'm not sure I believe that."

"All right. I'll sure check into it for you. Night, Craig."

"Thanks and good night," Craig said. But when he closed his eyes, sleep wouldn't come. He had to know the truth. Had he seen Margot before or not?

"You know you have to make your own choices in life," Steph said to Margot as they woke early the next morning to have breakfast with the tour group. "Create a bucket list. Really live."

"This conversation is about starting over here?" Margot asked. "I know you. You'll keep pushing me until I do it. But I mean, really, is it the best idea?" Having a fresh start after ending things with her fiancé did appeal. She was constantly seeing her ex-fiancé and the new girlfriend at places like retail stores, the movie theater, pubs, just anywhere. Even the library one day! And Margot didn't even think he read books!

"Are you kidding? I can't do it without you. And I want to live here with all these shifters."

Margot laughed as she hurried to dress, then helped Steph get dressed. Then they were out the door, while Margot was carrying their overnight bags, loving how close things were so they could just walk places and didn't have to drive to them. Otherwise, they would have had to leave their vehicle at the tavern for two days.

When they reached the tavern, Craig was there to take their bags and set them in the van, then invited them into the restaurant. Margot thought he was so charming, smiling, debonair, whatever he was dressed in. Today, he was wearing a rusty wool sweater and matching rusty cargo pants and she thought how well put together he was.

Steph looked at her like *he* was another great reason to make this their home.

"Come in and take a seat with the others," Craig said, offering seats next to him.

"Are you coming too?" Margot asked, hopeful.

"No. I would love to, but I have to make some deliveries. I'll have breakfast and then will head out. But when you get back, I'll have dinner with you. They always have a dinner afterwards and I'll join you," Craig said.

"Oh, okay." Margot really had hoped he would be taking the trip with them so she could get to know him better.

Craig introduced Edward and his twin boys as they came to the table.

"The boys are going to have breakfast in the playroom. I normally would go with the tour group, but with the young babies, I'm staying here for the time being," Edward said. "I still come in to see everyone off and have dinner with everyone upon your return."

"I don't blame you," Margot said. "And I'm sure your wife appreciates it. Robyn seems so sweet."

Edward smiled. "She is."

A man who looked like Edward joined them then and Craig introduced him as Rob, Edward's brother. He looked serious, not jovial like Edward and Craig. Rob said to Craig, "I need to talk to you."

Edward looked serious too then, like there was about to be some trouble and Margot sure hoped not, but he also appeared to want to go with his brother and cousin to hear the word. Still, he filled in for Rob, greeting the other tour arrivals while Rob and Craig left to speak in private.

"Well, that seemed ominous," Steph said to Margot, "don't you think?"

"Yeah." Margot was afraid there was some trouble, and the

tour group organizers would have to cancel the trip. She sure hoped not. She was really looking forward to this.

"Craig sure is heavenly on the eyes," Steph said.

Margot smiled, totally agreeing with her.

Then Casey MacIntosh arrived and welcomed everyone, smiling especially at Margot and Steph because they were single polar bears. Margot suspected the word had gotten to him right away once they signed up for the tour.

At least he was cheerful, but Margot suspected he didn't know about the concern Rob had about something.

"YEAH, WHAT'S UP?" Craig asked Rob, frowning as the tavern filled up with customers who were there for breakfast.

"I had a vision. We're going to have trouble on this trip. Edward needs to stay home with Robyn and the babies, and Ben is needed at the tavern. Andy is out on trooper business. I know you have to fly supplies out, but Casey and I could sure use your help if there's any way you can go with us."

"Yeah, I'll ask a buddy to help out with getting my supplies delivered. His plane was out of commission yesterday and I dropped off his medical supplies for him. I checked with him this morning and he said his plane has been repaired. What do you see is going to happen?"

"You know me and my visions. One of the shifters gets into trouble. She has separated from the group."

"One of the she-bears?" Craig was immediately thinking it was either Margot or Steph.

"No, an Arctic fox."

"Oh, okay. What happened?"

"I don't see everything, only that she is alone out in the snow and needs our help to return. We'll need someone to stay with the others on the tour while Casey and I look for the missing fox."

"Yeah, okay, sure." Craig would do anything to help his cousin out and help to protect the people on the tour.

"Another thing."

"I suspect the other thing is also bad."

"Yeah, Alicia couldn't see the vision well, but you know how she has visions of the past. She sees something about a young girl being in a coma."

"But you don't have any kids on the tour," Craig said.

"Right. It's a past vision. She doesn't know who it is, but she believes it's someone in the tour group."

"When it rains, it pours."

"Exactly."

"Okay, I'll join you for breakfast in a minute. I'll make a call and see if my friend can take my supply trip instead," Craig said.

"Thanks, cousin!"

"I always have your back." Just like his cousins had his. Craig got on his phone while Rob went back to the table and everyone was greeting each other, checking each other out, learning what kind of a shifter everyone was. That was the fun part of having a shifter tour. Normally, everyone just asked where everyone was from, maybe about what everyone did back home. But here, the main interest was whether they were the same kind of shifter or not.

"Hey, Johnson, can you take my supply trip today? I have a bit of an emergency." Craig had a million more questions to ask Rob about his visions, but he also knew his cousin would have told him more, if he had known more.

"Oh, absolutely. You've done this for me so many times after my wife got pregnant and had our baby girl, I'll never catch up on making it up to you," Johnson said. "And you were a godsend yesterday."

"No problem at all. I'm just glad your plane is fixed and ready to fly. Thanks. I so appreciate it." Craig was just glad his friend didn't ask him why he had to ask for his help. How could he explain that his cousin and her mate saw visions? When people were in trouble, Craig had to help them out. Not only that, but they were shifters, so if the fox was in her fur coat at the time, they couldn't ask for human help.

Craig rejoined Margot and the others at the table and ordered a breakfast of ham and eggs.

"Is everything all right?" Margot asked, both she and Steph looking curious.

"Yeah." Craig saw three female foxes at the table, or rather, could smell them. "Rob just wanted me to go with the group so no one gets lost. They usually have Edward with them."

Margot looked skeptical that that was all there was to it.

"I have a friend who said he would take my supply run."

Margot and Steph smiled at him.

He smiled back at them, figuring they thought he was just interested in going because they were going. Well, he was interested in that for sure too.

"So it says we'll be on a treasure hunt—going along with the pirate theme for Halloween," Margot said, changing the subject.

"Aye! This is the first year the tour group is giving Halloween wilderness tours—all Robyn's doing."

"Well, we can't wait. It's genius on her part," Margot said.

"I haven't been able to go on the Halloween tour before so I'm looking forward to it," Craig said.

"But you didn't pack to go on this trip," Margot said.

"I always have a bag packed for emergencies."

"Of course," Steph said. "Well, we're so glad you'll join us."

Craig just hoped this didn't turn out to be a disaster for the tour group. He wanted them to have fun, not experience something that could be disastrous if they lost the female fox for good.

He was glad to see that everyone was dressed in pirate costumes and were participating to the max on this adventure. They would all have more fun that way.

"You're not wearing a pirate costume," Margot said.

"Easily remedied." Craig left the table and went into a back room where everyone in the family had their coats and this case, costumes, if they didn't want to dress at home in them and show up here. He put his on and packed his other clothes in his bag, then returned to the table. "Better?"

"Aye, right smart for a pirate," Margot said.

They finished their breakfast, and everyone loaded up in the vans. Craig went with Margot and Steph. The three she-foxes and the two wolves were climbing into that van also. At least while they were on the drive to their first destination, no one would be lost. Rob was driving this van, while Casey was driving the second van.

Shifters were sharing stories about the trouble they had as shifters and keeping their secret. It didn't matter what kind of shifter they were, the problems they had were universal. Shifting and trying to make sure no one caught them at it. Rob had saved Alicia's life when she was a human and talk about not showing that they could shift and most of all, not biting someone and turning them! But Rob and Alicia had been perfect for each other, had all the chemistry, and their special visions that made them suit each other like no one else could.

They were talking about suffering an injury and healing up twice as fast as humans, like Steph would do with her fractured wrist. They mentioned seeing at night when humans couldn't. Or smelling scents that humans couldn't smell.

"Oh, yeah," Steph said, when a couple of foxes mentioned the scent issue. "Margot and I both got called on for jury duty at the same time. We could smell the defendant's guilt. Of course, we tried to ignore that part of our being and just concentrate on what the lawyers were saying, but we knew he was guilty."

"Did they find him guilty?" one of the wolves asked.

"Yeah. The prosecution was extremely persuasive, had all kinds of witnesses' testimony, and evidence. The defense team just tried to push the agenda that if there was any shadow of a doubt, we had to say he wasn't guilty. But we knew he was the murderer," Margot said. "He wouldn't talk on his behalf, but when he did at the final sentencing, he said someone else murdered his girlfriend. An ex-boyfriend. But the defendant already had a wife, was supposedly marrying the other woman, and then decided the only way to get himself out of this predicament was to murder the lover. He didn't want to have to explain to his wife of seventeen years how he had a lover he was marrying. The defense attorney tried to say the shirt he was wearing at the crime scene had been worn by his soon-to-be wife, but he lied about that. It had her blood on it, but it smelled only of his body sweat."

"Not to mention it wouldn't have fit her," Steph said.

Then they were talking about their best trick-or-treat memories as kids.

"We ran through the city as polar bears once, but disappeared before anyone caught us," Steph said. "Boy were our parents mad at us."

Margot laughed. "Yeah. We were fifteen at the time and we really weren't into trick or treating for candy any longer. We wanted to do the trick part of Halloween instead. It wasn't the smartest thing we ever did."

Everyone loved it.

"Oh, Fran wanted to be a veterinarian for Halloween, so she wore junior sized scrubs, a lab coat, and had Lenora wear her fur coat and walked her on a leash. Fran went around gathering candy for the both of them. Everyone loved Fran and her pet fox," Melissa said. "I was a beautiful fairy princess and didn't get half the attention that they got."

The three foxes were blonds, triplets, and they were cute. None of them had boyfriends and they had hoped a male fox would join them on the tour, but no such luck.

"I went as Red Riding Hood with my wolf," one of the wolves said. "That was my little sister, kind of the same theme. They thought she was adorable too. She had a ball. She always got tired of trick-or-treating, but as a wolf, not so much. And I took a buggy with me so when she got tired of walking, she rode in that. Everyone thought that was the cutest thing ever."

Everyone loved their story too.

Then they finally arrived at their first treasure hunt location. When they left the vans, Rob said, "Ye have an hour to locate the treasure chest. Beware the captain and his scurvy pirates who will skewer you if they catch you stealing their booty."

Everyone laughed.

"Ye be laughing, but this treasure hunt is serious business."

Craig thought this was great. Everyone in the tour group seemed to think so too. Rob divided the group up into two teams, the three fox ladies and the white bears and a jaguar stayed together. The others formed the second group.

Craig stayed with Margot and her group. He glanced at Rob, but he shook his head, indicating he hadn't seen any more visions. Craig suspected they would lose the fox when they shifted, not when they were in a tavern like this.

Then they went inside and waitresses in pirate costumes tried to distract the tour group members from looking for the treasure. It was too funny.

"If ye know what's good for you," one of the waitresses said, "ye be taking a seat and having some ale."

"Aye," another said. "The Jolly Roger will be docking soon.

Ye don't want to be getting caught looking for some worthless treasure."

"If it's so worthless, why would the pirate captain care?" Margot asked.

The woman gave her a big smile. "You'll be swimming with the sharks, dearie."

Margot and Steph laughed.

But then the ladies got around the gatekeepers and were searching for the treasure chest. A couple of men wearing pirates' garb patted their laps and said, "Come here, lassies, for a sit down. Join us for a rum."

"Thanks, but no thanks," Steph said.

Margot smiled. "I guess they're part of the 'show.' This is so much fun."

"Yeah, I couldn't agree more," Steph said.

"I wish we could have had a scent to follow," Margot said.

"It wouldn't give us the advantage."

Margot laughed. "Yeah, all of us could smell it then."

Craig asked Rob, "So have you had any more visions?"

"No. Nothing."

"Did you tell Casey about them?"

"Yeah. He's being a hawk too, watching over our flock."

"Good. Everyone seems to be having a great time."

"They are. And the shopkeepers who agreed to do this with our tour group, mainly because we bring groups through here on a regular basis, are having a blast." Rob got a call and said, "Yeah, honey. Any more visions? Okay... Uh, no, everyone's still accounted for. Thanks. I'll let you know when, or if, we run into trouble. Or if I see anything more. Love you. Bye."

Then one of the foxes whooped and held up the treasure chest. The tour group members all cheered and joined the fox to see what the treasure chest held. Inside the chest were minia-ture bottles of rum for everyone in the tour group.

Fran waved another scroll. "Our new location is a haunted house."

"Woohoo!" several tour group members said.

Patrons in the tavern were smiling at them.

"But it says we'll have lunch and a drink and then be on our way," Melissa said.

After everyone sat down at a long wooden table set aside for them, they ordered hot sandwiches, chips, and drinks of their choice.

Once they finished their lunch, they grabbed their personal items, including their little bottles of rum. The tour group had to leave in a hurry before the pirates came for their booty.

"Naughty," one of the waitresses said as the tour group started to leave. "I'll have to let the captain know who stole his booty or he'll have all of us walking the plank."

They laughed and headed outside, then got into the vans.

"Are you ready for the haunted house?" Margot asked Steph.

"For sure."

Craig was looking forward to it too.

Then they drove off again and Rob said, "We're going to find a treasure box in the haunted house. But this time, you might have to fend off pirate zombies and skeletons to reach the treasure."

When they finally arrived at the haunted house, the group got out of the vans. They did the same grouping as before and then they headed inside.

Craig wondered if this was where they would lose a fox. The place was dark, orange and black lights were flashing on and off, skeletons wearing pirate hats and vests were climbing onto the balcony to the second story of the house on the outside, and some were peering out the windows inside. This place was the coolest.

7

M argot was so glad Steph had found the brochure on White Bear. Everything that the tour group members were doing was so much fun. The other shifters all really added to the excitement, everyone enjoying this, eager to go on to the next phase on the Halloween tour— the haunted house. Margot got a call on her phone, and she glanced at the caller ID. Sheesh, her mother. She didn't go into the haunted house right away so she could talk to her mom. "Go in, Steph, so you get to enjoy everything. I'll join you shortly."

"Are you sure?" Then Steph whispered, "Oh, it's your mom calling."

Margot nodded, then answered the phone.

Craig was standing with them, waiting for them to go inside, but he elected to stay with Margot until she joined the others, which she thought was chivalrous.

"Yeah, Mom?"

"Where are you? I ran by the shop this morning, and Faye said you left on a trip."

Her mother had never come by the shop. What was up with

that? "I did. With Steph. It's a place where they do lots of Halloween stuff."

"Where?"

Margot never lied to her mom, but this time, she wasn't telling her the truth. Well, the whole truth anyway. "Kenai."

"Kenai Peninsula? I didn't think they had much going on there."

"Well, they do. What did you come by to see me about?" Her mom was usually to the point. No chit chat. And Margot still wondered why she would bother to drop by her shop.

"I thought if I talked to you about Howie, maybe you would reconsider trying to make up to him."

"Are you serious? If you're that interested in him, *you* go talk to him."

"Margot."

"I'm serious. He was seeing another woman! What don't you get in that scenario?" Margot glanced at Craig, who was listening to her side of the conversation. She hadn't meant to say all that in front of him, but for the moment, she had forgotten he was there.

"Men wander sometimes."

"This was before we even got married!"

"Right. So he was free to do it. Sowing his wild oats. You weren't even married yet."

"Oh, Mom, there's no talking to you about this." Margot realized her mother was never going to give up on her not marrying the guy. She guessed her mother, for whatever reason, really liked him and thought he was the perfect son-in-law. Maybe he was. But he wouldn't be the perfect mate for Margot. Even if he had any notion of the sort. "I'm just going inside a haunted house. I might need to rescue Steph. Talk to you later." Then she hung up on her mom before she could object about Margot wasting money and her life on this trip or say anything further about Howie. "My mother. I didn't tell my parents where I was going. I didn't think they would even realize I had gone. They're both lawyers and always busy. Besides"—she sighed—"they wouldn't approve of me going away to enjoy a week of Halloween activities."

Craig smiled. "Not fans, eh?"

"No. Not at all. They think if it doesn't help their social prominence, it's a waste of time."

"That's not fun."

"I agree." She was glad Craig didn't ask her about her ex-fiancé.

Then she and Craig went inside the haunted house and a pirate zombie jumped out at her. She screamed out loud with fright and fell backwards, not expecting that at all.

Craig caught her before she fell too far, which she was grateful for. Her heart was beating like crazy. She hadn't expected the fright—real actors moving freely about—and loved it.

She laughed and thanked Craig for the rescue. Before she could catch herself, she started kissing Craig, forget about looking for the treasure chest. She was probably too late anyway. And she was enjoying the kiss with Craig way too much. What if she did want to relocate to White Bear? She wanted to know if Craig was going to be someone who she wanted to see a lot more of.

Chilling laughter, pirates' banter, ghostly noises, screams, laughter, all of it faded into the background as Craig really got caught up in kissing her, their bodies pressed close even when a pirate zombie tried to break up the two of them. Until a glint of something gold caught Margot's eye and she pulled away from Craig. "Sorry. I just found the treasure!"

He laughed. "Thrown over for a chest of pirate's treasure."

"Aye. 'Tis a pirate's first love." For a moment, she stared at the tangle of dusty spiderwebs that looked like the real thing covering the treasure chest where it was mostly hidden on a pirate ghost's lap. She could envision a spider just waiting for her to poke her hand into it and bite her.

She finally took a deep breath and reached into the spiderwebs to grab the chest. The pirate that was sitting there suddenly moved, grabbing her arm and seizing the treasure chest! He wrapped his gloved hand around her wrist. She screamed again but yanked the treasure chest and her arm free. Her heartbeat kicked up ten notches.

Smiling, Craig served as her protector as he hurried her toward the others so she could show them that she had the treasure chest. All the way through the house, pirate women and men—actors dressed as zombies, ghosts, and skeletons—tried to grab the treasure chest, pretending to attempt to take it away from her.

"I've got it! I found the treasure chest!" Though it was too much fun just enjoying the trip through the haunted house, including the chilled smoky air and the "rats' tails" that whipped against their legs.

When they finally made their way outside, Margot opened the treasure chest. Inside were handmade pieces of coins to share with everyone. "These are so cool."

All the tour members had pouches or bags to carry their booty.

Margot pulled out a scroll and unrolled it. "And there's a note that states we have to go on a scavenger hunt next—in our fur coats."

"Aye," several cheered.

Then they got back onto the vans and Steph said to Margot, "You know we can see in the dark."

"Uh, yeah?" Margot didn't know what she was getting at.

"You were kissing Craig, why?"

Margot smiled. She should have known her friend was watching for her after her phone call from her mother. "He saved me from falling on my butt when a pirate zombie jumped out at me."

"Oh, yeah, that deserves a kiss. So what did your mom say about you going to White Bear?"

"I told her we were at a haunted house in Kenai, and she of course thought that was silly, but then I cut her off and Craig and I went inside and—"

"The zombie scared you so much that you had to kiss Craig like you were the best of pirate buddies. So you didn't tell her we're going to be in White Bear for the week, except for this little excursion?"

"Nope. It's best that I don't mention it. I can imagine them having a fit and wanting me to return home right away."

"Exactly. Which sure makes me wonder why they don't want you visiting White Bear."

"Yeah, me too."

CRAIG WAS SITTING with one of the foxes behind the seat that Margot and Steph were sitting, and he'd overheard the conversation about Margot's parents not wanting her to go to White Bear, which made him curious. He was surprised when she kissed him, but he hadn't wanted to let go of the opportunity and kissed her right back. From what he could make of the conversation she'd had with her mom, they were at odds over Margot and her boyfriend breaking up.

Then he thought of Rob's premonition. Every stop they made meant that they were getting closer to losing one of the foxes. He wished Rob could actually see the outcome of his visions.

Then they finally stopped at a couple of cabins in the wilderness. Tomorrow, they would continue until they reached the place where the whale carcasses were left for the polar bears to feast on—the wild ones, that was.

They all unloaded their bags, and the women went to one cabin, the men to the other. Except for the wolf couple. They weren't mated but staying together. Though Craig stayed with the women also since they needed someone who was "responsible" for the tour group remaining there with them. They got a big kick out of it. Casey had even tossed a quarter to get the chance to stay at the women's cabin instead. He had lost.

"Dinner, first," Rob told the group. "And then we all shift and run. Normally, if we're hiking, the fastest group on a hike who returns to the cabin first would start the dinner. But we're not hiking, and Casey and I will be making hamburgers and french fries for everyone. We'll eat in the women's cabin. After dinner, we'll clean up and then go to the separate cabins, shift, and then run. When we return, we'll have s'mores and cocoa, tell ghost stories at the men's cabin, and then be done for the night," Rob said.

"What about the treasure we find this time?" Margot asked.

"Oh, yeah, that's why we're running. We're going to be looking for something that has the scent of chocolate," Rob said. "So keep your sniffers on high alert."

Then Rob and Casey began to work on dinner while Rob asked, "So far, is everyone having a good time?"

"Yes!" everyone said.

Craig was glad for it.

"Are you going to do this again next year?" Amber, one of the lynxes, asked.

"Yeah. We've had a lot of interest. Of course we'll have to do new and different things for next year, but as long as everyone is enjoying the tour, we'll see what we can come up with."

"Did anyone get scared in the haunted house?" Casey asked.

"Yeah," one of the foxes said. "I didn't know they would be real live actors."

"Oh," Margot said, "they scared me to pieces. I wasn't expecting that either."

"Yeah," Wolfrun said. "I was ready to turn wolf."

Everyone chuckled.

"I loved the tavern too where the waitresses were trying to sidetrack us," Steph said.

"Not only that, but the pirates at a couple of the tables wanted me to sit on their laps," Erin said.

"Yeah, and he ignored the growly look I gave them too," her boyfriend said.

Then they all finished eating and the wolves headed into the kitchen to clean up after dinner. Then the guys went to the other cabin and Craig joined them, just so he could shift. Then everyone was racing out of the cabins in their fur coats.

Craig worried about Steph and how she was going to do while running as a polar bear on three legs. But she was getting along fine, and she looked thrilled to be running as a bear.

Craig walked over and nuzzled Margot and she appeared to get a kick out of it. He smiled at Steph.

Then Margot tore off when she smelled chocolate way off in the distance. There was a mad dash of wolves, lynxes, foxes, a jaguar, a snow leopard, and polar bears. Their tour guides and Craig were also keeping up with them.

But when they reached the location where Margot smelled the chocolate the strongest, she realized it had been a decoy. The wolves barked. Margot and Steph growled. The guides smiled. Craig was clueless as to where the treasure chest really was, and he was smiling to see how everyone reacted.

This time, Craig smelled the scent of chocolate coming from

several locations. The tour group members split up and took off in different directions.

Aww, hell. Craig was certain this would be when the fox disappeared. But he was supposed to be with the rest of the tour group while Casey and Rob went looking for the fox. He guessed they'd set this up too late for them to have a change of plans regarding the treasure chest hunt after Rob got his vision.

Craig saw at once that Casey and Rob were trying to keep up with the foxes, but they were fast and all three split up from each other. Craig was supposed to stick with the rest of the group. He couldn't keep after all of them. He raced in the direction the last fox had gone and hoped Rob's vision didn't change. He didn't think it ever would, but who knew? Or maybe it didn't happen now, but at some other time on the tour. Maybe tomorrow during the feeding of the wild polar bears.

Craig soon lost sight of the Arctic fox. She was small and blended in with the snow. Though an Arctic fox could run faster than a polar bear, if one hid in a den, the polar bear had a unique ability to dig him out. Not that one of these foxes was going to find a den to hide in. Craig smelled the distinctive smell of the fox going this way and of the chocolate. And he finally found her. But the chocolate wasn't there. It had been, which was the reason she had gone in this direction.

She acknowledged him with a little yip, and then tore off again. He hurried after her, hoping everyone else was fine and he hadn't screwed up by following her instead of some of the other tour guests.

One of the wolves howled, letting them know he had found the treasure. The fox and Craig ran in that direction, and he sure hoped everyone would show up so they knew they were all together. He saw the other wolf, Erin, heading for the male, and both lynxes on their way to join them. Then he saw Casey and the fox he'd been after. The jaguar and snow leopard soon followed. Where were Margot and Stephanie? Rob and the other fox?

As soon as Casey saw Craig was with the one fox, he inclined his bear head to him and went in search of Rob and the other fox. That's when Craig saw the she-bears coming out of the trees and he breathed a sigh of relief. Even though Rob hadn't seen a vision of them, it didn't mean that something wouldn't happen to them. Especially with Steph having an injured wrist and neither of the women were from around here and could possibly get lost.

Then they gathered together with the others. But they waited for Casey, Rob, and the other fox to join them. Finally, Craig shifted. "Let's get back to the cabins. They'll join us." He figured it was safer for them to do that and if they still hadn't heard from Rob or Casey, he would go out and help them search for the missing fox. At least once everyone was back at the cabins, they would be safe.

The treasure chest was sitting on a small sled and the wolf that had found it grabbed the pull rope in his teeth and headed back to the cabins. Even so, Craig smelled everyone's anxiousness and he assumed it was because the little fox and their guides hadn't shown up still. They had to know Rob and Casey were looking for the fox.

Before they reached the cabins, Casey and Rob and the fox came out of the woods. The little fox joined her sisters. They all greeted each other, and Craig was glad he'd made the right decision about following the one, and then having the tour group return to the cabins.

Once they were inside their respective cabins and had shifted and dressed, the women walked over to the men's cabin to see what the wolf had found. Though Craig was interested, he wanted to know what had happened to the fox. Had Rob's vision come true, or was it still to come?

When the ladies all arrived at the men's cabin, they got to see the treats in the treasure chest. Everyone had marshmallow ghosts, chocolate, and graham cracker s'more pops.

"These are so cute," Margot said.

"Oh, I love them," Steph agreed.

Everyone got one to eat while Casey and Rob made everyone hot chocolate with a marshmallow ghost Peep floating on top.

"Did someone get lost?" Erin asked the fox that had come late to the party while they were wearing their fur coats.

"Not me," Fran said. "Our tour guides were tricky. I found the scent of chocolate in four different places and I just kept going from one place to the next, checking them all out. Rob was with me the whole time. I guess he was afraid I would get lost. Then I heard Wolfrun howl that he'd found the treasure chest, and here Casey shows up. I figured that you all must have gathered around your boyfriend and thought Rob and I were lost."

Rob and Casey smiled.

Melissa sighed. "Casey was with me until Wolfrun howled and we joined him, then he went looking for you and Rob."

Lenora looked at Craig. "Yeah, and Craig was following me around like a huge lost puppy dog."

Craig smiled.

"Foxes have a great sense of smell. Just because we're smaller than the rest of you, doesn't mean we would have gotten lost from the group," Fran said.

But it wasn't that they were worried about that—still, Rob's vision hadn't come to pass and that was problematic too.

———

8

"We've never done a Halloween-themed shifter tour before. So we thought it might be fun for everyone if you would like us to share ghost stories," Casey said, as Craig and the rest of the group members settled down in the living room of the men's cabin to learn what was next on the agenda. "Even more so if you all have ghost stories—real or imaginary—to share."

"Yes!" everyone said.

"Okay, I'll start off." Casey stretched first. "This is a true story. We had taken a tour group out during the winter, and we had stayed in some cabins we hadn't been to before. That night, we were drinking cocoa and eating s'mores, like this evening, actually, and then we were about to split off into groups at each of the three cabins to retire for the night when we heard a man crying out for help. We were a shifter group on the tour like this one and with our enhanced hearing, we all heard it. Now, we were in the middle of nowhere, and you know if you hear a man calling for help, you have to go find him and bring him to safety." Casey took a sip of his cocoa.

Craig had never heard this story and like everyone else, he

was practically sitting on the edge of his seat, waiting to hear the end of the story.

"All we saw was something in the white mist of snow. Something white, ghostly, but we saw no footprints, and we couldn't pick up a scent. After about an hour of searching, we returned to the cabins figuring no one was truly out there that needed saving. For the rest of the night, we heard the man calling out, seeking help." Casey finished his cocoa. "None of us had a sound sleep that night. That was for sure."

Rob nodded, agreeing with him. "We didn't ever book those cabins again."

"That gave me goosebumps," Margot said, rubbing her arms.

"Me too," Steph said.

"Did you research the ghost? Did you learn if anyone else had sightings of it and had reported it?" Margot asked.

Craig was about to ask the same thing. He liked closure and if someone had died out there, then they might know who the ghost was.

"We could find nothing about the man. No missing persons. No one had died near the cabins. It was a total mystery," Casey said. "But yeah, we all checked into it. It was so real, we wanted to know if anyone had been lost in the wilderness recently, but we found no reports of it."

"That's a good one," Wolfrun said. "Can I go next?"

"Is it a true story or made up?" Casey asked. "Either is fine. You can share anything that you want to."

"It's a true story. A bunch of us wolves were running in the wilderness, watching out for bears and hunters like usual. It was nighttime of course, so we would stand a better chance at running as wolves and not see anyone we didn't want to. But then we all saw another gray wolf and howled at him, wondering if he was one of us or a wild wolf—a loner. He turned and looked at us and then he just vanished. Right before our eyes. You know when stuff like that happens, you don't believe your eyes, even though there were half a dozen of us who had witnessed it."

"Did you ever learn who it might have been?" Craig asked.

Everyone chuckled.

Craig smiled. He was like his trooper brother when it came to knowing when, why, how, who, what, where—everything.

Smiling, the wolf shook his head. "We never found out anything about him. It's hard to really research because he was a wolf. Was he a wild wolf? Even so, if someone had seen the wolf and it vanished like that, no one had reported it, so it was a mystery like in your case, Casey."

"Okay, I have one," Syliva, one of the lynxes said. "After my brother died, he haunted me for years. He was a trickster when we were growing up—snakes under my bed, turtles in my bathwater."

Several chuckled. One of the foxes said, "Eww."

"So after he died, several of my things would disappear and then reappear. Before my parents arrived to stay with me one time, I had put blue sheets on the guest room bed. Mom and Dad came down to breakfast and told me how much she liked the pink sheets. I didn't own any pink sheets. I figured in the early morning's light, she had seen what she thought were pink sheets—trick of the light sort of thing. When my parents left, I went to pull the sheets off the bed to wash them. The sheets *were* pink. But they had been blue!" Sylvia leaned back in her chair. "At other times, I would be washing dishes and feel a hand on my back. I could see a handprint on my back in the mirror." She waved her hand as if holding a magic wand and waving it. "My purse would just...vanish. I knew I had left it in the kitchen. But after a long search, I would find it under my bed. I never would have put my purse under the bed like that. I swore I could hear my brother snickering like he always did. He played pranks on Mom before he died too—buying her Guinea hens instead of turkeys like she wanted. So she ended up having to raise a bunch of noisy Guinea hens."

"He sounds like he was fun," Melissa, the fox said. The fox kind were said to be tricksters themselves.

"When you washed the sheets and put them in the dryer, were they pink or blue?" Margot asked before Craig could.

"They were blue."

"Ooh, he must have really loved you to visit you and play tricks on you all the time," Melissa's sister, Lenora said.

The lynx laughed.

"Okay, I have a story. It's a fun tale told by generations of our family on cold, dark, snowy nights. Because that's when this happened. It's said that cats have always had the gift of second sight," the other lynx, Amber, said. "But in this case, the lynx didn't have any visions, or he might have made different choices."

Now Craig wondered if that was true. None of the lynxes, the jaguar, or the snow leopards for that matter, had ever shared with him or the other polar bears that they had a gift like that. Definitely, Rob and his mate Alicia, had the gift of second sight, but they were polar bears.

"One cold winter day, a lynx shifter named Aiden, was bringing halibut home after a long, cold fishing expedition that he had struggled to catch for his mate and their young son's meals," Amber continued. "A sudden snowstorm forced him to take shelter in a dark cave, though all the while he feared for the safety of his family. Still, because of the blinding snow, he had to ride out the storm in the cave. The cave was cold and relatively dry, though the moss-covered walls glistened with ice. The cave appeared to go on and on, reaching deeper into the belly of the mountain. Upon further exploration, he discovered firewood and kindling stacked neatly into a pile, which he figured had been stored there by some earlier traveler. He promised that in the spring, he would add to the pile of firewood once he was able for some other person who might be in need of it during a winter storm in the future. After he started a fire, he warmed up a bit.

"Suddenly a loud, deep voice boomed within the depths of the cave. 'Who dares to invade the sanctuary of my home?'

"Aiden just about jumped out of his skin when he heard the male voice because he thought the cave was perfectly empty. He finally answered back, 'My name is Aiden. A blinding snowstorm forced me inside to take shelter. I would've frozen to death if not for this cave.'

"There was a pause, as if the person deeper in the cave was trying to decide what to do next. Then he said, 'Very well, then. You may share my cave. But leave the fish. You won't need it when you depart.'

"Now Aiden didn't have much of a choice. He was in someone else's dwelling without invitation, and he had to stay there to wait out the storm. He really wanted to take the fish home to his family because he'd worked so hard to catch it and they needed the food.

"Aiden sat by the fire forever, pondering how he was going to manage sharing his fish, just like he'd shared the man's cave, until he grew drowsy and fell asleep. Sometime later, he startled awake and was glad to see the snowstorm had spun out its fury. But his fish were all gone. He glanced back into the depths of the black cave but didn't see anyone. He guessed he couldn't even take one of his halibut home to share with his family then, which was what he had hoped to do.

"When he returned to the cabin, no one greeted him. He called his mate and his son's names but there was no answer. The door hinges creaked when he opened it. When he walked inside, he didn't hear a sound, not his wife playing with their son, no sound from the boy who would normally squeal and laugh and race around the cabin.

"The bedrooms were on the second floor, a room for him and his wife, and a second, smaller room for their son. 'Hey honey, I'm home,' he called out again, and to his surprise and relief this time, his wife finally answered him.

"She opened the bedroom door and she was as pretty as ever, almost glowing, he thought, her blue eyes bright and beautiful, her blond hair neat and orderly. She pulled him into the bedroom and sat him down on the bed. 'I'm glad you're home,' she said, but her voice had a strange timbre to it. Not metallic, but hollow, as if she were speaking from a long distance away. Before he could say anything, she added, 'I'll make dinner for you.'

"He hated to tell her he had lost all his fish to a man in a cave so he could survive the blizzard, but to his surprise, she said she had just enough halibut to feed him a meal. 'Where did you get it from?'

"She waved her hand in the air. 'A stranger brought us some fish. Our son fell asleep in his room, waiting for you to return home.'

"He told her about the bargain he'd made with the man in the cave. 'Was it the same man?'

"'Yes,' she said, but this time she looked close to tears.

"But Aiden was so glad the man from the cave had brought some of the fish to his wife and son while Aiden had been sleeping during the storm, and they wouldn't starve now. After eating, he felt like he'd been drugged. His head swam and he could barely keep his eyes open as he hauled himself to bed. He didn't even remember his wife coming to bed with him he was so groggy.

"At some point, he had the strongest feeling that something was wrong. When he reached for his wife, he was gladdened to feel her next to him, his fingers meeting fur. He was still in a dreamlike state, but he would recognize the feeling of his mate's fur anywhere.

"'Please listen to what I have to say,' she whispered in his ear after shifting into her human form. 'I gave my life protecting our son from a capricious spirit that lives in these mountains. The same one who took our fish from you. Protect our son and know that I will always love you.' With that said, she vanished."

"Oh, no," Lenora said.

"Aiden fully awoke with tears streaming down his face, but he knew taking shelter in the cave without permission had been the wrong thing to do. Despite never wanting to return to the cave, he did so one last time as he had promised himself. In the spring, he brought in kindling and firewood for anyone who might need to find shelter in a storm, though he was torn about doing even that. Then he reasoned that if someone took shelter in the cave, they would have something to warm themselves because they wouldn't stay there unless they had to. For months, he had raised his son alone, but that spring after he and his son left the firewood in the cave, he returned home with a bounty of fish and heard a woman singing sweetly inside the cabin.

"'Momma!' his son cried out.

"Aiden couldn't believe it. But when he threw open the door, there was his wife, smiling at him, giving their son and him hugs, telling him, 'You broke the spell. I don't know how, but with your kindness and your faithfulness, you did it.'

"He did it, he realized because he'd faced his fears and left firewood for some other poor soul should he or she need it, which made him wonder if someone else had done the same thing before him. The lynx and his mate lived to a very ripe old age, their son finding his own mate when he was grown, and fathered his own children, and so on until we have our family today."

"But that isn't a true story," Margot said. "Aiden could have turned into his lynx and made it through the storm to his home and never stayed in that haunted cave."

"And his mate would have been safe too," Melissa said. "Though I'm glad it had a happily ever after."

"Okay, so Aiden was a newly turned shifter and he couldn't turn into his lynx on demand," Amber said.

Everyone chuckled.

"I bet you tell that version the next time," Steph said, smiling.

"Yeah, I didn't expect a polar bear shifter to come up with the fur-coat scenario. Well, we haven't heard from any of the foxes. What's your ghost story?" Amber asked.

"Okay, so my sisters and I were close to our grandfather. He was the most fun ever. He loved to take us on fox runs, scare up fish dinners, and take us for rides in his old jalopy. And he loved to teach us outdoorsy stuff, like how to find a den or burrow to hide in"—Lenora glanced at Amber—"where no evil spirits lived."

Amber laughed.

"Or start a fire," Melissa said.

"Or how to learn if a fox is wild or one of us," Fran said.

"Oh, what did he say?" Wolfrun asked. "We're still trying to figure that out."

Everyone laughed.

"So we all went out with him to fish, and after we returned home to our parents, we got a call saying our grandfather had died the day before," Fran said.

"Yeah, talk about shocked. We thought we had a collective dream that we went fishing with him, but we ate the fish for dinner that night so we knew it hadn't been a dream," Lenora said.

"Maybe whoever was calling about his death got the time mixed up. Why notify you a day late?" Craig asked.

"He was home asleep in his bed. Our mom checked on him in the morning because we went with him fishing the next day, so she didn't check on him the next day because she knew he was spending the day fishing with us," Melissa said.

"Maybe she had the same experience. He appeared to be alive when she saw him," Wolfrun said.

Fran shook her head. "He ate blueberry waffles and had coffee with her, so I think he was fine."

"Did he catch any fish when he was with you and your sisters?" Wolfrun asked.

"No. He told us how to fish the right way for the millionth time. We just humored him. He was quieter though, more circumspect, not bothered by anything. Usually, he would be a lot more excited when we caught fish. But he had just nodded sagely. All three of us had seen the same thing and so to this day, we knew he had to have been with us one last time to share a fishing trip together," Lenora said.

"And repeat his sage advice. So that's our ghost story." Melissa folded her arms and smiled.

"That's a great one," Margot said. "Nice and spooky. I have one to tell too. It's more of a nightmare than a ghost story, but it seems so real."

Steph was frowning at her as if she didn't think she should say anything about it, which made Craig all the more curious.

Margot finished her second mug of cocoa. "I have this dream, nightmare, where I am in this car, and we are about to hit an oncoming car. It's at night and I was half asleep."

"You were driving?" Wolfrun, the male wolf asked.

"No, I was...I don't know, fifteen? I was in the back seat and felt the horrible jolt. I was seat belted in, but I was thrown forward with the impact and then caught by the seat back and fell back against the seat hard. The next thing I knew it was like we were in a hamster's wheel rolling, rolling, rolling, then slamming to a stop...upside down."

"Who was driving?" Craig asked.

"I don't know. It's like I'm keeping a wall between myself and the driver."

"And the front seat passenger?" Craig asked. "If you're sitting in the back seat, then your...the front passenger seat must be occupied."

Margot smiled at him. Craig couldn't help himself. He was a mystery solver at heart, even if it was just a dream—or a nightmare. Casey and Rob were smiling at him too.

"You're probably right. And then...I see a white light and people in the light."

"You were in the dark," Craig said. "A rescue team? Flashlights illuminating you?"

"You died," the wolf said as if he had the expert knowledge of what had happened in the situation.

"I...I saw my grandmother in the light, but she told me to go home. She had died when I was a little girl."

"You had died?" Craig asked, shocked. Hell, Rob had nearly died in an avalanche, but his brother pulled him out and revived him. After that, they learned, Rob had future visions. What if Margot had visions like that too but she wasn't revealing her ability to anyone?

"It was a nightmare. But I have it over and over again, as if I'm trying to figure something out."

"You had a near-death experience," Amber said.

"For real," Rob said, sounding so sure of it that Craig thought he must have had a vision about it, or maybe Alicia had. "It might be a reoccurring nightmare but it's about something that really had happened in your past."

"How would you know that?" Margot asked, sounding wary.

Not everyone knew Rob had visions, just their family and a few friends.

"I'm just sure of it." So Rob wasn't going to tell everyone his secret. But Craig suspected he would tell Margot when he could speak with her alone.

"So that's my weird story," Margot said.

"A near-death experience. That counts for me," the wolf said. "The added mystery of not knowing what had actually happened to you adds to the whole effect. What about you, Rob? Do you have any ghost stories to tell?" the wolf asked him.

Everyone looked at Rob to see if he had any other story to tell.

"We often see a boat on the water when we go on a particular tour, but it has no fishermen on it. When other fishermen tried to retrieve the boat, it was gone, enveloped in mists, and vanished," Rob said.

"For real?" Steph asked.

"Yeah," Craig said. "Lots of fishing boats have gone missing over the years. This one was different because it kept reappearing and then vanishing again. No one could ever identify it, so they don't know whose boat it was or who had been lost at sea. So that's a true story." But he really wondered if Margot had a near-death experience and why she wouldn't remember it.

Maybe she could have a hypnotist put her under and help her remember what had happened and then she could get rid of the nightmares. Maybe. Unless she ended up having new nightmares to feed into her old ones and that wouldn't be good at all.

But then he thought of Alicia's vision of the past concerning someone in their tour group. A girl who had been in a coma. Had that been Margot?

9

S teph told her story during their ghost-telling event next. "It's really not a ghost story but a true one. So last year on Halloween, Margot and I were having an overnighter. We'd given treats out to tons of neighbors' kids, eaten mummy dogs and spider deviled eggs, and watched *The Shining*. It was midnight by the time we were getting ready for bed. It had started snowing and it was frigid out. Suddenly, someone began violently banging on the door and it sure rattled us. A woman was screaming and crying out, 'He's going to kill me! He's going to kill me!'

"Of course as shifters we wanted to rescue her, but we were unnerved too. Margot and I each took a peek out the peephole and saw this woman with wild white hair covered in snowflakes. She was wearing a flowing silky white nightgown and slippers in the chilly wind, standing on my porch, no robe or coat or anything to keep her warm. Her blue eyes wide with fright, and we thought she looked like she was a wraith. But then she waved her arms frantically and said she feared for her life. We let her in, called the police, and they said both her husband and the woman got drunk, had their domestic fights, and they'd been called to their domestic disturbances several times a year," Steph said.

"Did the couple ever get help?" Melissa asked.

"Not that we heard of, but she never came to my door again. Thankfully," Steph said.

"That would be frightening," Lenora said.

"It was, but perfect for a wild Halloween night," Margot said.

Jasper Wright, the snow leopard, said, "I have one. I was staying with my brothers at a cabin we were renovating because it was so far out in the wilderness there were no other accommodations. After we retired to bed and fell asleep, I heard my sister calling to me and I went to look for her everywhere. William, my oldest brother, woke to see me peering into the bedroom he was staying in and asked me what I needed. I told him my sister was calling me.

"'Go back to sleep, brother. We don't have a sister. It was just a dream.'

"Which confused me because I was sure I heard a girl calling out that she was my sister. I had a fretful sleep after that. The next morning, William was telling our youngest brother all about how I thought we had a sister in the middle of the night. I expected Simon to laugh. But he didn't. His eyes widened and he said, 'Not you too. She had the prettiest blue eyes and said she missed us terribly.'

"'You saw her?' I couldn't believe that Simon had.

"'Yeah. It really shook me up. It gave me chills,' Simon said. William thought we were playing a prank on him, but when we returned to White Bear, we asked our mother about the experience. Neither Simon nor I could shake loose of what we'd heard, or in his case, what he had seen. Mom got all teary-eyed and told us we had a blue-eyed sister who was stolen from her at birth but no matter how hard she and Dad had looked for her, they were never able to find her. And being shifters, she couldn't contact the local police. There were no shifters on the force at the time. Learning we had a sister was a shock to all of us. My parents had never told us what had happened."

"Did your parents hire a private investigator?" Margot asked.

"Yes, several over the years, but she had just—vanished."

"Do you think she's alive and somehow called out to you?" Margot asked. "She must not have been a baby, but a grown woman if it was recent."

"It happened a year ago," Jasper said. "And, yeah, she's our age."

"She's telling you she's okay," Margot said.

"Or she had died and her spirit was trying to reach out to us, to tell us she was our quadruplet sister," Jasper said.

"Andy has been looking into it, but he hasn't learned anything, yet," Craig said.

"What about the cabin? What if she had lived there before and that's how come she made the connection? You know they say that renovating homes can bring out, uhm, spirits," Margot said.

"We kept the cabin and didn't sell it for that reason, and also because it's a good place for shifters to go to get away from town and run in their fur coats," Jasper said. "But we never have seen or heard from her again."

"Oh, wow, I want to help you find her," Margot said.

"Me too," Steph said.

Jasper smiled. "Thanks. We really want to find her too."

"Yeah, I think we all feel that way," Craig said, "once we learned of their missing sister."

Craig had heard Jasper's story before when he and his brothers learned from their mother that they truly had a sister, and he and his family had been trying to locate her.

The jaguar, Rex Manning, said, "Okay, I have one, if anyone wants to hear it."

"Yeah, I do," Margot said, everyone agreeing with her.

"Here goes. I was living with my mother when she was sick and before she died, and my girlfriend had moved in with us. Now, my mother knew my girlfriend was no good for me, but did I listen? Nope. She told me my girlfriend was catting around even though I didn't want to believe it, and there was no evidence of it. I just figured the two of them didn't get along for whatever reason. Maybe because I was close to my mother and she didn't like me paying attention to another woman, and the same thing with my girlfriend. I hadn't formally made any plans to marry her while my mother was so sick. But my girlfriend had put up a bunch of modeling photos of herself in my bedroom where we were staying. When my mother died that night, all those pictures were lying on the floor on the other side of the bedroom. Like they'd been pulled off and thrown there, but soundlessly. We hadn't heard a thing that night. But when I checked on my mother, she had died peacefully in the night."

"Ooh," Margot said, "a true story?"

"Yeah. It creeped out my girlfriend, but then she accused me of doing it because I never liked that she was modeling. And that's when she left me. Mom had been right. It sure was the best for all concerned."

"Do you think your mother appeared as a ghost to chase your girlfriend away?" Margot asked. "One last ditch effort to steer you right?"

Rex laughed. "Yes, for sure. She did a good job of it."

"I like that ghostly story," Steph said.

"Yeah, me too," Margot said.

"Does anyone else have a story to tell?" Rob asked. No one had any other stories to share and everyone looked like they were ready to turn in. "On that note, it's time to say our good nights."

After sharing the last of the ghost stories for the night, Rob went with Craig and the women to their cabin, saying to the guys who would be staying at the other cabin, "I will return."

Craig figured Rob was going to talk privately to Margot about how he knew she'd had a near-death experience. And that's just what happened.

The other ladies were taking turns having their showers while Rob sat in the living room with Margot, Steph, because she wanted to know what was going on, and Craig, because he already knew that Rob had visions. But Craig figured the other ladies were dying to know what Rob had to say about it too.

"Okay, other than Casey, my family and a few friends, people don't know this about me, but I have future visions," Rob said.

Margot and Steph's mouths dropped open.

"But," Margot said, "that doesn't explain how you saw what you believe is a past event."

"Alicia, my mate, sees past events. But once we mated, we've been getting cross visions—her seeing some future ones, me seeing some in the past. We're used to what we normally have been able to see but we're still getting used to the new visions we are getting. So sometimes we have a hard time figuring out what is going on in our minds. In any case, I couldn't envision anything for you in your past until you talked about the accident. To you, it's a nightmare, yet you still feel that it's partly true. I could see that you actually were in that accident."

"No way," Margot said. "I would have known about it. It wouldn't be just a nightmare. I could see having the nightmares after experiencing something like that, but I would still remember something about it."

"I agree, unless your mind blocked out the painful experience. We could look up car accidents reports through the police and news reports if we knew when it occurred and where," Rob said.

"I don't have any idea where it happened, or even the time of year. It's just all a blur."

"Since my brother Andy is a state trooper, he could look into it. What is your age?" Craig asked.

"Twenty-six."

"So he can look for an accident like that that occurred about eleven years ago when you were fifteen. Also, this could be a longshot, but what if someone could hypnotize you and learn what happened so long ago?" Craig asked.

"Do you know of anyone who is qualified to do that?" Margot sounded willing to try it.

"Melissa is a hypnotherapist. She has a degree and certification to do it. We can ask if she would mind doing it," Craig said.

"We are on a fun Halloween-themed tour group excursion. I'm sure she would instead just enjoy herself on the trip, rather than work," Margot said.

Craig understood her reluctance. What if she talked about things she didn't want anyone else to hear? "You and Melissa could use one of the bedrooms for the session if both of you are agreeable."

Melissa came into the living room and said, "I overheard someone might be in need of a session with me. I would be happy to do that with you free of charge, if you would like."

Margot let out her breath. "Okay. I'll do it, but somewhere private."

Her sisters came out of the bedroom they were staying in together. "The room is free," Fran said.

"Are you sure you don't mind doing this?" Margot asked.

"If it's about your nightmares, maybe we can uncover what you're blocking and you can be free of them," Melissa said.

Margot nodded. "That's what I hope for, certainly."

Steph said, "I'm going to take my shower then, unless you want me to sit in on it."

"No, go take your shower. I'll let you know if anything comes of it."

"All right, that sounds good."

Craig was dying to know about it too. If Margot could remember any more details through hypnotherapy, then they could investigate it further for her.

Margot thanked Rob for sharing his unique ability with her and they said goodnight and he left for his cabin. Then Margot left with Melissa and entered the bedroom.

Steph hadn't said anything in front of the foxes, but Craig was sure she wanted to ask Rob more about his second sight. Margot might have too, but she seemed to be lost in the knowledge that her nightmares were about a real incident and wanted resolution.

Craig made up his sofa bed while the fox sisters were in the kitchen making themselves some tea with chamomile and lemon, but he couldn't help wondering what Margot might remember and when one of the foxes would get lost on this trip.

MARGOT COULDN'T BELIEVE that not only was Rob and his mate both psychic, and able to see visions, but that her nightmares were of a real accident she'd been involved in. And to top that off, one of the foxes was a hypnotherapist who could actually hypnotize her and maybe she would learn what had happened to her and where.

She wasn't sure anyone could hypnotize her though. But once she laid down on top of Melissa's bed, before she knew it, she was in a dreamlike state, swinging on a swing at a park when she was about five. She was laughing, glancing back at the dark-haired man pushing her, vaguely recognizing him, but... then her memories fast forwarded to when she was about ten. She was talking, slowly, softly to a woman, who was asking her questions from far, far away.

Her mom and she were baking chocolate chip cookies. Margot accidentally dropped eggshells in the bowl and her mom dipped a spoon in and got them out. Before they could bake them, Margot was in a car and feeling the worst sort of dread. She could barely breathe. But something wasn't right. She wasn't supposed to be there, not there in the car.

It was night and Margot was half asleep. It was a long drive to get home and she couldn't sleep, yet she could barely keep her eyes open. Then she saw the oncoming lights. They were speeding in their direction, in their lane.

She remembered...her father...she thought...was incoherent. He was talking, but she couldn't understand his words. She was concentrating hard, staring out the windshield. Their car swerved and then it hit the shoulder, spitting gravel and lost control, left the road, and rolled, and rolled, and rolled. Tears dribbled down her cheeks.

Melissa woke her. And Margot realized she had been in an accident for real. But everything was so mixed up. Her mother... her mother wasn't there, Margot didn't think. It would be...it would be the only thing that made any sense. Margot had been half asleep in the back seat when the car came at them, and her father swerved to avoid a head-on collision.

"What do you remember?" Melissa asked.

Margot told her about the accident. "I don't remember what happened after that. It's like a black void. I couldn't even see my parents in the front seats before, like I had blacked it all out. My dad...he was my real dad. My biological dad. I don't know what happened to him." She wiped away fresh tears.

Melissa gave her a tissue.

"Thank you for helping me through this. I...I can't believe I couldn't remember any of this before—only in my nightmares."

"Physical and emotional trauma can do that to you. Do you recall anything else? Like what you were wearing? That might help to identify the time of year," Melissa said.

"No. It's like I'm just in the darkness in the seat, even though our kind can see in the dark. It's...it's just a void."

"It's completely understandable. If you would like, while you're in White Bear this week, we could do a couple more sessions, no charge. I would be happy to help a fellow shifter out. I mostly see humans to deal with their pasts. So it's refreshing to assist a bear with your issues. I'm sure you have all kinds of things planned for the week while you're here on vacation, but if it could help you, I would be more than happy to do it."

"I would like that. And I know Steph would insist I take you up on your offer. I think I drive her as crazy about the nightmares I'm having as much as they drive me crazy."

"Okay, just let me know. I'll work you in."

"Thank you."

Then Melissa hugged her, and Margot knew she had a new friend here. She hugged her back and then left the bedroom so her sisters could rejoin Melissa in their room.

Steph had finished showering and had retired to bed. Craig was waiting in the living room, sitting on the edge of the bed wearing a pair of pjs. The black top said Trick or Treat and the orange pants were covered in bats and pumpkins. Margot loved that he could be alpha enough to wear fun pajamas for Halloween.

The lights were on in the living room still, and she suspected he wanted to know if she'd had a breakthrough. She normally would have just retired to bed and talked to Steph about it, but she wanted to share what she'd learned with Craig, since he'd been the one to recommend Melissa to her.

As soon as she walked into the living room, Craig stood and

she joined him, then she sat down on the edge of his bed, being much more familiar with him than she normally would have been with a man she had just met. He sat next to her and took her hand and caressed it. "Did it help?"

She didn't know what overcame her, but she pulled him close and just began to kiss the daylights out of him. He didn't object—thank God—and placed his hands on her shoulders and began to kiss her back just as passionately—tongues tasting and stroking, mouths molding and lingering. Then she finally pulled away and shook her head. "I don't know what there is about you, but I just want more...to get to know you better and we only have a week." She meant to tell him about what she'd experienced, that the nightmare had been real. She didn't know why she was baring her soul to him, kissing him like she wanted this to go so much further. Which, truth be told, she did.

"I want the same. Hell, if I have to, I'll make deliveries to North, take people on sightseeing excursions up that way, learn if anyone needs rescuing and I'll be on my way, just so I can see more of you."

She smiled, and then her darn eyes teared up. "Sorry. My nightmares are about a real event, a real accident. It's still all mixed up, but I'm remembering some things."

Craig pulled her into a warm embrace and for the moment, that's what she needed. Someone to care about her more than her ex-fiancé ever had. If she had learned of this and told him, he would have said, "It's the past, get over it." That's the way he was. Just like ditching her at the wedding. His old life didn't mean anything. On with the new one.

But how could she do that when she kept having these awful nightmares?

"Melissa said I could see her for a couple of more sessions while I'm here."

"Are you going to take her up on it?"

"I sure am. I barely remember that my biological dad had even existed. It's like selective amnesia. I could remember how to eat and walk and talk, but big parts of my life were just gone. I didn't remember anything about friends or other family, just my mother was always there for me, and John was there. He's my stepdad. My mother married him a year after we moved to North. She wouldn't talk about my biological dad. Why wouldn't she?"

"To keep you from learning the awful truth? That your biological dad had really died? That you nearly died, and you couldn't remember any of it, so why make you go through all that pain and suffering when you had gone through so much already?" Craig asked.

"Maybe my mom and dad were at odds with each other. Maybe Dad had been in the wrong lane and not that the other driver had been. I couldn't tell. All I know was that the car was coming straight at us, the other car's headlights blinding me. Maybe I just didn't want to know that we were at fault for the accident."

"You weren't at fault. You were a kid riding in the back seat of the car."

"Mom should have told me."

"Maybe doctors told her not to. Maybe they thought you should gradually ease into your memories. That learning too much at once could...break you."

"White Bear!" she said.

"What?"

"My mother told me never to go to White Bear."

"Hell, you couldn't have been from there. We would have met you surely, at some point."

"Why would she tell me never to go to White Bear? I thought maybe it had a high rate of crime or something, but when I looked it up, it didn't. So I didn't know why she was so adamant about me never going there."

"We'll look into it. We'll learn whatever we can about it. Are you going to talk to your mother about it?"

"No. Not until I know the truth and then I'll confront her."

Steph padded down the hall in her witch's pajamas and said, "Do the two of you want the bedroom? I'm fine with sleeping on the couch." She smiled at them.

"No. I'm coming to bed." Then Margot kissed Craig right in front of Steph for good measure, not innocently in the least. "Night," she said to him and he looked like he wished she had said he could join her in bed and let Steph sleep on the sofa.

"Night," Craig said to both of them.

Then Margot took Steph's arm and hauled her back to the bedroom.

"Wow," Steph said. "I think you're really screwing this up by not taking him to bed with you. Okay, so tell me what happened with you and Melissa."

Margot knew that's why Steph came to offer their room to Craig and her. She really wanted to know what had happened during the hypnotism. "I need to shower and then I'll tell you."

Steph groaned. "If I'm asleep when you return to the bedroom, wake me up."

Margot smiled. Once Steph finally fell asleep, she could be a grouch if she woke her up, so no way was she going to do that. Margot grabbed her pajamas and headed for the bathroom and a short while later, she returned to the bedroom in her black cat on orange pajamas to find Steph sitting up in bed waiting on her.

"I figured you would be fast asleep."

"No way. I had to hear what happened."

After Margot told her the story, Steph shook her head. "Okay, you couldn't be from White Bear. Craig's right. If you had been, you would have met the other bears at some point. Unless your parents were real isolationists. But you couldn't have lived in a community where other bear shifters lived and not have ever met up with them. If the accident had occurred in White Bear, the bears would have learned about it, realized you were bears like them, and would have known you. You would have aged over the last eleven years, but they could still smell your scent and recognize it was you. When you described the accident in your nightmare to the others, no one knew about it. Wouldn't that have been significant enough for locals to remember about it?" Steph asked.

"Yeah, you're probably right."

"What if John really is your biological dad and your recollections are murky, muddied, mixed up?"

"No." Margot shook her head. "He's my stepdad."

"White Bear might not have anything to do with anything. Maybe there's some other reason your mother doesn't want you to go there. In any event, let Craig look into it, or his brother Andy check it out, do a couple more sessions with Melissa and you might learn more, or have a clearer version of what had happened, and we'll hopefully still have fun on our vacation here."

Margot let out a heavy sigh, then managed a smile. "You're right. We're here to have fun and we're going to continue to do that."

"You had better, but I know you and at the back of your mind, you're going to keep trying to sort his out. But others will too."

"You're right. Let's get to sleep or we'll sleep through everyone getting ready to go on the final part of our journey tomorrow morning."

"Yeah, and get left behind, but the way you and Craig were kissing, I would say there would be no chance for that."

10

Craig was glad that Margot had been able to get a little help with getting rid of her nightmares with Melissa's hypnotherapy session, but it sure made him wonder why her mother was so adamant that Margot shouldn't visit White Bear. And why, when he first saw her, he thought she looked familiar. But her scent was not.

He texted Rob with the news and then he texted Andy. Rob texted him back: *What's wrong with White Bear?*

Craig texted him: *I don't have a clue, but it's probably something her mother doesn't want Margot to learn about in the event she went there and discovered something about her past, possibly.*

Rob texted: *We'll have to clue Andy in on it and maybe he can uncover something with his trooper resources.*

Craig agreed. *That's why I already texted him and hopefully we'll learn something one way or another. Have you had any more visions?*

Rob texted: *No. We'll most likely lose a fox tomorrow sometime at one of the four stops we make. Just remain vigilant.*

Will do. Night, Rob.

Night, Craig.

Then Craig got a response from his brother.

Andy texted: *I'll look into it first thing in the morning. Night, brother.*

Thanks! Good night.

Craig settled back on the sofa bed. It was pretty comfortable as sofa beds went. He couldn't sleep right away though, thinking about all that Margot had told him. The business about her not going to White Bear had really piqued his interest. What if Margot had done something bad in White Bear and her mother was worried she would remember about it if she returned there? Or that law enforcement would catch up to her? A million scenarios raced across his mind.

Then in the middle of the night, Craig felt cold air swirling around his face as he was huddled under his blankets and thought he heard the front door of the cabin open. He sat up on the sofa bed and saw the door was wide open, the chilling breeze blowing into the living room. He threw his covers aside, bolted from the sofa bed, saw a pair of pajamas featuring orange foxes on black wearing witch's hats lying on the floor, and smelled the scent on them was Fran's, the youngest triplet fox. He peered out into the night. Immediately, he saw her fox's footprints in the snow. He hurried off to do a bed check in the room in case she had returned to bed by the time he had realized she'd gone outside. He was hopeful, but he figured it was not the case. Still, he didn't want to alert Rob and Casey that their charge was missing, or worry her sisters if Fran was in the cabin.

He walked into the room the fox triplets were staying in. Melissa and Lenora were sound asleep, but he saw that Fran was missing from her bed. Immediately, he called Rob on his cell phone. "We have a missing fox." He woke her sisters with his call. "Do you know where your sister is?"

They were sleepy as they sat up and then glanced at the bed

that she should have been sleeping in and realized she was gone. "Oh, no. Fran sleepwalks when she's overly tired," Lenora said.

"The sisters think she might be sleepwalking. No one was in the bathroom. The front door of the cabin was wide open, she had removed her clothes at the door, and I saw fox tracks in the snow," Craig told Rob.

"Casey and I are on our way."

At least she was in her fur coat and would stay warm. If she'd been in her pajamas and wasn't wearing any boots or gloves, he was afraid she would have suffered frostbite and hypothermia.

With all the talking in the cabin, Margot and Steph came out to see what all the trouble was. The two lynxes joined them then also.

Then when Casey and Rob showed up at the cabin, all the ladies wanted to join the guys in the search.

"No, I need you to stay here. We'll find her. We don't want to lose anyone else out there," Rob said.

But he was outvoted.

"She's our sister and we're looking for her," Melissa said.

"We want to help," Margot said.

Steph agreed. And then everyone got dressed and bundled up, then they headed out of the cabin, staying close enough to see each other so they wouldn't lose anyone else. The other guys and the wolf couple had all dressed warmly and gone with them. So much for Rob and Casey being in charge.

But Craig didn't blame them for wanting to help locate one of their kind. And he knew Rob and Casey were afraid they would lose someone else. With everyone's great scenting capability and being able to see in the dark, it didn't take them long to find Fran walking through the snow as a fox.

Once they found her and confirmed she was safe, they were glad her sisters had come with them because they knew how to handle her. Melissa said, "Come on, Fran. It's time to go back to bed."

Fran was glassy eyed and didn't look like she even noticed anyone there surrounding her. Not even Melissa who had talked to her. But she followed her back to the cabin, where all the rest of the shifters spread out behind them in case Fran decided to turn around and take more of a hike in her fur coat.

Craig had heard if a sleepwalker was suddenly awakened, he or she could be disoriented. He glanced at Margot, and she smiled at him. He smiled back. No matter what else was troubling him, or he was thinking about, when she smiled at him, that's all that was on his mind.

He moved in closer to Margot and she reached out and held his gloved hand.

Everyone else looked half asleep now that they'd found Fran safe.

Then they reached the cabin and Lenora and Melissa guided Fran back to bed. After a few minutes, Lenora came back out of the room. "We'll put a chair against our bedroom door. She usually only does that once a night when she's really tired, but just in case, we'll do that. She might have even been looking for the bathroom."

"Oh?" Craig asked.

"Yeah. When we've been on trips, she'll open the hotel room door and just stare out of it, like she forgot what she was looking for but whatever it was, it wasn't there. I asked her the next morning about the one time because she did it three times in the middle of the night," Melissa said. "She recalled that she was looking for a bathroom, but she didn't remember actually going to the door and opening it or coming back to bed. She most likely won't recall that she had stripped out of her clothes, shifted into her fox, and went for a walk in the snow."

"That's good to know," Rob said.

Then Melissa said good night and went into the bedroom to join her sisters.

Rob returned to his cabin, but then called Craig after that. "That had to be the vision I saw."

"Okay, good. So we'll be watchful, but we probably won't have a fox go missing tomorrow," Craig said.

"Exactly. I haven't had any other visions, so hopefully that will be our big excitement for this trip."

Craig agreed. "See you in the morning."

"Depending on how everyone feels after the excursion tonight, we might have a little later start in the morning."

"Sounds good." Though Craig would be up bright and early. He never could sleep in once he woke up.

"Night," Rob said.

"Night, Rob." Craig locked the door and this time, he put a chair in front of it just in case Fran still managed to leave her bedroom and thought of going for another nightly walk. At least if she tried to move this chair, he would hear it right away—unless he was totally dead to the world—and he would stop her before she left.

"HE HAD A VISION, Rob did, about Fran going missing," Margot whispered to Steph.

"Yeah, I heard that. Wow, that would be cool to have that ability, don't you think?"

"No, not at all. You would be worried about what was going to happen all the time."

"Unless you were used to it, and he seems to be. I still think you and Craig should have stayed together."

Margot smiled. "I didn't come here to pick up a boyfriend, just to spend some fun time with you."

Then Steph got a text message, and she pulled out her phone and frowned. "Well, Ames finally texted me! He said he couldn't find me at my place. Where was I? Serves him right. In all the time he has been gone, he hasn't sent me one message."

"What are you going to say to him?"

"I'm on a weeklong Halloween grand tour with Margot. See you when I get back." Then Steph began texting him and set her phone on the bedside table.

"I'm glad you didn't tell him we were going to be in White Bear."

"No. I didn't want him running into your parents someplace in North, which was bound to happen, and then him mention to them that's where we went."

"Did you ever tell him I wasn't supposed to go there?" Margot asked.

"Uhm, I don't think so. But I just wanted to be on the safe side."

Margot sighed.

"You know, when we get back to White Bear, I think you should sleep somewhere else."

Margot smiled, knowing just what her friend was getting at. "What if I ruined a good thing?"

"No way. Just think about it. Craig has probably got a place of his own. Maybe you could have dinner with him and then, you know, things could just...happen."

Margot closed her eyes. "He would have to invite me over for dinner and..."

Steph got another text. She checked her phone. "Damn, Ames wants to know where we are, and he wants to join us. He said I know he loves some Halloween stuff." But then she brightened. "Well, there we have it."

"We have what?" Margot was so tired. Running around in the snow to find a lost Arctic fox hadn't been part of her normal bedtime routine. As it was, she and Steph talked way too long at night with each other before they went to sleep.

"I invite Ames to stay with me and then you can stay with Craig."

"No. You just said you weren't going to tell Ames where we are."

"Oh, right."

"And we came here together to do this. Ames would spoil it."

"True."

"In no way do I want to impose on Craig's generosity to put me up for the few nights that we have left in White Bear."

"Okay."

"Night, Steph."

"Night, Margot. But—"

"Night."

Steph chuckled.

Margot did too. When they had been teens and had sleepovers, it was always like this. She'd missed doing stuff like this with her. And Ames would ruin that for sure. Unless of course Craig took Margot's mind off it. *No.* She was here with Steph, and they were having a great time. And she couldn't expect Craig to do stuff with her the whole trip when he had work to do at a minute's notice.

She just hoped she could wake up in the morning and not feel like she hadn't slept all night.

THE NEXT MORNING, Margot and Steph woke to the smell of bacon and eggs cooking in the kitchen, toast popping up in the toaster, and coffee and tea brewing.

Steph put her hands over her eyes and groaned. "I could sleep for another hour."

"I know. Me too. I guess we might as well get up and join the rest of the group." Margot got out of bed and dressed, then went to the bathroom, saying good morning to the foxy ladies who were the ones making breakfast. She wondered if they'd told their sister that she'd been sleepwalking.

Craig was setting the table and winked at Margot. She felt her cheeks warm, and she chuckled and shook her head. She wondered what Steph and Ames had been texting about last night. Margot had nearly fallen asleep when Ames had texted Steph again and again, probably because Steph hadn't texted him back.

Then Margot had finally fallen fast asleep, and she wondered how long Steph and Ames had been up texting each other back and forth.

Fran immediately apologized. "Sorry about last night. Melissa and Lenora told me I went for a walk in the snow and worried everyone. I rarely ever remember sleepwalking and I sure didn't remember doing that last night."

"No problem. It was invigorating and a little excitement never hurt anyone, unless you'd been hurt. It made the trip even more unique," Margot said.

Fran laughed. "I'll say."

11

When the other ladies joined them for breakfast, Steph still hadn't left the bedroom. Margot went to check on her. She opened the door and laughed. Steph had fallen asleep with her cell phone in her hand.

"Come on, sleepyhead. You kept me awake with all your texting last night. Come join us for breakfast." She hadn't, but Margot needed any excuse to get Steph out of bed this morning.

Steph just groaned. "I'll be out in a little while."

"No. You'll go back to sleep, and we need to get on the road after breakfast. Come on. You can doze in the van." Margot waited for her to get up and dress. She knew if she didn't, Steph would go back to sleep, but once she was up and dressed, she was ready—sort of—for the day. Then she realized she had to help her dress anyway.

Margot assisted Steph with dressing and the two of them joined the others and sat down to eat, everyone saying good morning.

"Sorry, about last night," Fran said to Steph.

"No, that wasn't the problem. My boyfriend texted me, wondering where I was, and we sort of texted each other back and forth way too late last night. It was my fault that I didn't get enough sleep," Steph said.

That was the thing about Steph. She was good at taking responsibility for her actions. Margot knew she'd be quieter today, and she probably would fall asleep in the van at some point.

"So you didn't tell him where you would be?" Melissa asked, then slathered blackberry jam on her toast.

"No. He never tells me when he's going to be home and takes business trips all the time. While he's gone, he never messages me, as if he forgets I even exist. So while he was away, Margot and I planned the impromptu trip and took it. I figured he would get home well after we got back anyway and he would never realize I had left North in the first place," Steph said.

"Good for you," Lenora said.

The other ladies agreed with her, and Craig smiled, looking like he thought he might be under the gun if he disagreed with the women.

"So what's the activity today?" Fran asked.

"We're going to an indoor miniature golf place that is all decked out in pirates, ghosts, spiders, skeletons, and more. They also have arcade games to play afterwards. Rob reserved the place just for our tour group. The treasure chest is somewhere in the building," Craig said, sounding eager to talk about the tour and not about wayward boyfriends.

"Oh, that sounds like fun. I haven't played miniature golf ever," Melissa said.

"I have." Fran lifted her cup of tea off the table. "I wasn't any good at it."

"Oh, me either," Margot said. "But I'm looking forward to it."

"Me too. I was as bad as you, Margot, when we played that one time on a lark," Steph said.

Craig laughed.

"What about you, Craig?" Margot asked.

"I'm just along for the ride."

"No way. You're not a tour guide so you can play." Margot wondered why he *had* come along. But before she could ask him, Rob called him on his cell phone.

"Okay, the others are ready to load up in the vans. Grab your things and we're heading out," Craig said.

After everyone cleaned up from breakfast and they loaded their bags, Casey packed up the food that wasn't eaten in an ice chest, then they took off for their next destination.

When they finally arrived at the miniature golf and arcade business, they all offloaded and went inside. Just like Craig said, it was filled with pirate stuff, spiderwebs, spiders, ghostly figures, and skeletons. They all loved it.

Normally, everyone would go in with family or friends in their own groups, but since it was a tour group, they just formed their own groups, and once that person finished, he or she would move to the next hole. Steph made sure Craig was with her and Margot and the two wolves joined them also.

Luckily, or unluckily, they were all bad at it. It meant they were taking longer for each group to get through, but everyone was having so much fun, laughing like crazy, watching how bad everyone was doing that it didn't matter. Some of the others even convinced Rob and Casey to play. They were laughing just as much, ribbing each other.

The last hole was the hardest and it took longer for everyone to get the ball in the hole at the top of an incline. But eventually they all started moving through that part of the course and finishing it and then heading out to the arcade.

There weren't any treasure chests in the miniature golf course, probably because it was too hard to find a place to hide it and the first person through might have seen it. Margot and Steph planned to look for the treasure chest in the arcade, but they soon got sidetracked. Margot found a Jurassic World game and Steph made Craig play with Margot. Talk about being a matchmaker.

Before Margot and Craig were ready for the engagement, the pterodactyls were going after the civilians and Margot and Craig had to fight the predators before they hurt the people. Man, was it intense! Of course the other predatory dinosaurs were going after the people in droves and after Margot and Craig also. It was terrifying as a pterodactyl flew right at her and she felt like sitting back, to get away from it as she was shooting away.

Then someone from their shifter group shouted, "I found the treasure chest!"

But Margot was too busy trying to keep other people and herself alive in the game to see what the treasure chest held this time. Then a pterodactyl got her. *Aww*. She glanced at Craig, he was still working at taking down the meat-eating dinosaurs, trying to stay alive. She loved it. He was quick and decisive, much faster than she was.

Then he finished the game and he smiled at her. "Do you want to begin a new game?"

She smiled. "I sure do."

But before he paid for it, he leaned over and kissed her. Their game was located inside a mostly enclosed vehicle and fairly private. She kissed him back. "For good measure?"

"To give me luck."

She laughed. Then they began playing again, having a ball. She was doing better this time, staying in the game a lot longer and nearly to the end, but she finally managed to get herself killed again. She laughed. He smiled. And then she got to watch him finish, but he didn't quite make it to the end.

"Three's the charm, right?" he asked.

"Yeah, let's do it." She wasn't even thinking about the tour group, if they needed to move on, or if anyone else wanted to play the Jurassic World game too. "Do you think we have time?"

"Yeah, we do. We have to save the world. Everyone will understand that we have to do this."

And then the fight was on. It never got any easier. But she was getting more used to it, and she was racking up more points and getting further. Yes!

Then her warrior partner fell in battle. "Oh, no!" But she had to concentrate and keep going. So she fought to the end and made it! She couldn't believe it.

He kissed her again. "You did it."

"I did. It's really a game of skill and chance. You were much better at it than me."

"But you did a remarkable job at the end. And I've played a lot of these shooter games. It just takes some practice."

"Are you ready to go?" Rob asked them, poking his head into their Jurassic World vehicle.

Margot laughed. "Sorry. I hope we weren't holding everyone up." She and Craig climbed out of the vehicle and saw everyone watching them, smiling.

Margot wondered if anyone had seen them kissing each other. "What was in the treasure chest?"

"Oh, these beautiful coffee mugs with octopuses on them declaring 'seize the day,'" Steph said.

Margot looked them over. "Oh, they're beautiful."

"Next on the tour is snacks and drinks. We'll be stopping at a restaurant that has just about anything you want to eat and great appetizers. And yes, it's dressed out in Halloween decorations," Rob said. "For this tour, we made sure everywhere that we stopped at is, and also that they would be willing to hide our treasure boxes. Everyone's been so agreeable because they know we'll be bringing in lots of customers. Goodwill for everyone all the way around."

"That's fantastic," Wolfrun said.

And then they were on their way.

"Wow, the two of you sure find a way to share a moment," Steph said to Margot.

"What do you mean?" She was sure then that Steph had seen them kissing.

"You were playing that game together in privacy. The two of you are so cute together. You can't deny it."

"It was a fun game."

"Yeah. I saw."

Margot chuckled. She should have known Steph would have peeked when they were kissing, if she had.

"When we return, we have to talk about sleeping arrangements."

"Not that again."

"Yeah, that again."

12

In the worst way, Craig wanted to do some things with Margot—alone. Dinner out, or at his place. But he couldn't ignore that she was with Steph on this trip and that they'd come together specifically to enjoy their vacation. But then he realized he could still spend more time with Margot. He would just ask her to his house for dinner—and he would invite Steph too. Then he could get to know both ladies better since Steph was Margot's good friend.

As soon as they left the van, he planned to ask them both over for dinner. They would have dinner with the group when they arrived back in White Bear tonight, but tomorrow night, he could have them over. If they agreed, he needed to ask them what they would like to eat first and then he would go to the grocery store and pick up whatever he needed.

Then they arrived at the restaurant for lunch, and he wanted to wait to be able to talk to the ladies alone. The restaurant had several empty tables, and everybody moved inside to pick a table. Craig said to Margot and Steph, "Would you both like to come to my home for dinner tomorrow night?"

"Oh, I couldn't," Steph said.

Margot frowned at her.

Steph took her seat at a table and Craig and Margot joined her. The lynxes followed them in and sat at their table. "I have a confession to make. Ames is showing up tomorrow night. He was going to have dinner with us, but this works out great. I'll have dinner with Ames, and then you can have dinner with Craig," Steph said.

Margot's jaw dropped. "That was why you were saying we might need to have different sleeping arrangements?"

Craig's ears perked up. "I've got two extra rooms. A few of us do in case all the lodging is booked in White Bear and travelers need an emergency place to stay."

"Well, I think we have an emergency, if you could put—" Steph said.

"Steph and her boyfriend up for the night or a few nights," Margot said.

Steph laughed.

Craig smiled. "I would be glad to have you stay with me for however long you want, Margot, if it's something you wouldn't mind doing."

"Well," Margot said in an exaggerated way, "it seems I'm in need of a room."

"Sorry," Steph said. "You know how persuasive Ames can be when he wants to see me."

"Yeah."

Craig was thrilled about the change of plans, but he hoped Margot wasn't put out about it. "Okay, then dinner tomorrow night with me, Margot, and then you'll be staying with me."

Then the server came and gave them menus, and everyone was eager to decide on what to eat for appetizers.

"You're really all right with this, aren't you?" Steph asked Margot.

Margot said, "Of course. You and I have known each other for eleven years. I'm glad he wants to see you so badly."

"I...I think he's going to propose."

Margot raised her brows. "Oh, wow. Then yes, of course, you've got to be with him! Why didn't you say that to begin with?"

Steph shrugged. "Because you know him. I get my hopes up and then nothing comes of it."

"Then you propose to him."

"I'm going to. This time, I am." Steph sounded serious. "I think."

Craig wondered if Ames was going to ask her this time. But no matter what happened, he was glad he could spend some more time with Margot.

The lynxes were both listening in on the conversation, of course, though looking over their menus as if they weren't. Everyone in the tour group would know about the polar bears' sleeping arrangements in record time, Craig figured. His brothers would tease him. His cousins too. Craig smiled. He could take all the cheerful ribbing they wanted to dish out.

They soon were talking about one of the golf pros in the bunch, not a real pro, but apparently Jasper, the snow leopard, had made a hole in one on all of the miniature greens. "Yeah, he kept swearing he just had a keen eye for making the hole," Sylvia said.

"Ha! I bet he goes out and golfs all the time. He took his time playing but he still beat everyone's time at every green because he knocked the ball into the hole on the first shot," Amber said.

"He was good-natured about having to wait for the rest of us as we fumbled around with our balls though," Sylvia said.

Margot, Steph, and Craig chuckled.

"So we really don't know Jasper that well. What's the truth? Do you know if he is out golfing all the time?" Amber asked.

Craig smiled. "Not that I know of. But now I'm curious. He and his triplet brothers have gotten into the business of flipping houses. So they're usually pretty tied up with that. But he wanted to go with us on a shifter tour and see what we were all doing for a Halloween-themed one. His brothers stayed home to work on another house."

"Oh, cool," Margot said. "I watch all kinds of house flipper shows. There's even a haunted house series, a murder house one, and a zombie house series, which all are perfect for Halloween."

"Now those sound like cool shows to watch. I can guess at the haunted house one. People who have lived or visited there say the house is haunted," Craig said.

"Yeah, someone has died in the home," Margot confirmed.

"But that would be like the murder house show," Steph said.

"That one may or may not have a ghost, but someone was actually murdered in the home. The other could be just someone who died of a natural death or an accident," Margot said.

"Ahh, okay," Steph said.

"You know in Alaska, a real estate agent has to disclose the information about a murder or suicide that has taken place in the home within the last year that they're trying to sell to a potential buyer, but if they don't know about it, they don't have to and they're not liable," Margot said.

"That sounds like an easy out," Sylvia said. "They could just say they didn't know when they really did and didn't want to jinx the sale of the house."

"Yeah, that's what I was thinking," Steph said.

Then their salmon, halibut, and shrimp dishes were brought to the table, and everyone began eating.

"So what about the zombie house?" Craig asked.

Margot laughed. "That show caught my attention just

because of the name. In most cases, you would think the best thing would be was to just condemn the house and remove it from the land and start from scratch. But they will take these zombie houses that are like the living dead—and revamp them from the foundations to the rooftops and voila, they're beautiful. You would never know they had been beat-up old places, with rotting, termite-eaten wood, with mold throughout, water pipe issues, broken ceiling trusses, sagging, leaking roofs, water damage, just amazing. They were total eyesores in the neighborhood. But what I find is just as fascinating is that they take overgrown vegetation and clean it up and the place just isn't the same any longer."

"That's not all she watches," Steph said, as if she was going to tell about another of Margot's obsessions. Everyone waited to learn what else she watched. "Besides zombie shows and house flipper series, she watches hoarder shows."

"Oh," Sylvia said, "I watch those. I see all that new stuff being tossed out because it has been water damaged, or rodent chewed on or worse, and I want to take some of it—I mean a few items—home. Some of them have beautiful paintings, or sculptures, birdbaths, water fountains. But all the treasures are buried under piles of stuff, most often just trash. They don't have a long time to get these peoples' homes in order before they're kicked out and the homes are condemned—only a couple of days, so they don't have time to find homes for all that stuff. But still, I keep thinking how some of that hoard could be shared and make someone who needed these things —especially in the case of a hoarder who has tons and tons and tons of new stuff still in boxes, never opened—given to them."

"I agree," Margot said. "In other cases, the stuff is so bad, so filthy, it's best just having it thrown out."

"True."

Margot glanced at Craig and smiled. "I like tons of different things to watch, not just those things."

He laughed. "I was going to see if you wanted to go to a movie tomorrow night after dinner."

"Sure, I would love to." Margot said to Steph, "See what you're missing out on?"

"Yeah, and if Ames doesn't propose to me and I decide I don't want to propose to him, I'm going to be annoyed with him." Steph took a bite of her salmon.

Margot laughed.

Craig was curious how it would all work out but he planned to make it up to Margot for losing her friend on this trip to her boyfriend.

"So where are we going to find the treasure chest this time?" Sylvia asked.

"Oh, look under your plate after you've eaten," Craig said. "Someone has the ticket to the treasure chest."

The lynxes both lifted their plates high, even though they still had shrimp and stuffed mushrooms left to eat, but they couldn't wait.

"Not me," Sylvia said.

"Not me either," Amber said.

Craig knew he wasn't supposed to get one so he didn't look. But Margot and Steph had to look under their plates. Steph whooped! "I got the magic ticket!"

The rest of the tour group clapped. Even others in the restaurant did, just to add to the comradery. A server brought the treasure chest to Steph, and everyone waited for her to open it to see what they got this time.

"Jolly Roger T-shirts for each of us," Steph said.

Then Rob handed them out to everyone.

The prizes made the cost of the trip totally worthwhile.

After lunch, they drove to where the wild polar bears had

their dinner. Even though they were polar bear shifters, Margot and Stephanie had never seen a wild polar bear eat on a whale carcass. It was amazing to see all the eagles there looking for good eats and lots of polar bears, when normally they were territorial over their area and their food. But there was so much food for them, they didn't need to quibble over it.

"This makes me think of how we're not supposed to feed wild bears, or they get used to being around people and become dangerous," Margot said, taking lots of pictures.

"Yeah, I know, right? But all that's left over from the whaler's hunt would go to waste, so it's good that the wild animals can have a feast. The whalers aren't actually hand feeding them. They drop them off and then they're gone," Steph said.

"That's true."

Craig agreed with both of the ladies.

Everyone was thrilled to have a chance to see this firsthand. Then after an hour, they finally gathered back at the vans for the long trip back.

"We'll be stopping for ice cream at an ice cream parlor on the way back," Rob said, "and to find another treasure chest. And then there will be one last treasure chest at the White Bear Tavern when we return and have dinner."

ON THE TRIP to the ice cream parlor on the way back home, Steph said to Margot, "You're not sore with me, are you? I know I should have told you that Ames wanted to see me, but it was in the middle of the night, and when it comes to seeing him, you know me. I just can't say no."

"Of course. What if he really is coming here to ask you if you'll marry him? No way would I want to stand in the way of that. Though you have to know I'll be missing our time together once you're mated and busy with him."

"No way. He isn't giving up his job, which means he'll continue to travel and I'll have the same amount of time to spend with you. Well, in the evenings or any free time I have, once I have a job."

"So I guess that means no moving to White Bear if you end up mating him." There were other bachelor polar bears here and Margot had thought maybe Steph might even be intrigued with one of them if things weren't ever going to work out between her and Ames.

"Oh, well, nothing's decided until it's decided, you know. We have to wait to see what happens with Ames. Hmm, so does this mean you are seriously thinking of moving there permanently?" Steph raised her brows and smiled.

"No, I'm just mentioning it in case something happened to change my mind."

"Well, I believe there's someone here who's eager to see more of you while there's no one back home like that. And if things don't work out with one, there are more brothers to consider."

Margot laughed. "You're too funny." She wanted to ask Steph if she was interested in one of the single polar bears, Craig's brothers, or Casey, if things didn't work out with Ames like Steph was hoping for. But at least Steph didn't sound like she was going to be terribly surprised if Ames didn't propose a mating this time either.

"If you decide you don't want to stay with Craig—and I'm serious about this—maybe he could put Ames up at his place, you and I will continue to stay at our bed and breakfast, and Ames and I will meet up for dinner still."

Margot smiled at her. "I'm sure Craig isn't put out about it and I'm fine with it. I would feel more uncomfortable if you and I stayed together when Ames wanted to be with you, possibly to propose to you. Okay, so what if I ended up moving down here—"

"I knew you were seriously considering it!"

"And you stayed back in North with Ames? We wouldn't be able to see much of each other then."

"Oh, well, if that happened, I might have to rethink my situation with Ames." Then Steph chuckled.

Margot would miss her. She was always fun to be around.

"So when are you going to have your next hypnotism session with Melissa?" Steph asked.

"I guess when she has some time available. She's not seeing me as a paying client, and it's really late to be making appointments, so she'll have to tell me when it's convenient for her."

"Okay. Well, be sure and tell me what happens during the next session."

"I will. Unless you're too busy."

"No way. I'm never too busy for something like that. We need to take care of these nightmares you're having."

"You know, last night was the first night I didn't have one in a long time. Maybe that one session really did the trick."

"That's great!" Then Steph got quiet, and Margot began thinking about everything she'd dredged up during the therapy session.

Something just wasn't right about it. She kept feeling like she was hiding in the back seat of the car, hiding from the truth. But what was the truth? She couldn't figure out why she couldn't remember what had happened to her. Worse, her mother refused to take her to see a psychologist for the gaps in her memory when she was younger and by the time Margot was old enough to do it on her own, she didn't care. She'd lived so long without knowing, why dig up the past?

She supposed it was because she was a coward and really didn't want to know. Still, she felt better about it now that she'd tried to come to grips with it. Especially since the nightmares had been plaguing her for so long and for the first time in forever, she hadn't had a nightmare terrorizing her sleep.

She glanced at Steph and saw she was leaning against the van window, sound asleep. Margot smiled. Steph hadn't gotten enough sleep last night, too busy texting Ames. Margot didn't know how she felt about him. He was a likeable guy, had a good job, but Margot didn't like how he just wouldn't make a firm commitment to Steph. She knew her friend tried to pretend it didn't matter, but Margot figured it did.

When they finally arrived at the ice cream shop, Steph was wide awake, smiling. "I guess I nodded off."

"It's probably good that you did."

"Right. I still want to go with you to the Halloween party and all, by the way. I told Ames we would be together sometimes, but when you and I wanted to go and do our Halloween stuff, he had to figure things out for himself. He said he would get some work done online."

"He could go with us, if he wants."

"He might do some of it."

"Okay, that works for me." Margot didn't want to be a third wheel if the two of them were having a great time.

13

The tour group members all went into the ice cream shop that had Tiffany-style, stained glass hanging lanterns, stained glass windows featuring ice cream cones on narrow side windows, faux marble tables, and wrought iron chairs with floral vinyl seats and booths all along one wall. The shop was so cute and quaint, all decorated in pumpkins.

They took seats in the various booths and tables and then two woman dressed in pirate costumes were taking orders from each of the tables. Jasper suddenly said, "Ha! The server has a little tag of a pirate's chest on her pirate's hat."

She smiled and gave him the tag.

Jasper turned it over and said, "We all are receiving a pirate's deck of cards, maties!"

A bunch of "arghs" were heard from several of the tour group members, all of them raising their water glasses in salute, and everyone laughed.

"We normally wear any costume we want for Halloween, but Rob convinced us that a bunch of pirates were visiting from the far corners of the earth, so we're glad we dressed just right to receive ye," the one woman said to the shifters there.

"There be tips in it for ye, lass, for sure," Jasper said and winked at the server.

She promptly blushed.

Jasper was a charmer.

Then everyone's ice cream treats were being delivered to each of the tables.

Steph got a text and smiled. "Ames will be at the bed and breakfast tomorrow sometime before dinner. I need to be there before he can go into the room. He said he would wander through town and meet up with us if we're off doing stuff. He has to see what is so special about it that we wanted to come here."

"I didn't think he was all that into Halloween."

"He goes to some of the Halloween stuff. Not all the time, but sometimes he's in the mood. Sometimes he's out of town on business. I think he just wants to see what we're up to."

"And a proposal too?"

"Maybe."

Margot started eating her maple ice cream, hot fudge sundae while Steph was spooning up her cherry ice cream. Craig had a hot fudge sundae with smores ice cream, and he smiled lots.

"Good, huh?" Margot asked Craig.

"Yeah, I haven't had ice cream in way too long. So what's next on your agenda, ladies?" Craig asked Steph and Margot.

Steph pulled out the brochure and pointed to the listing for zombie paintball.

Margot laughed. "Oh, absolutely. You know that I'm game."

"I knew you would be as much as you love to watch zombie flicks," Steph said. "What about you, Craig?"

"Yeah, count me in."

"Yes!" Steph said. "I already told Ames about it, and he said he wants to do that for sure. Me? Not so sure, but I'll go along with the party."

"What about your wrist?" Margot asked Steph. She kept forgetting about it.

"Oh, fine. It's not hurting, and I've been careful with it."

"But what about firing an air gun?" Margot felt bad that she hadn't taken Steph's injury into consideration.

"Oh, I'm good. I'll be careful. I can do things with both hands, like steadying something. I just have to be careful. No lifting heavy objects with my left hand, not until my wrist is properly healed. Don't worry. I'm doing this no matter what," Steph said.

Margot did worry about her and now wished they were doing a different activity that wouldn't hurt Steph's wrist. But she understood how she felt. She wouldn't have wanted to give up the opportunity either.

Then Steph pointed at the listing for the Wine and Candy Tasting Party. "And we can do this too."

Margot looked at the listing and said, "Really? Wine and candy together?"

"Yeah, my grandmother always combined red wine and chocolate, for instance. She swore by it."

Margot laughed. "Have you ever been to anything like this, Craig?"

"No, I'll go to it. I like both, but I've never had them together."

"Good. That's one thing about Ames, he won't try anything, so he won't go with us to that, I'm sure. I was so tired last night, I forgot to mention it to him when I was texting him," Steph said. "We should visit the haunted house. Is it really haunted? It says it is."

"Yeah. It's a 50,000 square foot building that used to be a hospital," Craig said. "It's used for all kinds of things, but they always turn it into a haunted house for Halloween. It has twenty-seven escape exits for anyone who can't handle the scariness of the place."

"For real?" Margot said.

"Yeah, for real. Maybe we could go as a foursome to it and watch each other's backs," Craig said.

"Ames will definitely want to go to that. What do you think, Margot?"

"We have to, or we'll wish we had, wondering how good it was. What about you?" Margot asked.

"Yeah, to be a good sport, but I don't know if I'll make it to the end," Steph said. "I might have to make a quick escape through an emergency exit."

Margot thought it would be fun to go as a foursome—safety in numbers, sort of thing.

Then they finally headed out to White Bear for the conclusion of their trip. She had thoroughly enjoyed not only the trip, but being with Craig for longer, having fun with Steph, and meeting all the shifters in the area who had come with them. It was a really nice intimate group, and she hadn't expected to run into so many different kinds of shifters.

When they finally arrived at the tavern, a group of greeters—including Craig's brothers Ben and Andy, and their parents—cheered them as they entered the place. Margot thought it was a really nice way to end the tour that way, well, before they had their dinner. The dinner would be the finale.

They all sat down at the two tables reserved for the tour group to have their dinner. They chose what they wanted to eat and then began to talk about their favorite parts of the tour.

"The polar bears at the whale dump," several said.

"The ghost stories," Sylvia said.

"Oh, yeah, they were good," Margot agreed.

"The ice cream shop. That was fun," Steph said.

"Saving Fran," Erin said. The she-wolf seemed to be really compassionate when it came to all of the shifters.

Everyone laughed.

"The pub was great," Jasper said.

"Yeah, they had delicious food and terrific decorations," Margot said. "Really, the whole tour was delightful."

Everyone agreed.

"We're back to work soon, but we have three more days to do some activities. What is everyone else doing while you're here?" Wolfrun asked.

"The zombie paintball," Steph said.

"Sign us up," the wolf said.

Then the foxes wanted to join them. The lynxes too. The jaguar bowed out, needing to return to Houston, Texas.

"It seems we have another 'tour group' lining up for some Halloween after-the-tour fun," Margot said.

Rob and Casey smiled. Rob said, "That's the thing that's nice about these tour groups, making new friends."

"That's for sure," Margot said. "We're going to the haunted building too."

"We'll go with you," Wolfrun said, everyone else agreeing.

Here, Margot thought she was going to be missing all these people after the tour was done.

"What else?" Melissa asked.

"Painting with a Halloween Twirl. It's for groups," Steph said.

"Count us in," Fran said.

Everyone looked at the lynxes and the wolves. They were all enjoying their food. Amber raised her hand, indicating they were in.

Wolfrun finished swallowing his food. "I can't draw stick figures even."

"That's what's fun about this. You don't have to have any knowledge of painting. Just go with the flow," Margot said.

"Okay, we're in," Erin said.

"Uhm, learn a Halloween dance," Steph said, lifting a rib off her plate.

"We don't have partners," Lenora said.

"No problem. It's like group dancing, not like couple dancing," Margot said. "Can you dance all right with the splint on your wrist, Steph?"

"Sure. I'm just going to keep my arm close to my body and not swing it around. I think it would ache if I did that."

Jasper had been quiet, but then he said, "I'll join in on anything I can if my brothers don't need me, though I have to admit that they'll probably want to come to the haunted house. The zombie paintball too, but we'll see."

"Okay, if it's a group thing on the dancing, we're in," the foxes said.

The lynxes said they would be too. The wolves laughed and said they would also.

After dinner and dessert, Rob and Craig thanked them for going on their tour and wished them all the best.

Then Craig took Margot and Steph to their bed and breakfast and wished them a good night.

THE NEXT MORNING, Margot and Steph went to breakfast at the bed and breakfast while John Snow made fresh omelets and his wife was working on other dishes for their guests. They had lots of fresh fruits—grapes, melons, apples, and oranges, and omelets made to order. Margot got a cheese, bell pepper, ham omelet and Steph opted for French toast.

"Okay, first up today is the Halloween dance. Are you ready for it?" Steph asked, then took another bite of her toast.

"Oh, yeah, this should be entertaining. We're meeting everyone over there, right?"

"Yeah. Before you got up this morning, I checked in with everyone," Steph said.

"Oh, good." Margot was glad someone was in charge of all the planning and communicating with everyone. She figured once Ames got here, Steph would drop the ball, but for now, she was glad her friend was taking care of things. "What about Ames?"

"When it comes to dancing, he would prefer skipping it. He always says he has two left feet so he has no plan to get here in time for it. I'm glad that Craig wants to go with all of us. But I'm sure it's because he really wants to be with you. Now see? That's the difference between Ames and Craig. Craig will probably do anything with you to spend time with you. Ames? Only if it's something he wants to do."

Which was why Margot wasn't sure about Ames when it came to mating Steph.

Then Margot got a call and answered the phone. "Hey, Craig. Are you going to meet us at the banquet room of the club where they're having the Halloween dancing lessons?"

"Yeah, I'm headed over there now."

"Okay, we're just finishing up breakfast. We'll see you in a few minutes." Margot was thrilled Craig could do this with them.

"I can't wait to see you."

"Me either."

She and Steph had dressed in their long pirate skirts, blouses, corsets, and pirate jackets, figuring that it would be more fun. When they arrived at the banquet room, she saw Craig all dressed up for the part. He smiled and immediately joined them and gave Margot a hug and kiss as if they were already an item. He was definitely a dashing pirate, and she enjoyed his hugs and kisses as if she was his ladylove and he was her debonair pirate lover. He made the experience of being here even better. After Howie's betrayal, Craig was a breath of fresh air.

Steph was smiling at them, not at all appearing to be disappointed that Ames hadn't arrived in White Bear yet. She just looked like she was thoroughly ready to have fun.

Most of the tour group showed up dressed in their costumes. The lynxes were the only other ones who weren't wearing pirate dresses. "Oh, we didn't get the memo," Sylvia said.

"No, we would have dressed up too," Amber said.

"We'll have to make that part of the dialogue when we're getting ready to go to the other activities," Steph said.

The dance instructor welcomed everyone to the dancing lessons. "We're going to first start with Michael Jackson's *Thriller*. I'll even have the video he was in displayed on the wall in front of us and you can do the steps as best you can. But remember, this is all for fun. Are you all ready to give this a shot?"

"Yes!" everyone shouted. They were an enthusiastic group.

About ten humans were at the Halloween dance, some of whom were dressed as pirates or gypsies, one in a ballroom gown.

Then the music began.

CRAIG WAS SO glad Margot was here and that he had agreed to do this. He was having such a great time with her. He started to laugh as he was trying to keep in step with the teacher and the others. It was infectious and the rest of their shifter group was laughing. The non-shifters there were also having a great time.

But then the male wolf was facing the wrong way when they all turned, and he laughed. They all followed suit. Even the instructor was smiling. Craig was glad it was all just for fun and not taken too seriously.

They'd had so much fun watching the video and trying to learn the steps that they wanted to do it again and the teacher said, "Yes. We'll do whatever you want to do."

And then they danced to *Thriller* again. It was as fun as the first time. Maybe more so because they had a little experience at it now.

Then after semi-mastering the dance moves, the dance instructor said, "Great job everyone. We're going to take a five-minute break, get some water, and then we'll start the *Monster Mash* by Bobby "Boris" Pickett & The Crypt Kickers."

Craig had seen Michael Jackson's Thriller choreographed dance so he kind of knew what to expect but the dance instructor had created his own choreographed dance for this one, so it was more of a challenge. Not that the *Thriller's* dance moves hadn't tripped him up. But this one was a ton of laughter too. He bumped into Margot more times than he wanted to admit, and she just smiled at him every time.

He noticed that Steph was keeping her injured wrist close to her body, not moving it to the dance steps, which he was glad for, and hoped it didn't hurt too much after all of the exercise they were getting. He also hoped she wasn't too disappointed that her boyfriend wasn't there.

Then it was time for *Witchy Woman* by The Eagles, and they had just as much of challenge dancing to that. He was really enjoying dancing with Margot and the others. Dancing wasn't really something he was normally into. But with Margot? He was sure interested in dancing with her as a couple at other affairs.

After another short break, they danced to *The Skeleton Scat* by The Wiggles. All of this was great exercise. He tried to keep his mind on the dance moves, but he couldn't help but think of being with Margot tonight. He couldn't wait to have dinner with her and then see a movie.

When the dance instructor announced *Hungry Like the Wolf* by Duran Duran was up next, the shifters all howled. The instructor laughed. Because the shifters were so enthusiastic over that song, the next one the instructor had them dance to was *Werewolves of London* by Warren Zevon. They were the two really popular tunes for the shifters that afternoon.

Again, the shifters all howled while they danced to the song, amusing their instructor who said he'd never had such an enthusiastic group.

After another drink break, *Don't Fear the Reaper* by Blue Oyster Cult was next on the agenda. They danced to *The Devil Went Down to Georgia* by the Charlie Daniels Band for the last part of the class.

All of the songs were perfect for Halloween, and everyone, shifters and humans alike, had a blast.

When they were done with the dance session, they all thanked the instructor who said they had been the best group ever.

Then the shifter group gathered together outside of the building. "How about lunch together? We're trying to hit all the shifter-run shops," Melissa said.

"Yeah, that sounds good. Where does everyone want to go?" Margot asked.

"The White Bear Deli has really great food," Craig said.

"Let's go there then," Margot said. "Steph and I have already been there, and we really enjoyed the food and the atmosphere."

Then that was decided, and they all headed over in their vehicles to the deli. The bear owners were surprised and delighted to see the group of different shifters arrive en masse.

But it was later than the usual lunchtime break, so luckily, they had some free tables, and no one had to wait for one.

"I think of all the songs we danced to, the wolf ones were the most popular with our group," Craig said as he sat down with Margot, Steph, and the lynxes at one of the tables.

"Yeah. Everyone howling really added to the fun. I was thinking we need to have shifter bands that write award-winning songs for the rest of our kind," Margot said.

"Right, and songs like *Cat Scratch Fever* aren't wild enough for us lynxes," Sylvia said.

"There are plenty of teddy bear songs," Steph said, "but not the right category for us either."

They all ordered sandwiches and then talked about what they did in real life.

"I'm finishing up college work to become a hotel manager," Steph said.

"Oh, that's cool. I'm friends with the owner and the manager of the Commodore Hotel and could put in a good word for you if you're interested in settling down here," Sylvia said.

"Thanks," Steph said and cast a smile at Margot.

"I own a dress shop in North," Margot said.

"Oh, see, you should join us too, open up your shop, and enjoy everything we're doing here," Amber said.

"I would be all for both happening," Craig said.

The ladies smiled at Craig.

"Yeah, I could see it would be fun having a shop here." Margot reached under the table and squeezed his hand.

"I'm the manager of a dating site for shifters," Sylvia said.

"Oh, wow, how do you manage that? I imagine it's hard to ensure only shifters sign up for the site because you can't just ask if the person is a shifter or not. Even if you did, crazy non-shifters would say they were one, just to check out what kind of a dating site it is. Not that they would realize it was really all about people who shift into various kinds of animals," Margot said.

"You're right. Truly, I had to go by word of mouth. Kind of like signing up for the MacMathan tour. There was one listed on the brochure, but if you were a shifter, Rob and Casey assigned you to the shifter tour, unless you really wanted to go on the other," Sylvia said.

"Aww, okay," Margot said. "I wondered how that worked."

"Yeah, Rob and Edward and their mates, and Casey knew you were polar bear shifters already," Craig said.

"Sure, because you came to aid us and then they gave us a free meal at your tavern," Margot said.

"Right," Craig said.

"So for my online dating service, I would just spread the word among shifters to let them know we have this available. Everyone knows not to share the information to non-shifters. Since you and Steph aren't living in White Bear, I didn't mention it to you on the tour. If you had been, I would have. Though we welcome everyone from all over, it just makes it more difficult for the shifters to actually get together if they are from other cities or states."

"That's true," Margot said.

Which was the problem with Craig dating Margot.

Amber said, "I run a daycare for shifters."

"Oh, I bet that's interesting," Margot said.

"Yeah, it can be a challenge at times—you know, kids having a fight and then instead of telling me or the other dayworkers so we can deal with the dispute, the quarreling kids start to strip off their clothes and shift. But we have fun working with the different kinds of shifters."

"Have you even had one of them bite another kid?" Margot asked.

"A few times. Even human kids will bite each other until

they learn not to. I worked in one before I earned my certification to have my own daycare."

"Oh, wow," Margot said.

"But we stop them pretty quickly before anyone gets hurt."

"Well, we know what your occupation is," Sylvia said to Craig.

"Yep, I'm a seaplane pilot," Craig said.

"Oh, yeah," Sylvia said, "we all know who *you* are. You take care of people all over the place."

Craig smiled. "I love doing it."

"Well, Steph and I sure appreciated your help," Margot said.

The lynxes shared conspiratorial looks like they knew there was more to what was going on between him and Margot. He sure hoped so. He was really looking forward to spending some time with *just* Margot.

They enjoyed their meals and once they were done, they all headed over to do the Halloween Painting with a Twist.

Craig figured it would take him a third of the three hours to do his painting of a black cat in the woods, the moon glowing behind it, fireflies shining around it in the Halloween Party with a Twist. The art teacher's example was amazing. They had plenty of space to spread out in the art studio and enough room for each of the groups, in their case, their shifter group, to feel separated from others who had paid for the session.

He and a few of the others in their group had brought bottles of wine so they could enjoy their wine while they painted. Maybe their artwork would improve with a couple of drinks.

"Oh, my," Margot said, sitting on the seat next to him and staring at the cat portrait the teacher had done. "Now if I had some really good luck, mine might even look halfway like a cat, and not like a boogeyman."

Craig laughed. He'd had a knack of being able to paint animals and backgrounds since he was a kid, but he didn't mention it to the others. He poured them each glasses of wine and some for Steph too and they clinked their glasses together. "Ready?"

"Yep." Margot drank some of her wine and he did too. "Let's begin."

"I'm right on it," Steph said.

The instructor started playing music like *Hotel California* and other Halloween type songs while they began working. She came by and gave each of them tips on painting with the acrylics as they created their own interpretation of the black cat in the woods.

"This is quite the experience, isn't it?" Melissa asked nearby. "We get to have fun socializing, learning something new, and creating something with friends."

"Yeah, I agree," Steph said.

Margot glanced at her. "Ames hasn't arrived yet, right?"

"No. He said no to painting. He wasn't interested in it."

Craig thought she sounded disappointed that he didn't want to do most of the things Steph was interested in doing. He was beginning to think the guy wasn't right for her. She was vibrant, fun-loving, and seemed to enjoy life to the fullest. Ames sounded like a drag.

Craig had painted the background of his masterpiece. It wasn't the same as the teacher's, but he didn't want it to be. He glanced at Margot's and thought it was even as nice as the teacher's background. He began to layer in the next part.

Then Steph got a call, and she answered her phone. "I'm in the middle of painting a black cat for Halloween. No, I told you that's what I was doing next. You could have joined us but you said you didn't want to. I'll see you at the bed and breakfast afterward and we'll have dinner. We're done here at five. No, I can't leave any earlier than that. I'm painting a cat! Okay, see you soon." She got off the phone and shook her head.

"Did he get in early?" Margot asked.

"He thinks he'll be here around four, but he doesn't want to come here. I mean, I don't blame him. If it were me, I couldn't paint anything in just an hour and sitting around for all that time watching others paint wouldn't be much fun. He wants me to just leave and meet him at the bed and breakfast as soon as he gets in, but I'm not going to. I paid for this and we're having fun. I don't want to rush through the painting either."

Craig sensed Steph's animosity toward Ames and maybe regret that she had said he could meet her here in White Bear instead of just doing things Halloween related with Margot. She'd been having the time of her life until Ames had called.

Margot had painted the blue sky and yellow and orange glow from the sun setting that would be behind the cat, but then her paintbrush was raised midair, and she was just staring at the glow.

"Margot, are you okay?" Craig asked.

Steph glanced at her and then her painting. "What's wrong, Margot?"

Margot broke free from the trance she seemed to be in and said, "Uh, nothing."

But she looked a little flushed and he didn't think it was nothing at all.

Then she began painting the trees on either side of the cat and he went back to work on his trees too. Okay, so a lighter shade of tree in the background as if the mist was cloaking it and a darker tree in the foreground because it was closer to him. He smiled at his work so far.

He refilled the ladies' glasses with wine and then his own. He was doing a lot of pondering in between applying layers to slow down his pace. When everyone was beginning to work on their cats, he started on his, making it fluffier than the teacher's, adding more details, shadow, making it richer. He assumed the teacher had made hers simpler so that beginning students could follow along.

Then he noticed Margot was watching him paint. She began

to copy what he was doing on his cat to make it fluffier, but her cat's eyes were greener, his cat's eyes were more golden. Her cat was taller, thinner, even with fluffier fur. He liked her painting. She did a great job on it.

Steph's cat was even skinnier with bright blue eyes. The three hours were nearly up. Once they were done with their paintings, everyone went around the room to check out the other shifter's paintings.

Everyone had done a great job. Yet each of the "artists'" paintings were their own. It really had made for an entertaining Halloween activity, one he would remember forever. He would never have done this if it hadn't been for wanting to do it with Margot and he'd had a blast.

The shifters all said their goodbyes. Craig followed the ladies to the bed and breakfast in his vehicle so he could take Margot and her bags to his place for dinner. He hadn't discussed with Margot what she would like to eat. She might want to go out even.

He was willing to do either, anything to make her trip here special.

∿

MARGOT COULD SMELL Craig's eagerness to have her stay with him, and she was sure he could smell hers in return, but she swore he already had known how to paint. His picture was far beyond what the teacher had directed them to do.

"Don't do anything I wouldn't," Steph said to Margot. "Forget that. Do everything I would and wouldn't do. Just have the time of your life."

Margot laughed. "We'll have fun, and I'm sure I'll do everything you would and wouldn't do."

"That's the spirit! By the way, do you think Craig knew how

to paint already? I thought his painting was more detailed and nicer than the teacher's."

"Yeah. I thought the same thing. I'll ask him and let you know."

Then they parked at the bed and breakfast and Steph took a deep breath. "Okay, Ames's truck is here."

"Good luck with whatever you decide to do." Margot was glad he was here and didn't disappoint Steph if he hadn't shown up.

"Thanks. I'll let you know how it goes, however it goes." Steph and Margot got out of the car and waited for Craig and they all went inside the bed and breakfast.

Craig said to Margot, "I'll help you with your bags."

"Okay, thanks. I just need to pack them," Margot said.

Ames was waiting in the lobby and surprise, surprise, he had a bouquet of red roses for Steph, her favorite. He gave her a hug and kiss like she really was the only one for him. Margot sure hoped it would work out for them one way or another. Margot smiled at him.

Then Margot and Craig went up the stairs to get her bags. So far, so good, she was thinking since Ames and Steph seemed to really be into each other still. Sometimes she wondered.

Margot opened the door to their room, and Craig went inside with her. The two queen size beds wore primrose bedspreads, and the room had a couple of mahogany chairs and a table, a dresser, bedside tables, a TV—very nice and comfortable. She packed her bags and then Craig grabbed them up. Then they left the room and walked down the stairs to the lobby.

Steph joined Margot and gave her a hug. "See you at the zombie paintball tomorrow."

"Yeah, see you. Have fun you two." Margot hugged her back.

"Both of you too."

Then Margot and Craig went out to his Bronco, and she just stared at his vehicle.

"What's wrong? You look like you've seen a ghost."

"I...I don't know. I just felt chills running all over my body when I saw it."

"Are you sure you're going to be okay?"

"Yeah. Sorry."

"No, no, I'm here to help you remember. You don't have anything to feel sorry about it." He pulled her into his embrace and just hugged her, letting her know he was there for her while she was going through whatever she was experiencing.

She wrapped her arms around his waist and kissed him thoroughly. "Thank you for being here for me. You don't know how much that means to me."

"Of course. Always." And he meant it. He got the door for her and put her bags in the trunk. Then he drove her to his house surrounded by woods and privacy. "I have nearly twenty-five acres out here," Craig said. "I was living nearer town, but when Edward and Rob mated and began having families—"

"You decided you needed more room for a family?"

He smiled. "Yeah. I'm ready. I know most guys wouldn't say that, and truly I haven't ever spoken to any woman about that before, but with you?" He smiled again. "The house is nearly 3,700 square feet and I have four bedrooms and four baths."

"Four baths."

"Yeah, that way when I have kids and we're off running around, then return home, we'll all have a bathroom."

"If you have twins and not triplets."

He chuckled. "Uh, yeah. But at least no one has to wait that long for a bathroom."

"Did you have some issue about this during your child-hood?" Margot asked.

"Yeah. When Mom and Dad took Edward and Rob in when

their parents died, we only had two bathrooms as it was. So then we had the five of us boys waiting to use a bathroom."

"I had to share one with..." Margot stopped speaking.

Craig glanced at her as he pulled into the two-car garage of his one-story log cabin, the green metal roof sporting a bit of snow on the sides of the two gabled dormer windows on the roof, but at least the covered wraparound deck was clear of snow.

"Uh, sorry. We had two bathrooms when I was growing up and...I just remembered someone being in the bathroom when I needed to use it. We'd both been sick with the flu. Well, Mom and Dad too. So another bathroom would have been welcome."

"Someone?"

"I...I don't remember."

"Another elusive memory."

Margot nodded. "Yes. It seems that knowing some of my past is helping me to remember more of it, yet it's still hard to pin down. But, oh, I just love the exterior of your home. You must get a lot of use out of your deck."

"We do. We all take turns having the family out to our homes, so it helps to have enough room to spread out."

"Do you take a walk on your acreage in your fur coat?"

"Yeah, because it's so treed, we can do it. Especially with the little ones, it's fun to go out and play with them in the snow."

"The six-year-old twin boys."

"Right." They got out of his Bronco. "They need some space to play. And when the babies grow up, it will even be more important to have the room." Especially when Craig had his own kids too.

"Well, your place is truly beautiful."

"Thanks. Okay, so now the big question is what do we eat and what do we want to watch in the line of a movie?" He carried her bags inside.

She grabbed their cat paintings and followed him inside. "What's your specialty that you like to cook?"

"Chili, ribs, steaks, fish, and fried potatoes."

"Oh, we're pirates, matie. Fish and fried potatoes sound good." She set both their cat paintings on the mantle over the fireplace, in between the ceramic jack-o-lanterns and ghost statues.

He laughed. "We don't have to go grocery shopping then. What movie do you want to see?"

"Let's watch something at your house. Maybe we can find a good Halloween story to watch. I love a bunch of different ones. If you have *Practical Magic* that would be great. That's one of my favorites."

"Okay, I haven't seen it in years. I really like it too. We'll watch that one."

"What can I do to help?" Margot asked.

"Pour us some wine?" He got a bottle of Marsanne out and opened it for her. "I'll get all the food started."

"Sure." She pulled out some wine glasses, poured the wine into them, and placed them on the table. Then she set the table, adding glasses of water at their place settings.

He was frying up the potatoes, green beans, and fish when she asked, "So you've painted before."

He smiled. He figured it might come out sooner or later. "Yeah, but I didn't want to mention it to anyone in case it made anyone feel they couldn't do as well."

"I knew it." Margot got on her phone and texted someone.

"You're telling Steph on me?"

"Yeah. Though I'm sure she's too busy to read my texts right now."

"I hope you don't mind."

"Nope. I watched you paint and made my picture a notch better using a couple of your techniques."

He thought of putting the movie on while they ate, like having dinner at the theater, but he really wanted this time to visit with Margot.

"So, you're moving here now that you've been to our fair town, right?" Craig asked.

She laughed.

Well, subtle he wasn't. He smiled. "I'm serious."

"That's what's so funny. I know you are. I'm having a ball here, but thinking of moving my business here, getting a place, all of that, it's such a job. Even though I don't spend a lot of time with my parents because they're so busy, or I am, I know they would be against my moving here."

"But ultimately, it's your choice."

"Sure. It is. So convince me that I should do it."

"Hell, yeah, I'll work my darndest to make it happen."

She laughed again, clinked her wine glass against his, and said, "To missions impossible."

He smiled and drank some of his wine. "The thing is that I'll take any challenge on. And believe me, not only would my family help to relocate you, the shifters in the community would do it too."

"Okay, so that's good to know. Before we watch the movie after dinner, I want to change into something more comfortable," she said.

"Pj's?"

"Yeah, that's the best way to watch a movie at night at home after having such a fun day," she said.

So now the question was would she want to stay in his bed tonight, or would she decide to stay in a room of her own?

"Dinner was delicious," she said after they finished eating and she helped him clear away the dishes.

"Thanks. How about some hot buttered popcorn for our movie night?"

"Oh, perfect. I really do love your place, by the way. It's understated elegance. The beige stone fireplace is beautiful. The settees that you can actually lie down on look so comfortable. With four bedrooms fitted for sleeping, you could still have another couple of guests in here."

"The settees are really comfortable, perfect for sitting and lying down on. I've been known to fall asleep on one of them while watching a movie after having a late-night seaplane run, but still too wound up to sleep."

"Oh, if you fall asleep on the sofa while we're watching the movie, do you want me to wake you or just let you sleep?"

He smiled at her in a way that said that would never happen! "No way am I falling asleep when I've got you here for company. And yeah, about the other rooms, they're perfect for emergency accommodations." He finished popping the popcorn and she refilled their glasses of wine and set them on the dark, smoky glass table. Then he brought the big bowl of popcorn into the living room.

"I'm going to change into my pajamas." She pulled out a pair of pajamas from one of her bags in the living room.

"Go ahead. I'm going to find the movie and then change." He found *Practical Magic* on one of his streaming channels and then he headed into the master bedroom. She was changing her clothes in the main bathroom. He pushed off his boots and then pulled off his pirate's jacket, vest, shirt, and pants. He yanked on a pair of Halloween pajamas.

He rejoined her in the living room, thinking how sexy she looked in her orange and black buffalo plaid pajama bottoms and a long-sleeved black shirt with a smiling pumpkin on it.

"We match," she said, running her hand over his shirt. "I love your buffalo plaid pajamas and black pajama T-shirt with a large frowning pumpkin."

He touched the pumpkin on hers. "I love your smiling pumpkin. Well, and the rest of you."

She smiled and they settled down on the couch and he grabbed a fluffy, orange and black buffalo plaid blanket off the back of the sofa to cover them. Then he started the movie, and they cuddled together while they watched it and snacked on popcorn and sipped their wine.

"This is so great," she said. "The perfect end to a perfect day."

"I agree." Craig sipped some of his wine.

"Everyone is so mean to them because they are witches," Margot said, about the women in town who shunned them in the movie.

"Yeah, can you imagine if humans knew that we were polar bear shifters? They would ostracize us too." He grabbed a handful of buttered popcorn.

"Absolutely. I was so sad when they were cursed to lose the men they loved though." Then Margot grew quiet for quite a while. "Oh, this is one of my favorite parts."

"Where the sheriff questions the women about the missing guy?"

"Yeah, he was such bad news." She got some more popcorn.

Then the bad guy came out of the grave that the two witch sisters had buried him in and Margot was shaking her head. "This is so not good."

He smiled. She was cute. He'd forgotten a lot of the movie, but he was amused at how much she got into it.

"At least the non-witches in town got behind the ladies and helped them to get rid of the villain in the end," she said later in the movie.

"In our case, probably some would really accept us if they knew what we were and that we're really good guys and just like them, in many ways, while others would want to burn us at the stake."

"I agree with you there. But don't you think that some would want to be like us? And want to get bitten?"

"Oh, I'm sure some of that would go on. You know Rob had to bite Alicia," Craig said. All the bears and many of the shifters knew about it so it wasn't like he had to keep the news secret.

"What? On purpose?" She sounded so surprised that he figured she'd never known anyone who had done that.

"Yeah, but he had to."

"She saw him shift?"

"She was accidentally pushed into the frigid water. Rob had to shift and bite her to save her. She was suffering from severe hypothermia."

"Oh, wow. I don't know anyone who has ever been turned. Everyone was born that way that I know of."

"Yeah, same here. No one really had any real protocols in place to deal with it. They were on a tour too, so that made it problematic," Craig said.

"Oh, no. That's even worse."

"It was. On another topic, do you think Ames will propose to Steph?" Craig grabbed another handful of popcorn.

"I don't know. They've been together on and off for about three years, so I don't have a gut feeling that says they are perfect for each other, or not. They seem good together when they *are* together, but..." She shrugged. "By the way, I was engaged to marry a guy, but he was a no-show at the wedding. That was this summer and my parents are still mad at me for chasing the guy off since they had paid for the wedding arrangements. Anyway, I just wanted to tell you that I had planned to marry, but the deal fell through."

"The guy must be an idiot."

She smiled, appearing pleased that Craig would said that.

"He found another ladylove. Truthfully, I was relieved. I would rather he stray before the marriage than leave me in the dark after being married to him."

"Yeah, me too. I'm sorry you had to go through that." He knew she had dodged a bullet on that one, but she must have felt bad about the betrayal.

"What about you?"

"I haven't found anyone that I've been halfway interested in dating long-term, not to mention marrying."

The movie ended on a happy note—like he knew it would.

"Good. So we're both happily single." She finished the last of the buttered popcorn. "These were great. So was the movie and the company. Are you ready for bed?"

"Yeah." He just hoped she would join him in bed! He carried the wine glasses and empty popcorn bowl into the kitchen and then he moved her bags down the hall to the bedrooms. "These are the guest rooms, but you are more than welcome to stay in the master bedroom with me."

"No one will believe I am staying in a separate room while I'm here, and if you're truly going to convince me to move here—"

"Say no more." He smiled and hauled her bags to the master bedroom, and she followed him in.

"Oh, lovely. You have a thing for beige, but I really like it. It's light and cheery."

"I like it that way. When we have so much darkness in Alaska, it feels lighter out, even though it isn't. And when we have no darkness, I love the lightness anyway."

"I agree. I love the big suede chest at the end of the bed. It would be great for removing boots or shoes." She sat down to take her slippers off, but he crouched down and did the honors. Then he pulled his socks off.

"Come, I'll show you the bathroom," he said.

"Ooh, pretty marble counters, double sinks, walk-in shower, whirlpool bathtub, and a separate private toilet. I love it." She glanced at the shower. "Do you want to take a shower or a bath?"

"With you?" He was so ready for either.

"Yeah, we can save water."

He smiled. "Let's take a shower this time."

"All right. Let me grab my shampoo and body wash."

"I'll start the shower." This day couldn't get any better as it had turned into night.

Then she came back, and she set the shampoo and body wash on his shower shelf as if she was moving in for good. He really liked the idea. He couldn't believe he would meet a woman and fall for her at first sight. He always figured that was some kind of romantic myth, no matter how many other shifters that he had known that that had happened to and they had been happily married from the beginning to this day.

He kissed her full lips and slid his hands up her pajama top and felt her luscious breasts. She moaned against his lips. Their pheromones were going crazy, synced with each other's, coaxing each other to keep on going. Then he slid her pajama top off and she eased his pajama pants off.

Man, he was ready for her.

She tongued his mouth and sent his hormones spiraling. She was a keeper, as far as the sexual attraction went. She rubbed her sexy body against his, stirring him all up. Before he could remove his pajama shirt, she was sliding her fingers up his torso, her hands warm against his skin. Then she was pressing the palms of her hands against his nipples, making them so sensitive and eager for her touch. She began massaging them.

Hell, he was afraid he was going to come before they even got into the shower.

Then she pulled off his pajama shirt and he continued to kiss her while pulling down her pajama bottoms. She separated from him and took his hand and moved into the shower. He shut the door, and they began kissing each other under the shower spray.

This was heavenly. He'd never made love to a woman in the shower before, and with Margot, he didn't want it to be a one-time occurrence. They began soaping each other's hair up. His was citrus mint scent. Her shampoo was peach. Together, they were a fruity mixture of something divine. The shampoo and water mixed and ran down their bodies. They pressed together, sliding against each other, their hands caressing through each other's hair, their scalps.

He cupped her buttocks, and she wrapped her legs around him. He slid into her narrow sheath, wet and warm and welcoming. She groaned with pleasure as he ground into her. She was rocking her hips against him, kissing him, her hands clinging to his shoulders. No matter how hard he was trying to hold off from coming, he couldn't. He came in an explosive way. God, she felt great. He set her down on the shower floor and began to stroke her between her legs.

"Oh, Craig," she moaned, her hands clinging to his shoulders, their lips pressed together in a never-ending kiss. "You are so...ahhh..."

He smiled and kissed her deeply, his fingers rubbing her between her legs. She was holding onto him while he continued working to bring her to orgasm. She was shivering with anticipation, gripping his waist harder, and he thought she was about to come she was concentrating so hard, moaning in a sexy way.

"Yes!" she screamed out.

He loved how exuberant she was. How passionate she was. Then they began washing each other again. He was so glad Steph's boyfriend had shown up to be with Steph and Craig got to spend this time with Margot.

They finally finished up and then they left the shower, and

they dried off. She dried her hair while he considered pulling on his pajama bottoms.

"Don't bother wearing them. Unless you think you're just going to sleep," she said, over the hum of the hair dryer, her smile wicked.

He laughed and picked up their pajamas and laid them on the chest at the foot of the bed. And then she came into the bedroom, naked, beautiful, her burgundy hair soft, curly, hanging over her shoulders and he pulled her into his arms and kissed her. "Which side of the bed do you want to sleep on?"

"Either side is fine with me as long as we're together."

That's just what he wanted to hear.

Then they climbed onto the bed and gravitated toward each other. They cuddled and kissed. She was someone special and he hoped they could keep developing the relationship. He thought his life had been complete, loving the job he had to do, the family he had, though he loved seeing his cousins living the married life with their children and how much they enjoyed each other.

He knew Margot was someone he needed in his life.

Wow, that's all Margot could say. Craig was an amazing lover. He could have stopped once he'd had his own orgasm, but he wanted her to feel the pleasure too and she thought the world of him for it. She realized then he was so much more spontaneous than her ex-fiancé who had never wanted to have shower sex with her. She thought it would be exciting for her first time with Craig. And yes, she was looking forward to doing it again with him, in bed this time.

Steph wasn't going to be the only one who was having fun with a guy tonight. Besides, the way Craig and she had kissed before, Margot knew this was where it was headed, so she wasn't going to delay taking it to the top.

She loved that Craig would snuggle with her like this, as if he really wanted more of this, something further. Sure he did. Because he already said he and the others would help her move to White Bear. She loved his house too. She wouldn't want to make any changes. It was beautiful. But she was probably getting a little ahead of herself there.

She really needed to learn what she could about her past—about the accident, why her mother hadn't wanted her to go to White Bear, mysteries that she didn't want to take into a relationship that she hoped might become permanent.

At some point, she finally fell asleep, but then sometime in the night, Craig was nuzzling her face, his hand massaging her breast. He was gently trying to wake her to make love to her, and she smiled and wrapped her arms around his neck and began to kiss him again.

They didn't have to get up at the crack of dawn for anything, which was good, because she was enjoying this time with Craig way too much. And she wanted it to last. Which it did! After making love, they finally fell asleep in each other's arms like this was where they were meant to be.

When they finally woke again, they got up to have breakfast. For the zombie paintball, they were wearing jeans and sweaters, jackets, boots, no costumes.

"About last night..." Craig said, pouring the coffee for them.

"It was amazing."

"You weren't annoyed with me for waking you up last night?"

She laughed. "I would have been disappointed if you hadn't."

He smiled. "Good. I was worried about that."

"Don't be. I had a wonderful night—dinner, popcorn and the movie, and you, *especially* you."

15

Craig was looking forward to doing the zombie paintball with Margot when he got a call, and he was afraid he would be needed to go on a flying mission. He was always up and ready for anything they threw at him, but now? Hell, now he wanted to be with Margot all week, enjoying all the things she wanted to do. "Hey, what do you need?"

"Next week, we need a supply run done."

"Okay, yeah, sure, you can count on me." He was thrilled it was for next week! Then he ended the call.

"Do you have a job to do?" Margot asked.

"Next week."

"Oh, good. I was afraid you weren't going to be able to go to the paintball game, and I would lose my partner." She really sounded grateful he was going to be with her.

"No way." He wanted to do this and all the rest of the activities this week with her.

～

MARGOT WAS SO glad when Craig didn't have to do the seaplane delivery. She really wanted him to go with her to the paintball fun. Even though she totally understood if he had to go.

But then she got a call and she looked at the caller ID. "It's Rob." She wondered what he would want to talk to her about and answered the call. "Hi, Rob."

"Hey, Andy got a hold of me and said that he looked into any accidents that had occurred in White Bear and the surrounding area. He didn't find anything about a man driving a car that had rolled off the highway or streets anywhere during the year that this would have happened. Could you have been older or younger?"

"Possibly. But I don't think so."

"Okay, well, no one on the police force back then was a shifter, so if anyone had been, they would have smelled your polar bear scents and would know about it."

"Well, thank Andy for me. It was a longshot. It probably happened somewhere else then. I don't know why my mother wouldn't want me to go to White Bear."

"Did you ever ask her?"

"I did. She wouldn't tell me. I didn't figure I would ever be in your area, so it just didn't matter."

"Wait, did your stepdad adopt you? I'm only asking because if you had taken his name, we were looking under accidents for the wrong family name."

"Oh, I'm so sorry. I don't know why I didn't think of that. My biological father's name was Benjamin Rider."

"I'll tell Andy about his real name. If he comes up with anything else or any of us do, we'll let you know."

"Okay, thanks, Rob." Then they ended the call and she said to Craig, "Your brother couldn't find anything about the accident I was in, but I forgot my biological father's name isn't the same as my last name now."

"We knew it was probably going to be difficult to research if it didn't happen around here," Craig said. "But it would help to have the correct name. I don't know why I didn't think of it."

"Yes, I agree." She let out her breath. "You know, I'm really worried about what I will learn."

"Why? Because your mom was adamant about you not coming here?"

"Yeah, and I keep feeling like my memories are wrong, distorted, mixed up somehow." Then Margot didn't want to talk about it any longer and changed the subject. "So...are you ready to paint some zombies?"

"I sure am. I have to say I never expected to be doing this and certainly not with a beautiful she-bear too."

"Me either. I mean, I figured I would be doing this with Steph, not a hunk of a male polar bear." She got on her phone to talk to Steph. "Hey, we're headed over there now. Do you want us to meet you there?"

"Yeah, we're on our way. We're wearing just regular clothes, right?"

"Yeah, we don't want to get paint on our pirate costumes," Margot said. "Besides, I think we'll be better able to maneuver if we're wearing jeans and boots instead of long skirts."

"I agree. We'll see you soon."

When they arrived at the facility, they all greeted their fellow shifters who had signed up to do this. Then the people running the show gave them a safety briefing, explaining about the special air rifles that fired paintballs. "Wearing safety face masks is required at all times. Paintballs can injure an eye, teeth, or an eardrum. So never take off the mask. Also make sure it fits your face." Then the instructor explained how to adjust the mask. "Don't pick up paintballs on the ground and insert them in the hopper. They could have dirt or other debris on them and clog up the air gun. The paintballs are in the hopper and fall into the gun with their own weight. So if you turn the gun sideways or upside down to make a shot, the paintball isn't going to fire. Watch your air pressure also. If it drops down to one or zero, ask an instructor to fill it back up with air or you won't be shooting anything. The air guns are semi-automatic. This means you fire one shot at a time. The red frame on the safety means the gun is in shooting mode. Press it to put the safety on when leaving the range. Also, a special safety plug should be placed on the end of the rifle when leaving the site.

"The zombies are your targets, but the only difference is they'll be shooting back. I know. Not fair, right? Real zombies don't know how to shoot anything. But these zombies were created in a lab and so they are weaponized zombies. The good thing about that is they won't eat your brains if they capture you. The bad part is that they don't growl or snarl to give away their position. That would make it too easy for you to target them."

The instructor didn't know the half of it. With their enhanced shifter hearing, they could even hear their wildly beating hearts, though the shifters' hearts could be beating just as hard, so that might not clue them in.

"Now, if you get hit by a ball that forms paint on your body that is at least the size of a coin, you're out of the game. Same thing for the zombies. They're…uhm, dead again, for the duration of the game this time. If you are shot, you raise your hand up and shout, 'Out!' The zombies don't talk. They'll just drop down dead. If you're not sure if you've been hit with a paint ball, ask your instructor. He'll decide if you have or haven't been. You can't shoot through holes in the walls. You both must be visible to each other."

"Aww," Erin said.

Everyone chuckled.

Then their instructor said, "Does anyone have any questions about the safety rules?"

Everyone shook their heads.

"All right then. We're heading into a zombie-infested area, and everyone needs to be on the lookout. Our goal is to clean out the infestation. Is everyone ready?"

"Sir, yes, sir!" Wolfrun said.

Margot smiled. He must have been former military.

"Take your rifle's safety off."

Everyone pressed on the safety button to take it off safety.

"Remember you're aiming for zombies, not your own people. Believe me, things get so wild, that has occurred before. Ready? Go."

Margot couldn't believe how nervous she was to do this. She was so afraid she would let down their team. But then she heard a zombie moving around a stone facade and she whipped around and saw one seriously scary-looking zombie with shedding skin, yellow eyes, and scraggly, unwashed hair appearing surprised to see her and she immediately fired on him. He cried out and collapsed on the ground, his reign of terror coming to an end before he'd probably had time to take anyone down. He didn't stand a chance against a shifter, she thought to herself.

Her team members had disbursed, looking for other zombies and she quickly began searching behind rock walls, listening. None of her team members had called out that they were out yet, so she figured they were all in the game, when she heard someone sneaking around the end of the wall. She came around the wall ready to shoot if the person wasn't any of her team members, and it wasn't. This one was a female zombie, and she was as hideous as the other, but slow on the draw, thankfully. Margot shot her. Margot might not have ever played this before, but she realized she could hear the zombies before they reached her and even smell them, once she was in sight of them. At least in the last two cases.

She wondered how the other members of her team were

doing. She wished she hadn't lost Craig, but she should have realized that when they were faced with zombies, they might end up splitting up to solve the mission. Then she heard someone else coming and she ducked behind the wall, peeked out, and saw it was Craig. She smiled, but then saw a zombie coming up to get him and she shot the zombie. Craig whipped around and fired on another.

Once the zombies were out, Craig hurried to join her. "I think we have the advantage," he whispered.

"We can hear the zombies sooner than they can hear us," she whispered back.

"Yes. I'm sorry I lost you back there but when I saw a zombie a little ways away, I went after him. He moved back behind a wall and then when I got him, I came back for you, but you were gone. So I went out looking for you and ran across a couple more zombies. Thanks for getting the one behind me," Craig said.

"You're welcome…there's another one."

Before she could target the zombie, Craig shot him. The zombie collapsed in a nice, crazy zombie way.

Margot loved zombie movies. She never thought she would be in a situation where she would be clearing out an infestation of zombies herself. This was just too much fun.

She heard someone else coming, and she turned. *Steph.* She smiled at her. Ames wasn't with her. Steph probably had lost him like Margot had lost Craig during the first part of the hunt as soon as they were engaging zombies.

"No kissing between the two of you," Steph whispered.

Margot smiled. This was not the time to kiss anyone for sure. Not like in the movies where the bad guys would be after the couple, and they would have a kissing fest before getting back to evading or fighting the bad guys.

"No one from our group of zombie fighters has called out

that they're out of the game," Steph said. "I think the shifters are winning."

Margot was thinking the same. The organizers of the paintball probably had never had a group who was so successful against taking down a common enemy.

Then they moved on, searching for more of the zombies, but they ran across one of the lynxes, and then the other. They shrugged, letting them know they weren't finding any zombies.

One of the foxes showed up. "Where are they?" Fran whispered.

"Maybe we got them all," Margot said.

Then her sisters showed up. Lenora whispered, "We couldn't find any more."

The wolves soon joined them, and Ames finally found them.

One of the instructors joined them. "Well, that's the quickest a team has cleared out all the zombies and without any casualties on your side." He frowned. "Have you done this before?"

They all smiled at him and shook their heads.

"We had a blast," Margot said.

All the rest of the shifter team said the same.

They put their air guns on safety and put the safety plug on them, then turned their air guns and their masks in.

Everyone thanked the instructor for a great time. The zombie actors were really super, their makeup, their actions, but they had been at the disadvantage.

Margot asked how Steph was feeling. She was holding her left arm against her body, smiling. "I'm good, thanks, Margot."

"Okay, good." Margot was relieved Steph wasn't feeling a lot of pain.

Then Craig took Margot's hand and asked, "Do you all want to meet up for lunch somewhere?"

"Your parents' tavern," Wolfrun said.

"Yeah, that would be great," Fran said.

Steph looked at Ames and he nodded as they all walked out to their cars.

"Shifters rule," Craig said.

"And zombies drool," Margot said.

They all laughed.

Then Margot said to Melissa, "Can you see me after lunch for a session?"

"Sure. I scheduled off the day from sessions because I didn't know how long our zombie paintball game would last."

"Oh, great." Margot sure hoped she might get further with recalling her past. She glanced at Craig. "Does that work for you?"

"You had better believe it."

Margot was happy that Craig was so agreeable. "Okay, we'll do that then," Margot said to Melissa. She was so glad they were going to do this again, especially since Andy couldn't learn anything about the car accident that she'd been involved in. Though maybe now that he knew her father's name, he might make some progress. Maybe she would get somewhere with the hypnosis again also.

Craig made a phone call as he got into his Bronco. "Hey, Ben, Rob and Casey's shifter tour group is coming in for lunch. Can you save us a couple of tables?" He smiled. "Thanks, brother. We just finished up our paintball zombie session." He laughed. "The zombies and the staff weren't expecting a bunch of shifters with enhanced hearing and an enhanced sense of smell."

Margot laughed. She imagined the group in charge would talk about them forever. She wondered what the normal ratios were for good guys who survived against the zombies.

"Okay, see you in a few," Craig said to his brother.

"I'm glad your brother could get us some tables ahead of time for a group this size."

"Yeah, that's why I was glad we were having lunch at my family's place."

"I sure loved playing the zombie paintball game," she said.

"I've watched a couple of zombie shows. I don't remember any of them being able to operate weapons."

"I know, right? And they would have grunted and snarled and warned us they were coming."

Craig laughed. "That would have really helped."

"But just hearing their footfalls and their heavy breathing did the trick. Plus, I smelled the scent of a couple and knew they weren't our shifters."

The whole group of shifters filled the two tables and ordered lunches. Craigs' parents dropped over to thank them for coming in to eat there after their paintball game.

They had a lovely time and when they finished their lunches, Melissa said to Margot, "Do you want to meet with me now for another session?"

Margot glanced at Craig to see how he felt about it.

"I'm going to work at the tavern until you're through." Craig handed the keys to his Bronco to her. "You can follow Melissa and meet me back here."

"Okay, thanks. I'll do that." She was a little surprised he would just give her the keys to his new vehicle. Her ex-fiancé had never allowed her to drive his new car. That said a lot about Craig and how he trusted her.

Then Margot followed Melissa to her office and when they went inside, she thought it was cute that Melissa had decorated everything in foxes. A couple of pumpkins had hand-painted white foxes on them even.

"Okay, we're going to try this again," Melissa said as Margot got comfortable on the couch in Melissa's office. "This time, I want you to think only about the accident," Melissa said as Margot went under. "When your father was driving..."

"No," Margot said, slowly moving her head back and forth. "It's...it's not right."

"What's not right?"

"The steering wheel is so hard. My fingernails were digging into my skin."

"While you were half asleep in the back seat. Your father was driving..."

"It's...it's...the light. The blinding light is in my eyes. I can't see."

"But you're in the back seat. You could close your eyes. You could duck behind the headrest to keep the light out of your eyes."

"It's...it's headed straight for me. I swerve."

"Your father swerved."

"I swerved too hard and...and the car left the road."

"You were only fifteen. Did you have a learner's permit?"

"The car rolled and rolled and rolled. And then I was upside down."

"Was your father in the car?"

"He...he was...he was...I don't know. He didn't make any sense."

"Was he injured?"

"I was gone. He was gone. The car was gone. The bright light was there. I saw the light, but it was different from the one I saw before the car swerved."

"Were you driving?" Melissa asked.

"He couldn't."

"Your father?"

"He couldn't."

"So you had to drive the car and the bright light blinded you from an oncoming car."

"So bright. It was my fault. My fault. I shouldn't have swerved the car so hard."

"Were you in your lane then?"

"On the shoulder. The car hit the gravel and then it rolled and rolled and rolled. I didn't see him again. I never saw him again."

"Your father?"

"I was in my lane. I was."

"So the other car was in your lane. You've said your father didn't make any sense. Was he injured? Incoherent?"

"He was...he was drunk."

Melissa didn't say anything for a moment. "Your father was drunk, and he asked you to drive the car."

"No...no...no...no. He wouldn't give me the keys." Margot sobbed. "The accident wouldn't have happened if I hadn't been driving."

"No, if your father was drunk, he could have gotten you killed. You did the right thing. If the other car was in your lane, they were at fault. There wasn't anything you could do about it."

"I made him give me the keys. I made him."

"It's not your fault. I'm going to count backwards from one to three and you will remember everything we've talked about. Three, two, one, you are awake now and feeling refreshed."

Margot opened her eyes and stared at Melissa. "I was driving the car?"

"That's what you said. Did you have a learner's permit?"

"At fifteen, yes."

"Then your dad would have been the responsible adult driver who was supervising your driving."

"He was drunk."

"Which is why you were actually driving that night."

"I fought with him over the car keys. He didn't want to give them up. He was slurring his words. He couldn't have driven us home."

"Exactly."

"I shouldn't have either."

"It wasn't your fault. You remember hitting gravel as soon as you swerved the car out of the path of the oncoming vehicle. You wouldn't have been on the shoulder if you had been in the wrong lane. You would have swerved and been in your lane. If you'd lost control and continued in that direction, you would have hit gravel then. But every time you mention it, you hit gravel right away. To the right of your vehicle, correct?"

"Yes. It was to the right of the vehicle, and we rolled to the right."

"So that clarifies that you weren't in the opposite lane and ended up hitting the shoulder of the other lane and then rolled off the shoulder on their side of the road."

"Okay, so then what happened to my father? My mother said he just left us. I asked her where he went. Mom said she didn't know. That he just took off and left and she divorced him."

"If your mom didn't want you coming to White Bear, do you think that means he ended up here?"

"It's possible. Now that I know more of the story, I'll certainly look for him."

"Ask Andy. He'll look into it and locate him if he can."

"I will." Actually, Margot would ask Craig and he would ask his brother. She figured he would be more willing to do something his brother asked of him than her since she wasn't even from here. "Thanks so much for doing this for me free-of-charge. I probably never would have tried something like this if it hadn't been for you and since you're a shifter, that makes it easier to do."

"I'm so glad we did it. I hope it's helping with the nightmares."

"Oh, absolutely." And of course the night spent with Craig didn't hurt. "Again, thanks."

"If it's not too much of an intrusion asking, how are things going between you and Craig?" Melissa asked.

Margot smiled. "We're really enjoying the time together. I was glad that Steph and I came here and that she's having a good time spending it with Ames, so being with Craig is an unexpected pleasure."

Margot felt better to have some of the mysteries solved, though she hated to think that she was the cause of the accident, and maybe she had even been the one to make her father go away.

16

C raig was at the tavern delivering orders to the tables, waiting to hear from Margot. He hoped she would get more information during her hypnotherapy session that would help her learn what had happened during the accident. If she did learn more, he hoped the knowledge wouldn't upset her. He hoped, too, that she would talk to him about it if she wanted to and not bottle it up.

While Craig served meals, he'd been half watching the door, waiting for her. Ben teased him for door watching. "Margot will be here before you know it."

Yeah, Craig knew it, but he couldn't help himself. Then he saw Andy come in to have a late lunch.

"Hey, brother." Andy slapped him on the back.

"Do you have any news?"

"Yeah, with the correct name I discovered an accident a few miles out of White Bear that involved a fifteen-year-old girl named Margot."

"That has to be her case," Craig said.

"Right." Andy showed him a picture of Margot taken when she was fifteen, but right before the crash, that was featured in a brief newspaper article about the accident. Andy headed to the counter to order his lunch.

"Hell, that's why I remembered seeing her. She has the same smile, same eyes, just a fifteen-year-old version of herself."

"Exactly."

Craig walked with Andy to get more details about the case. "So did you learn anything about where her father is?"

"No. The report said that the girl was the driver and the only one in the car, and that Margot was in a coma for two months from the injuries she had suffered."

"Hell."

"Yeah. That's what I was thinking." Andy ordered a cheeseburger from his dad.

"Coming right up. And french fries."

"Like always." Andy smiled at their dad.

"Who caused the accident? The car in the other lane or Margot?" Craig wanted to know because once Margot knew the truth, she might feel a lot of guilt about the accident.

"From checking out the skid marks, the accident investigators confirmed the driver of the other car was clearly at fault, not Margot. It was a wonder, when they swerved to avoid her, that they hadn't gone off the road on the other side. The hospital did a blood-alcohol test on her, and she hadn't had anything to drink prior to the accident."

Craig was glad for that. At least he knew a little bit more about the situation and could talk to her about it if she was willing.

"But the other car left the scene of the accident. Luckily, another car was some distance behind her and saw the whole thing. The driver was human and called it in to the police and stayed with her, talking to her, afraid to move her. Unfortunately, he died of a heart attack a couple of years after that so I couldn't speak with him to learn any further details."

"That's a shame."

"Yeah, I would have liked to have learned more from him if I could have."

Then Craig heard the tavern door open and glanced in that direction, expecting to see more customers wanting a late lunch. Margot walked in, looking for him and smiled to see him. She warmed up a chilly late October day with her sexy smile.

He hurried off to greet her, amused that his brother was chuckling and saying he never expected Craig could dump him so fast to see a she-bear. Craig figured Ben was watching them too like he always was when something interesting was going on with the family.

Craig reached Margot, pulled her into his arms, and kissed her. Maybe he shouldn't have done so in the tavern and in front of his family and customers, but she kissed him back, showing she was just fine with it. And he was glad for that. "Andy has some news about your car accident." He hoped she would be all right with it when she learned she wasn't at fault, but that her dad hadn't been in the car with her.

"Oh good, I do too."

"Do you want some dessert and a drink, and we can join Andy and talk? He's getting a cheeseburger for lunch."

"Yeah, sure, that would be great."

Margot sat down with Andy at the table. Craig asked her what she wanted to have to drink and eat.

"Hmm, that double chocolate cake looks terrific. I love the little orange pumpkins on top too."

"Okay, I'll get us both a slice of that. What would you like to drink?" Craig asked Margot.

"Earl Grey tea."

"I'll go get it and Andy can tell you what he learned."

"Thanks."

Andy began telling Margot about the accident while Craig

was cutting some slices of the cake. His mother smiled at him. "Have you convinced her to move here yet?"

"I'm working on it. The slices of cake should help."

His mother laughed.

Then he carried the tray of slices of cake and the teapot of hot water, teacup, and a couple of packages of tea to Andy and Margot's table.

"Hey, where's mine?" Andy asked, brows raised.

Craig laughed. "You could have said something when we decided we wanted a slice of the chocolate cake, and I went to get them."

"I didn't think about it when I was eating my cheeseburger, but that looks like it will hit the spot."

"Okay, eat one of these. I'll get another slice of cake." Craig returned to the counter and pulled out the chocolate cake from under the display counter again and cut another slice.

"I could have told you Andy would want one too," their dad said, "as soon I saw you get a couple slices for you and Margot."

"Yeah, but I thought he would say so." Craig smiled at his dad and then headed back to the table with the last slice of cake.

"I was waiting to talk about what had happened to me in the hypnotherapist session until you returned, Craig," Margot said. "I don't understand why the accident report said I was alone. I couldn't have driven the car without an adult present."

Craig and Andy exchanged looks and smiled a little because they often had done that when they were that age. Sometimes, the three brothers and their two cousins were together and would take turns driving. And they were all the same age.

He noticed Margot had waited for him to bring his slice of cake to the table too before she started eating hers. She'd already made her tea and was sipping it.

"What did you learn through your hypnotherapy?" Craig asked.

"I was the driver of the vehicle," Margot said, her voice hitching.

Andy nodded. "Okay, so the accident report confirms you were driving the black Ford Bronco."

"That's why you suddenly reacted to my Bronco," Craig said, the light dawning as to why she had acted strangely all of a sudden when she saw his vehicle.

"Uh, yes. I guess I was regaining my memories. Your Bronco is a much newer model of the one my dad had owned. His was an old 1996, the last of the line until they began making them again. I only had a learner's permit. I swear my...my dad was slurring his words, incoherent, drunk. I fought with him over..." She paused.

Craig wondered if this was too much for Margot to deal with right now, especially at the restaurant.

"He...he bruised my arm and threw me up against the car. I... I didn't remember that before. But I wouldn't let him drive. I knew he would kill himself and maybe others. I couldn't let him do it. I managed to grab the Bronco's keys and wouldn't let him have them. He..."—she rubbed her temple—"I thought he finally just collapsed in the back seat of the car, and he was yelling at me, but I couldn't let him drive no matter what. I'd driven him home several times before when he was inebriated like that. I'd never had any trouble getting Dad home before that time. How could I be so mixed up about him being there if he wasn't?"

"You said you had to drive him home before. Maybe because of the memory loss, you're thinking of the other times that you drove your father home," Craig said.

"That could be." She took a steady breath and continued. "I saw the light shining in my eyes. Headlights and they were in my lane, headed straight for me. I swerved to miss the other vehicle and lost control of the car."

"By the time the witness stopped for you, he said you were alone. He told the police that he knew your car had been in the right lane, but the driver of the other vehicle had fled the scene and hadn't reported it or come to your aid," Andy said.

"What hospital was I at?" Margot asked.

"The one here. No one on the police force who worked the case was a shifter. No one at the hospital was either so no one knew that you were a polar bear shifter. If someone had known, they would have contacted someone in the bear sleuth. They listed your home address as Anchorage." Andy finished his cheeseburger and drank some of his coffee. "Your mother was reported to have shown up to see you at the hospital and then you were transferred to a long-term care facility in North. Your dad never came to see you. I don't know where your dad is still, but if you want, I'll keep looking for him, if you want me to."

"I do."

Craig didn't know how she would feel if she found her dad, but he would be there for her as her support system if she needed him.

"I will then." Andy ate his cake in a hurry. "I've got to run."

"Thanks so much for all you've done so far," Margot said.

"Of course. Anything I can do to help, just ask me." Then Andy winked at her. "I hear the zombie paintball went well."

"Oh, yeah, we tromped the zombies. Score: one—shifters, score: zero—zombies," Margot said.

Andy laughed. "Good. I'll have to do that with a bunch of us some other time." Then he said goodbye and left the tavern.

"What do you want to do this afternoon?" Craig asked Margot.

"We have the candy and wine tasting event."

"Ahh, right. I forgot all about it. And after that?"

"What's playing at the movie theater? I still want to watch *Hocus Pocus* after dinner tonight though."

"You've got it." He pulled out his phone. "What do you want to see?"

She looked at his phone and smiled. "The thriller. And it will start right after our candy tasting party."

He took his phone and purchased tickets. "Are you done with your tea?"

She looked at her empty plate. "Yeah, man was that cake good."

"It sure was." Then he drove her to the candy tasting event where they met up with everyone who had wanted to do that.

The lynxes, foxes, and wolves were there. Jasper had skipped out on it, probably to work with his snow leopard brothers. The jaguar had left for his home in Houston, but those who were left were eager to test this out.

"I'm Wendy Wolfson, owner of the White Wolf Gourmet," a she-wolf said, greeting Margot and Steph. "I know everyone else but haven't met the two of you yet. I want to see if I can offer some candy with wine samples at my shop instead of just cheeses."

"It's great to meet you," Margot said, thinking that they needed to drop by her shop at some point too. "And that's a great idea for your shop."

"Yes, it's nice to meet you," Steph said.

Margot said to Steph, "Ames didn't want to do the taste tests?"

"Are you kidding? He's a stick in the mud. He eats blueberry everything. Blueberry waffles, muffins, cheesecakes. He would never mix wine with his blueberries," Steph said.

Margot smiled. "I forgot that you said that about him. He never likes to try anything new."

"Exactly."

Margot was a bit like that, but for the special Halloween event, she was willing to try different things. Who knew if she might really like some combination of candies and wines. And she loved that Craig was willing to try out the different combos too.

They started out with sherry and peanut butter cups. The lady in charge of the demonstration said, "The sherry has a raisin, nutty, caramel flavor so paired with the nutty, chocolate taste of the peanut butter cups, it makes a wonderfully tasty blend."

She had everyone eat a little sherbet to cleanse the pallet, then said, "Next, we'll combine a sweet and sour gummy candy with an aromatic wine like Riesling. The citrusy, acidic taste works well with the sweet and sour candy."

Margot wasn't into sweet and sour candy, but she was amazed at how well it tasted with the wine. Likewise, peanut butter cups weren't her thing. But the sherry took it to a new level of different.

"Now, one of my favorite Halloween candies is candy corn. Combining it with Chardonnay, which has kind of a buttery, vanilla flavor, if aged with oak and it mellows the sweetness."

They all tried that. Margot loved candy corn and she thought the combination tasted pretty good.

"Malty chocolate goes great with a fruity Merlot," the lady said.

Then she had them taste other kinds of sweet and sour candies with different kinds of wine, and more peanut butter, chocolate, caramel candies with other types of wine that gave the experience a whole new taste.

By the time they were done, Margot was ready to go to the movies and have hot buttered popcorn—all salty and buttery.

Everyone loved the experience and when they left the event, Wendy said to Margot and Steph, "I've got some more fun things to offer at the shop. Not an event like this because it's hers, but I can just offer samples to test out. Sometimes customers don't care for cheese, so candy might help to sell the wine instead."

"Oh, that's a great idea," Margot said.

Steph and Craig agreed, and then they said good night to everyone, and Margot got into Craig's Bronco and drove to the movie theater.

"So what did you think of the candy/wine combos?" Craig asked.

"I liked the candy corn ones the best but that's because I love candy corn. I love chocolate malted candies too, so that one was good with the fruity Merlot. It would be fun for parties, but I prefer drinking my wines with dinner, and having my candy for dessert. What about you?"

"That's the way I felt. They were interesting combinations for sure. I was thinking solid dark chocolate with champagne might be good," he said.

"Oh, yeah, we'll have to try that sometime."

He turned down another street. "But for now, I'm craving hot, buttered popcorn."

"You read my mind," she said.

When they arrived at the movie theater, he got them a big bucket of buttered popcorn, and they found their seats. They both silenced their phones.

"This is so much fun. I can't tell you how glad I am to have come here and met you and had such a great time," Margot said.

"Me too. I would have just been on a routine seaplane run if I hadn't glanced down at the woods from the window of my seaplane and seen a couple of polar bears running through the woods. I just don't want this to end."

She leaned over and kissed his mouth. "I know. Me either. It's like a fairy tale romance. Bear meets bear. Bear loses bear. Bear gets bear back."

"Is that how this is going to play out?" he asked and kissed her back.

"Yeah, I think that's exactly how the story is going to go." Then she cuddled up to him and ate some of the popcorn from the bucket he had gotten them. "This is just perfect."

"But I don't want to lose the bear, even for a second."

"I have to return home after this."

"Yeah, I know. I don't want to think about it." He was afraid when she left, she would forget about him. That she would go back to her old way of life, her store, her friends, and her parents and decide this *had* been a fairy tale. That she wouldn't want to commit to that big of a change in coming here. Or even that she might meet someone else back home and start dating him. Likewise, he didn't want to leave his home, his family, or his friends, either. They had a great shifter community here. Plus, he would probably run into her ex-fiancé and Craig would want to deck him for leaving her at the altar for another woman.

She smiled. "Just enjoy the moment."

He was, every moment that he was with her. Tonight, he wanted to really know how she was feeling about all this news about her father and the car accident. He really thought she was combining times that she recalled of driving her father home but that for whatever reason, he hadn't been in the car with her that day. The coma and her memory loss had a lot to do with it, he figured. He wanted her to know that she could talk to him about it. The movie theater wasn't really the place to do so.

It seemed that every time he reached to get some popcorn out of the bucket at the movie theater, she was reaching at the same time. They chuckled when they bumped fingers again.

"Great minds," she said.

Then they were engrossed in the movie and once they finished their popcorn, he wrapped his arm around her shoulders, and they snuggled together. The movie was really good, fast paced like he liked them, and Margot seemed to be enjoying it just as much. But he especially liked that he was with her on a date.

Because of the late afternoon hour, the theater was pretty empty. He didn't see anyone he knew in the theater. It felt like it was almost a private showing. He wanted to be able to do this with Margot in the future too.

She was holding his hand now as if she was afraid that the villain would get her next. He smiled. He liked being her hero. The last woman he had dated hadn't liked thrillers or horror. She had been all right with Halloween, but no haunted houses and the like. So Margot was a lot more like him in tastes and interests.

At the conclusion of the movie, Margot smiled. "Good. I love it when it has a happy ending. I don't mind if it has a twist, as long as the characters I'm totally hooked on are safe."

He smiled and they left the theater. "Yeah, like *The Cave*, where the creature from the cave made it out in another woman's body?"

"Oh, yeah, I saw that movie too. But at least the guy who made it out didn't have to deal with her anymore in that dark cave. Others would be at risk, sure, but he was safe. Now, if I got to know the others she targeted, I would feel the same way about them."

"You don't think he would go after the threat to humankind and take her down?" Craig asked.

"Ah, yeah, he would. He was like you. Truly a nice guy."

He chuckled. "Thanks. When we eat dinner, do you want to go out or have dinner at home?"

"Dinner at home, if you don't mind making something. We'll be having dinner at the tavern for the Halloween party. If you're tired of cooking, I can make something, if you would like."

"How about pizzas?" he asked. "I've got frozen ones and we

can add a bunch of ingredients to them. I have lots of different fixings."

"Oh, that would be great I haven't had one in weeks. All right, so we'll have pizza, wine, and *Hocus Pocus*."

He laughed. "That sounds good."

"Okay, show me the town."

"Walking or driving?"

"Let's walk. We need to work off the cake we had earlier at the tavern with your brother Andy and the popcorn."

"Deal." He wanted to do anything he could to convince her to return here for good but he didn't want to appear pushy or controlling. She had to decide something like this on her own. Not that he wasn't hoping to influence her a bit, but...

They parked downtown and then they began to walk down the sidewalk on Main Street and saw all the decorations in the windows—black cats, witches, ghosts, pirates, skeletons, spiderwebs, and big black spiders, and the black and orange lights on most of the buildings made it all very festive.

The owner of the White Wolf Gourmet greeted them and said to Margot, "I don't think I mentioned that Wolfrun is my brother. He and his girlfriend, Erin Wilden, were on the tour with you. And I got to see you at the candy and wine tasting event." Wendy motioned to them to come into her shop. "Come in and get some free samples of our gourmet cheeses. We have sausages, jerky, coffees, jams and jellies. Fudge and other special candies. And we have a variety of beers and wines."

Margot smiled. He wanted to laugh, since she wanted to walk off some calories, not eat any more before dinner.

"Sure, thanks," Margot said, and she and Craig went into the shop. "Oh, it smells delightful."

Craig knew she would feel she had to buy something. Well, so would he. If they didn't have their own tavern here, or they weren't shifters and all knew each other, he wouldn't have felt obligated.

"We have a big wine and cheese party in an hour, but it's quiet right now. Of course, you could attend, but it's not Halloween themed," Wendy said, showing them all the shelves of gourmet spices, cheeses, meats, and jellies.

"Oh, thanks but we plan to have pizza tonight and watch *Hocus Pocus*," Margot said.

"I love that movie. *Practical Magic* first. But I have to say I love *Stardust* too."

"That was our first movie night. *Stardust* will be next on our witch's night out shows unless Craig wants to watch anything different," Margot said.

Craig thought she was cute. "No, I love the ghost brothers in that one."

"Especially the one in the bathtub," Wendy said.

Craig and Margot smiled.

"My brother said he and Erin are visiting the haunted house with the two of you. That should really be fun," Wendy said.

"It should be. I haven't been to one in years," Craig said.

Margot laughed. "Me? Every year. But not one like this. So I'm looking forward to going with everyone."

Then Margot and Craig sampled some cheese and wine, and they decided on a bottle of wine and a couple packages of cheese, bought them, and then said goodbye to Wendy before her wine and cheese party guests arrived.

Margot and Craig left the shop and continued on their way, checking out the other stores and just having a delightful walk in the chilly night air.

"We weren't supposed to be eating anything before dinner," she said.

Craig laughed. "That's just what I was thinking." Then he got a call and answered it. "Yeah, Mom? Uh, hold on. I'm with

Margot and we're just down the street seeing all the shops. Let me put this on speaker."

"Your dad and I need to go to an emergency bear council meeting. Ben's here, of course, but we really need your help with the grill."

"I can help with the cash register," Margot said.

"You are a godsend."

"We'll be right there." Craig was so appreciative and gave Margot a big hug.

Someone honked and they turned to look. It was Edward and he pulled up beside them. "Are you going to the tavern to help out?"

"Yeah, we both are," Craig said.

"Hop in. I'm helping out too."

THEY GOT into the van and Margot was surprised to see Robyn and the two-month-old babies had come with him. Their six-year-old twins were in the back seat coloring cute little monster pages. "When the babies are asleep, I can help," Robyn said, smiling. "Their parents have a special room for the kids to play in, or in this case, sleep in."

"I'm going to work the cash register because I manage one at my shop," Margot said. "No one wants me to carry platters of food to the tables. I did that when I was a teen and totally made a mess of things."

Robyn laughed. "I can help serve the tables. This will be fun."

Margot thought so too and really felt like she was becoming part of the family. Unlike with her own parents who were so distant from her.

"So did Mom tell you what it was all about?" Edward asked Craig.

Margot thought it was sweet that Edward called his aunt mom since she had raised him and Rob after their parents died.

"No. We had the phone on speaker on the street so she might not have wanted to reveal what the matter was that they had to convene an emergency meeting for," Craig said.

"She didn't tell us either, just asked if I could help out," Edward said, "but it has something to do with"—he glanced back at Margot—"someone Margot knows and the mess he has gotten himself into."

"My father? My biological father?" Margot was feeling shaken and didn't know what to say or do.

"If Mom didn't tell you about the case, how do you know?" Craig asked. Then he snapped his fingers. "Rob had a premonition."

17

C raig was dying to know what Margot's father had done that their bear sleuth had to deal with in an emergency bear council meeting.

"Rob doesn't think it's your father," Edward said to Margot.

"What? Who? Steph? Ames?" Margot sounded a little panicky.

Edward pulled into the parking lot of the tavern. "The person was about your age, maybe a little older. Rob didn't know his name. But he's close to you. Rob doesn't know who this guy is, but he got the feeling he's related to you in some way. He could even be your ex-fiancé."

"If he has gotten himself into trouble, that's on him. So what has happened?" Margot asked before Craig could.

They got out of the vehicle and walked across the parking lot, Craig carrying the packages of cheese they had purchased at the White Wolf Gourmet, so he could refrigerate it at the tavern while they worked.

"Whoever this guy is, he got some girl pregnant. He's a polar bear shifter and she isn't. So her dad wants him to make this right and marry her. Of course that would mean he would have to turn the whole family, which, understandably, he doesn't want to do."

"I...I've never heard of a shifter impregnating a human," Margot said.

"Me either," Craig said. "Not anyone that I've known personally, though I've heard stories, rumor, myths about it. I always thought it was a case of trying to scare shifters out of having relations with non-shifters. I had always thought the only way a person became a shifter was through a bite or was born to shifter parents."

"We'll see what happens. Mom said she would let the family know as soon as she learned all there was about it. I think she didn't want to say until she was certain about it. Or because she was in such a rush to contact all of us to see who could come and help out at the tavern," Edward said.

Craig wrapped his arm around Margot's shoulders and kissed her cheek as Edward carried one of the babies in a carrier and Robyn carried the other. Craig quickly got the tavern door for them. He knew Margot was feeling uneasy about this whole mess, and he wished Edward hadn't told them about Rob's vision. They would learn more when their mom and dad told them what was going on. He hoped it wasn't anything that would impact on Margot and her life.

MARGOT COULDN'T BELIEVE that someone close to her had gotten a human pregnant! She didn't think it could be her ex-fiancé because she was no longer close to him. Though she didn't want him or any polar bear shifter in a mess like that, she just couldn't imagine her ex would do that. He had an aversion to dating humans, for one thing. But the last she knew, he was still with the new girlfriend. The one he had dumped Margot for, and she was a polar bear. So unless it was Margot's biological father, she didn't know who else it could be and how he was related to her What if...what if it was a cousin that she didn't know or hadn't remembered having?

Craig showed Margot how to work the register, though she worked one that was similar to it at her shop.

Then they began working in the tavern and Margot really felt like she was part of the family already and she liked the feeling. His whole family was so close to one another. Not like she was with her mother and stepfather. She loved that they were there for each other when they needed assistance.

She was glad they had wanted her to help at the tavern, and not treat her like she shouldn't because she was a visitor to White Bear and here just on vacation. Everything she did here made her feel more and more like this was where she belonged.

She rang up her first customer, smiling. The woman told her that she and her family would be back and they would tell all their friends about the wonderful atmosphere and the great food.

"You're so welcome. I'll let the management know." Margot smiled again and said, "Happy Halloween!"

The three ten- to twelve-year-old kids chanted, "trick or treat," as she handed them each some chocolate candy from the pirate's treasure chest.

She saw Craig wink at her before he delivered a tray of meals to one table. She smiled but then she was so busy after that, she didn't even notice Craig's parents return to the shop so Genevieve could take over the register and Ned went back to the grill to work.

"Thanks so much for helping us out," Genevieve said to Margot.

"It was no trouble at all. I was glad to." Margot noticed Craig going back into the kitchen and she suspected that he was learning from his father what had come out of the bear council meeting, while she really couldn't ask his mother because she was busy handling customers who were paying for their meals.

Robyn went back into the playroom and Margot followed her in there to see the babies. "They are adorable." She picked up one of the babies, who was starting to fuss, and gently rocked him in her arms while Robyn sat in a rocking chair and started nursing the other baby boy.

"Thanks. They were so good. They have been sleeping for most of the time tonight. Which was good as far as us managing the workload at the tavern, but I hope they'll sleep okay through part of the night now."

Margot smiled. "I don't blame you."

The twin boys were watching an animated Halloween movie.

"Rob said Alicia has visions of the past. Do you know if she has seen anything about the accident that I was in?" Margot asked.

"About your accident, yes. I'm sorry for not mentioning it to you earlier. We were so intent on getting to work at the tavern and the business with the man who got a human pregnant, I forgot about it. Not to mention lack of sleep with taking care of the babies gives me brain fog for sure."

"Oh, sure, I bet. Did she see my father in the car?"

"Not your father, unless he was your age, or close to it."

Margot frowned at her. "I don't understand."

"Did you have a boyfriend back then? Maybe the two of you had gone for a car ride and then the accident occurred."

"I...I don't think so. Unless he was much older, I wouldn't have been able to drive the car."

"What if he had been, but he switched places with you after the accident and—"

"No. I remember holding onto the wheel. Are you sure Alicia's vision was of me?"

"Yes. Margot Rider."

"But the witness said I was the only one there."

"What if whoever was with you escaped the vehicle and ran off into the woods? He might have done so before the witness's vehicle reached you and he didn't see the other person."

Margot patted the baby's back in her arms. "I don't know. I mean, I remember fighting with someone over driving the car and finally managed to get the keys away from him. I was sure it was my dad."

"Okay, so what if you did get the keys away from your dad and he had been drunk. But he didn't get into the car with you."

Margot's lips parted and then she closed her mouth and nodded. "But then who was the other guy?"

CRAIG'S FATHER grilled steaks while Craig grilled up some hamburger patties. "So what happened at the council meeting?" Craig asked his dad.

"Does Margot know she has a brother?" his dad asked.

"Hell, no. Or at least not that she has mentioned to me. That's who got a human woman pregnant?"

"Yeah, by the name of Kyle Rider. His girlfriend had told him she was on birth control pills but apparently it didn't work, she lied, or she didn't take them on purpose because she thought being pregnant would convince Kyle to marry her."

"But how do you know he's Margot's brother and not just someone unrelated to her?"

"We asked him because Margot is a polar bear shifter and has the same last name before she changed it to her stepfather's."

Craig let out his breath in a huff. "Okay, great. So how come she doesn't know he exists?"

"She had the accident and was in a coma for two months."

"And he never visited her in the hospital? He never saw her afterward?" Craig asked, astounded.

"Yeah, that's what he said."

Craig thought that over and wondered why? Hadn't he cared for her at all? "Why?"

"He wouldn't say."

"He must not have lived with his mother after the accident then, instead staying with his father."

"He did."

"So what's going to happen with the woman and her baby?" What a mess Kyle had gotten himself into.

"On rare occasions, a human female will have a baby by a shifter. We've checked with all the sources we could find on the subject. Not all situations are known though, which makes it all a big case of guessing."

"Okay, but the baby can't shift, can it? It won't be a shifter like us, right? With both parents being shifters, or one of them turned like in Alicia's case before the babies are conceived, the babies will be shifters. When she shifts, the babies shift. But a human woman can't shift, so the babies wouldn't be able to."

His father shook his head. "Not until they are older, if they can. We just don't know."

"Wait. Andy said a Kyle Rider had his vehicle stolen from him a couple of days ago and then returned to him. Man, I never made the connection once Margot said her dad was Benjamin Rider." Craig finished the burgers he was grilling and plated them. "So what does the council want to do about it?"

"Take the babies from her and have a shifter family raise them. Or Kyle can. But it's going to be troublesome because the woman won't want to give up her babies. I can't imagine being in her shoes and having her babies taken away from her. The babies will have to be watched until they're able to shift on their own and then taught how to get along with others as shifters."

"Which can be between five and ten years of age. That's a lot of years to watch over them when they could shift at any time. There's no set age. All shifter kids develop at different ages in life."

"Right," his dad said.

Craig started working on another order of burgers. "What if the babies aren't shifters and can't shift?"

"Or what if they have an affinity toward our kind but can't shift? There's a case like that where the wolf shifter genes were in part passed down to a twin brother and sister. They have some of our senses—enhanced hearing and sense of smell—but they can't shift. In that case, the parents were human, but the grandfather on the mother's side was a shifter and the grand-mother was a human. Things just get really complicated and there's no telling how something like this might turn out. We're still considering what to do about it, short of kidnapping the babies when they're born and raising them as our own—not our family in particular"—his father said quickly—"but some family."

"Or Kyle turning her?"

"The woman in question has a large family and they're really close to each other, Kyle said. If we turn her, it's going to cause a lot of problems."

"Okay. What should I tell Margot?" Craig wanted to tell her everything, and yet he was afraid it would really upset her, especially when she must not have remembered her brother at all.

"Tell her what we know. Though I hope it won't be too much of a shock to learn of it. But I wouldn't keep it from her. She'll know you know something, and she'll likely resent it if you with-held the information."

Craig plated the burgers.

His dad said, "Go talk to her. I saw her go into the playroom with Robyn. Thanks for helping out. And thank Margot for assisting us too."

"I will. Thanks." Then Craig took off his apron and left the kitchen and soon was walking into the playroom where he heard Robyn and Margot talking about the accident Margot had been involved in.

"Oh, so what happened?" Robyn asked before Margot could speak to Craig.

"The guy who got himself into trouble with a human woman who is now having his twins is—" Craig said.

Robyn gasped. "Margot's brother!

"WHAT?" Margot saw Craig's serious expression, but she didn't have a brother! Or at least that she remembered.

"He was the one in the car with you, Margot," Robyn guessed. "Now that the pieces are coming together, I can see the situation more clearly. I may not have Rob and Alicia's gifts, but I'm pretty good at solving puzzles." She swapped babies with Margot, though Craig offered to take the well-fed baby.

But Margot wanted to hold onto that one for a bit. She guessed her maternal instincts were kicking in. The babies were so sweet. She frowned at Craig. "What's his name?"

"Kyle Rider." Craig was watching her for any sign of recognition in her expression.

And she reacted! "Ohmigod, Kyle! He's...he's my twin!" She couldn't believe she wouldn't recall anything about him for all these years until now.

"Do you remember him being in the car with you when you had the accident?" Robyn asked.

Margot tried to envision her brother being in the car with

her, but she couldn't. "Why can't I remember that much about him? Some details are coming back. Like I remember our fights and Mom breaking them up when we were kids. But...but I can barely remember anything else about him."

"The accident?" Craig asked.

Margot let out her breath. "I don't know. Maybe." She shook her head. "I don't know." She rubbed her temple. It was hurting while she was trying hard to come up with memories of her past. "I need to know where he is. I need to see him. Maybe that will help me to regain some of my memories."

"Yeah, I should have thought to ask my dad where Kyle is living now. I can't believe the mess he has gotten himself in with a human female," Craig said.

"I know. I guess it makes all of us shifters more conscious of the fact that it could happen to us if we got involved with a human and how it could turn out for us, if a baby is conceived," Margot said.

"Exactly. I'll be right back after I see if Dad knows what his address is, and we can go home and have dinner, or—"

"Maybe see Kyle first, if he's agreeable." Margot had to know the answers to her questions—if he'd lived with their father and why. If he'd been in the car with her, or not. If he had, what had happened to him? But then she didn't want Craig to believe she was dumping him to see a long-lost brother, whom she might not want to see once she met up with him.

"Absolutely, and I want to go with you, if that's okay with you."

"Oh, perfect." Margot didn't want to do it without him, and she realized just how much he meant to her when it involved a situation like this that could be traumatic.

Craig leaned over and kissed her cheek. She turned her head to get a kiss on the lips. He smiled and kissed her as she kissed him back. Then he left the playroom while Margot cuddled the baby further. She saw Robyn watching them, smiling. Margot sighed. The whole family would know she was already hooked on the bear.

Margot didn't know what to think about all this concerning her twin brother though. "Do you think Alicia could see anything else in a vision, Robyn?"

Robyn said, "Maybe if Alicia saw a picture of Kyle when he was fifteen, she would know unequivocally that he was the one in the car with you when you had the accident."

"I would show her one, but of course I don't have any since I didn't even remember he existed. But then what had happened to him all those years since the accident?" Margot still couldn't wrap her head around the whole notion.

"When you meet up with him, you can ask him. You know, if things work out between the two of you, he could probably really use someone to give him moral support, concerning the twins and all."

Which made Margot wonder if he was living with the woman and what her name was. Even though she was human, she was the babies' mother and Margot wanted to refer to her by name. "Right. I can't understand why my mother wouldn't tell me about my brother or why he wouldn't have lived with us all those years."

Then Craig returned to the playroom with Edward in tow.

"Are you ready to go home, Robyn?" Edward asked.

"Yeah, let's take the babies home. Do you have to return to the tavern to help out further?" Robyn asked.

"I'll come back for a couple of hours. Business is brisk, but I'll make sure you and the twins all get settled at home first," Edward said. "Good luck, you two, with speaking with your brother, Margot. Craig, see you when I see you."

"I'll give you a call when we learn what we can," Craig said, grabbing the cheese they had purchased from one of the fridges in the kitchen.

"Okay, good," Edward said. "Oh, could I give you a lift to your Bronco?"

"Nah, we were enjoying the walk," Margot said.

"Sounds like a winner." Then Edward took the baby from Margot and settled her in her carrier. He and Robyn carried the babies out of the tavern, while their six-year-olds hurried out after them and Margot and Craig followed them outside.

Edward got their wine out of the van and handed it to Craig.

"Thanks, night all," Craig said.

Everyone wished everyone a good night.

Then Margot and Craig walked down the street to where he had parked his vehicle.

"So is Kyle living with the woman who's carrying his twins?" Margot asked as Craig pulled onto the road and began driving.

"No. Dad said she lives with her parents. Janice wanted to move in with Kyle, but he wouldn't go along with that because he's a shifter and he had no plans to turn her. He never thought he would get her pregnant," Craig said. "How are you feeling about all of this?"

"That it's so unreal. I mean, I still can't fully picture him. It's like he's there, but elusive and I can't dredge up the memories about the accident or so many details about him no matter what."

"Memory loss can be like that. At first, Rob had the same condition. When the avalanche had buried him, and his brother had dug him out. He had forgotten some of his memories, but they came back. But he wasn't in a coma for two months either."

"But we both died, right?"

"Yeah, and Rob had second sight after that. Though I always wondered if he had them earlier and had just been afraid to let on that he could see future visions, or maybe didn't even trust in them himself."

"I could see feeling that way." Margot folded her arms. "About my brother, does he even love her?"

"I don't know. Even if he does, it's a mess of a situation no matter how you look at it."

Margot bit her lip. "I can't believe this. I would call my mother and ask her, but I would rather talk to my brother and see if he'll be more honest with me. Wait, did you or anyone else let him know we're coming to see him?"

"Dad gave me the phone number." Craig handed her his phone. "We can call him on Bluetooth, or you could call him directly."

She put the phone number in her own list of phone contacts. "Let's call him on Bluetooth and we can both hear what he has to say."

Craig called him up then and when someone answered on the other end of the line, Craig said, "Hi, you don't know me, but you met with the White Bear council members about—"

"Yeah, hell, so what do you want?" Kyle asked, sounding angry and she suspected it was because he was in a lot of trouble with the bear sleuth, and he figured Craig was going to give him more grief over what he had done.

"Kyle? This is your sister, Margot."

Kyle didn't respond and she was afraid they'd lost the connection.

"Kyle? My boyfriend and I are coming to see you."

He still didn't respond.

"Are you still there? I need some answers. I was in a coma for two months after the accident and I didn't even remember I had a twin brother. Not until now. The memories are coming back piece by piece. I need you to help me recall more of my past life. We're coming to see you."

Then the call disconnected.

She wiped away a couple of tears. She wasn't prone to weeping, except, okay, if she saw something that saddened her in a movie, she did, though she always tried to hide that she did, not wanting anyone to think she was silly for doing so.

Craig reached over and took hold of her hand and squeezed. "He's under a lot of stress right now. Learning you're here and wanting answers from him too is probably more stressful for him."

"I don't care if he can't handle it. I need answers and I'm not waiting to learn the truth."

"Oh, I so agree. He owes it to you. He'll have to deal with it." Then Craig smiled at her. "Boyfriend, eh?"

"Yeah. I figured if anyone could help unravel the mysteries of my life and be there as my support through the whole thing, you earned the role of boyfriend. As long as you're okay with it."

"Hell, yeah I am." He sat a little taller in the driver's seat. "Now we just need to find a place for you to open your new shop."

She laughed.

"I'm serious."

"I know you are. You're a man of action."

"You bet I am."

She was so afraid they would arrive at her brother's house and find he had left so he wouldn't have to speak with her. Or that he wouldn't open the door to them. To take her mind off it, she began to do searches on her phone for a possible retail store for sale that she could purchase and found one right down the street from the White Bear Tavern. If she could sell her shop, she could buy this one.

"This looks good," she said. "A place that is just down the street from your parents' tavern."

"I know one of the real estate agents, a wolf shifter. I'll call her and see if we can set up an appointment to see the shop that's for sale tomorrow. She'll make sure you get a good deal on it if it looks like a place you would like to buy. We can even buy it for you until you sell your own store in North to pay off the zero-interest loan."

She laughed. "Wow, okay, sure."

Craig got on Bluetooth and called her. "Hey, Paige, this is Craig. I've got a client for you. A polar bear shifter also. She's interested in relocating her dress shop from North to White Bear. She liked the one down the street from my parents' place."

"Yeah, sure. Do you want to see it tomorrow?"

"In the morning, yes," Margot said. "I'm Margot Anderson."

"I'm Paige Stanford, and I would be happy to show it to you. I'll take you to a few more locations also so you can have some other options to check out."

"Thanks. Would eight in the morning be all right?"

"It sure would be. Do you want to meet at my office, Craig knows where it's at, or meet me at the first shop and follow me from there?"

"We can follow you there. Thanks again." Margot was really doing this. She was going to make a big change in her life, and she felt good about it. She loved being with other shifters, and just holding onto Alicia's babies and wanting that for herself, she knew this was where she needed to be. Even if Craig ended up standing her up at the altar, which she didn't believe would ever happen, at least she knew there were other bachelor males she could date. Three other eligible male bachelor polar bears lived in North, but all were good friends of her ex-fiancé, and no way did she want to date any of them.

She had the passing notion that she should check in with her mother first. That she should even talk it over with Steph also. But she knew what they would both say. Her mother would say no. Steph would say do it.

She wondered how Steph and Ames were getting along. Steph would have told her what was what if she'd wanted to but Margot suspected Ames hadn't asked Steph to mate her yet. And Steph hadn't done so with Ames yet either.

Craig finally pulled into the driveway of a small, red brick, one-story house, the lights on in the main part of the house. She took a deep breath as Craig parked the vehicle.

He took her hand and squeezed it, giving her moral support.

They got out of the car, and he took her hand as they walked up the front walk to the door.

18

Craig couldn't believe that the man who'd gotten himself into so much trouble with a human woman was Margot's twin brother, whom she hadn't even remembered having. Maybe visiting with him would help her get her memories back or at least some of them back. He was also shocked when Margot told her brother that Craig was her boyfriend, and she was ready to move to White Bear! He couldn't wait to tell the rest of the family. He was absolutely ecstatic.

He always felt great when he rescued someone needing help, but this time, he got a girlfriend he adored out of the deal. He wondered what Steph would say about it. And Craig was glad Margot had wanted him to come with her to meet her brother. He hoped he would be her emotional support if she needed it. Not to mention he wanted to get to know her brother, and this business with the twins was personal now. His whole family would be there for him, trying to work this through as if he was already part of the family.

Margot took a deep breath, her heard pounding as she rang the doorbell. A few minutes later, the door opened, and she just stared at the man standing there. Craig had a sinking feeling that she didn't recognize him. Maybe because he was all grown up, just as she was. Kyle was dark-haired and had dark brown eyes, tall like Craig and his male kin.

"Come in," he said. "I take it you're Margot. You look like her, except older. I'm Kyle Rider. Do you want something to drink?"

"No, thanks," Margot said. "Yeah, I'm Margot."

"I'm Craig MacMathan."

"So you have a boyfriend," Kyle said to Margot.

"What happened to you that night?" Margot asked, not playing around with small talk.

"I got a woman pregnant."

"Damn it, Kyle. What happened the night of the accident that I was in? Where were you? What happened to you? Did you live with Dad? What happened to Dad?"

Kyle took a seat on a chair in the living room and Margot and Craig sat together on a sofa. "Okay, niceties aside, I thought you came to ask me about Janice."

"Her too, but I want answers about the accident where I ended up in a coma and you...?" Margot asked.

Craig had never seen Margot angry, but he could understand her frustration. Her brother was only thinking of his current predicament with no thought of what had happened to Margot in the past.

Kyle hadn't hugged his sister, and she hadn't acted like she wanted to embrace him either. Again, Craig wondered if she even recognized him. He really had thought this would be more of a happy reunion. But Craig knew the siblings needed to clear the air. Craig hoped that as much as he cared about his brothers and parents and his cousins, that Margot and Kyle could come to terms with their differences too.

❧

MARGOT UNDERSTOOD that Kyle was faced with some real issues with this business with the woman he got pregnant, and she could understand how that was still foremost on his mind, but hers was about the accident and wanting to know what had really happened that night.

"What about the accident?" she asked again.

"The accident." Kyle rubbed his whiskered chin.

"Yes!" she said.

"I had too much to drink that night. I don't remember much about it."

"Oh, that's just great. I took the keys from you. You were going to drive. You were drunk. You fought with me over driving the car, but I managed to win and grabbed the keys from you. So much for winning. You got in the car and fell asleep, but I didn't remember that. I thought of Dad and how many times I had to stop him from driving drunk. I thought it was him. But it was you! I was driving home and then the car was in our lane, and I swerved to miss a head-on collision."

"I don't remember."

"I was in a coma! I don't remember all of it. I'm trying to recall what had happened to me. I've had terrible nightmares about it. No one said anything about you being there! The eyewitness saw only me there. Not you. So what happened? How did you end up not getting picked up by an ambulance at the same time as me, if you had been there and injured also?"

"I...I was thrown from the car. I don't remember anything about it. I swear to you." Kyle threw his hands up in exasperation. "When I was found, it was later, and the car, you, none of it was there by then. I didn't know how I ended up in the brush. I couldn't remember how I got there, that you were driving the car, none of it. I don't even remember who had found me."

"But Mom knew about it?"

"She...uh, learned about it when the ambulance brought me

in and then she had a big fight with me—one-sided. You know
how she is. Our family was all sorts of dysfunctional. When Dad
sobered up, she told me I could live with Dad. She was divorcing
him, for the same reason she disowned me—drinking too much.
She said it was my fault for the accident. Hell, I wasn't even
driving."

"Which was a damn good thing," Margot said.

Kyle cleared his throat. "You're right, but I swear I don't
remember any of it."

"So what happened to Dad?"

"Five years ago, he died fighting with someone in a barroom
brawl. He was drunk as usual. When I was sixteen, a year after
the accident, I finally left home, unable to deal with Dad's
drunken bouts. After the car accident, I never drank like that
again. It wasn't my fault that you had the accident. It wasn't
yours. Mom said that the police reports identified that the other
driver had been in our lane and was the reason for the accident.
The truth of the matter is Mom feels guilty about the whole
thing."

"Why?" Maybe that was why their mom never wanted
Margot to see a therapist about it.

"Because she hadn't divorced Dad sooner. If she had, none of
that would have happened. Dad was at the bar that night and
gave me too much to drink. Not that he forced it on me exactly. I
just went along with it to be cool, you know. I was sicker than a
dog. Before I was found in the brush, I'd thrown up all over the
place where I had been lying. Thankfully, I had been on my
stomach, or I could have choked to death. I'd had alcohol
poisoning. But that night, you had tried to get Dad to go in the
car like you always did. He wouldn't go but you managed to get
the car keys away from him. Then I guess you were trying to
convince me to get in the car. You were trying to get me home
that night. And no, I didn't remember any of it. Mom told me

that's what had happened. That's why she disowned me, because she thought I was going to be just like Dad, and she didn't want to have to deal with Dad *and* me."

"But you didn't drink like Dad?"

"A couple of drinks and I'm done." Kyle shrugged. "I'm not anything like Dad was."

"You...you could have talked to me after the accident."

"Mom told me you were in a coma. She was worried that you would never come out of it or that you could have been brain damaged. Once you came out of the coma, she said you didn't remember that night. She told me that if I explained what had happened to you, you could be further traumatized. But I only made her madder when I told her I didn't know what had happened that night myself. I...I tried to see you at the hospital, but she was always there, and she told me I wasn't welcome, and she would call security if I showed up there again. She didn't have to tell me that twice."

Margot could understand how Kyle had felt, stuck with their dad, the drunk, having to go it alone at only sixteen. Their mom should have given Kyle a chance to prove he was okay, that he wouldn't become like their dad had been.

"Okay, so what's the deal with this mess you got yourself in?" Margot honestly wanted to know what was going on with her twin brother and his girlfriend, even if it meant helping him to raise his twins.

"What do you care?" Kyle asked, his eyes suddenly glassy with tears.

"I care. All right? I love you no matter what, and I'm so glad we've been able to reconnect. We have to figure out what to do about this baby situation. Do you think your girlfriend will be agreeable to giving up the kids to you after she has had them? Giving you full custody rights?" Margot asked.

Kyle shook his head. "No. She wants the babies."

"But when they're able to shift, it will be an issue since she's human," Margot believed someone would have to kidnap the children at some point to take them and raise them as shifters for their own safety.

"She's not exactly human," Kyle said.

"What?" both Craig and Margot said, both of them sounding shocked.

"She's a tigress."

Margot and Craig just stared at him.

"Uh,"—Kyle scratched his head—"we thought we couldn't conceive since we're different kind of shifters. I mean, yeah, if we had been different kinds of bears, then yes, we could. But different species? In the wild, it wouldn't happen. Except in the cases with some wolves in a wolf pack mating with coyotes. But a tiger and a polar bear? No way. Tigers and lions? Sure."

"You said she was human." Craig sounded just as surprised as Margot was.

"No, I said she wasn't one of us. I guess everyone assumed she was human. I was embarrassed to say what she truly was and left it to everyone's imagination. I guess that wasn't a good idea."

"No, it wasn't a good idea," Craig said. "There's a hell of a lot of difference between her being human or being a different species of shifter. Her parents can't want you to wed, if they know what you are. And my parents, who are on the bear council, didn't realize this. No one on the council did."

"Her parents don't know that I'm a polar bear shifter. They've never met me. She didn't want them to see me. Everything was fine until she told me she was pregnant, and then the dynamics changed, and she wanted me to marry her. Her parents think I'm a tiger like Janice. But the other two guys that I know of that she has been with don't have jobs and they're perfectly fine to live off her income. She can't have that because she'll be taking care of the twins when they're born."

Margot shook her head.

"I've got to tell my parents. This changes everything." Craig pulled out his phone and made the call. "Hey, Mom, we're seeing Kyle right now, Margot and me, and he says the woman he got pregnant isn't human. No." He glanced at Kyle. "She's a tiger shifter. Her parents want him to marry her because he got her pregnant, but they don't know he's a polar bear. I know. That's what we all thought. Different species couldn't have offspring. Even if their offspring were a similar species, like the combination between a lion and tiger, the babies should be sterile so they can't have children of their own. All right. Talk to you—oh, another thing. More great news. Margot and I are dating and...uh,"—he looked over at her and smiled—"I haven't yet, but she's looking at a place to buy to put her new dress shop in. Yeah. I really lucked out. Okay, talk to you and Dad later. Bye."

"Another emergency council meeting?" Kyle asked.

Craig shook his head. "We haven't eaten dinner yet. Have you?"

"No. I don't have much in the line of groceries in the fridge," Kyle said. "And half of my stuff is still in boxes. I just left them in the garage to empty out as I had time and organized my living room and kitchen."

"We can order out. What does everyone want?" Craig asked.

Then they ordered individual pizzas and Craig said, "All right, Mom said that there isn't any way that you could have gotten Janice pregnant. So you say there's a tiger shifter in the area that she had been seeing?"

"Yes, and a lion. This happened in Anchorage, and then I moved to the outskirts of White Bear," Kyle said. "A few weeks later, which would have been the right timing for me getting her pregnant, she calls me up and said I'm the father. So maybe it's the bachelor tiger in Anchorage. I know there was a lion shifter who was sniffing around her all the time when we would go out too."

Craig snapped his fingers. "We have a wolf doctor here who can determine if you're the father. The two of you just need to do the test."

"How much do you want to bet that Janice won't go along with it," Kyle said.

"Well, because of the circumstances, she'll have to or you're off the hook," Margot said. "I bet you anything she was with one of those big cats and when she got pregnant, she didn't want to be with him as in married and actually being with him."

"But it wouldn't make any sense to her parents either when they learn Kyle is a polar bear. They'll think the same as us. That there's a mistake as to who the father of the twins would be," Craig said.

"What if she thinks Kyle would be a good husband and father to the kids even knowing full well that they would be tiger shifters, or even ligers if she got mixed up with the lion." Margot was so hopeful that her brother wasn't responsible for the babies. She couldn't imagine how he could be. And they would need one of their kind to really raise them right. What did Kyle, or any polar bear shifter for that matter, know about tiger cubs and how to train them?

"You're not off the hook yet," Craig said, "but things are looking up."

Kyle suddenly got up from his chair and crossed the floor to Margot and reached his arms out to her. "I'm sorry for not trying to get in touch with you later, once you were awake. I figured Mom would have told you how awful I was and that I would be a bad influence on you."

She stood and hugged him. "She didn't tell me you even

existed. I just never had any memories of you. But some of them are coming back. Besides, from the sounds of it, you had your own demons to deal with. I do remember that you and I would go polar bear fishing and had a blast at it."

"Right. We did. And you were always trying to set me up with one of your girlfriends."

"At least they were bear shifters," she said.

"True."

"So you really don't have a drinking problem?" she asked her brother.

"No, I'm good. Truly."

"We bought some wine and cheese at a gourmet shop," she said.

"I'll go get it," Craig said and headed out of the house.

"So what's this business between you and him?" Kyle asked, jerking his thumb toward Craig as he returned with the cheese and wine.

Margot smiled. "My friend, Stephanie, and I had to duke it out with a mother grizzly bear and Craig came to help us. The grizzly bear broke Steph's wrist. I was a lot luckier. Anyway, we're here for the week doing a lot of Halloween activities and we would love it if you joined us."

"Ouch, a fight with a grizzly would be bad. Yeah, I would like that." Kyle got a plate out and a knife to cut the cheese and then pulled out some wine glasses. They had some of the wine and cheese.

"Good. You can go with us to the haunted house," Craig said.

"For sure," Kyle said.

They were enjoying their wine and cheese when their pizzas arrived.

Craig answered the door and paid for the pizzas. They all sat down to eat at the dining room table.

"So Craig rescued you and now you're moving here?" Kyle sounded surprised.

"When I met Craig, I knew right away that we had something special going on. And I love the bear community here, not to mention all the other shifters that I've met." Margot took a bite of her pizza.

"We're all thrilled that Margot is in our lives, especially me." Craig pulled off a slice of pizza.

"When did you end up in White Bear?" Margot asked Kyle. "No one knew you before this."

"I just moved into the house a week ago. I bought it after some house flippers—a bunch of snow leopards—renovated it and flipped it. I needed to get away from Anchorage after the deal with Janice."

"I don't blame you. What are you doing then for an income?" Margot asked.

"Dad had a bunch of stocks and bonds that had made over five million dollars. They were in a separate account from the joint ones Mom and Dad had. Mom's name wasn't on those so he never gave her any of the money. They divorced on bad terms. Understandably. He died five years after they were divorced and even though I had abandoned him to live on my own, he had left all his investments and properties to me. You know, even though he was a drunk every night, during the day, he worked hard. Because he had done so well financially, I became an investments councilor, and I got a job at the White Bear Bank. I'll be starting work on Monday."

"Oh, great. You missed the zombie paintball and the Halloween dancing. But you have to go with us to the haunted house." She knew that would be one of his favorite activities, but she was surprised that she remembered that. She thought it would be a great way to connect.

"Yeah, sure. It's too bad I didn't know about the zombie paintball. I would have enjoyed that."

"You would have. Give me your email address and I'll send the list of things we're doing and the times to you."

He did and she sent the itinerary to him in an email. She hoped he would really do some of the activities with them. "I'm sorry we didn't get to know each other over the years." She would have a hard time forgiving her mother for giving up on her son and not telling Margot about her brother.

"We'll make up for it." Kyle gave her a hug.

"Yeah, and this is a good way to start." Then Craig got a call. "Yeah, okay. Kyle says there's a possibility that Janice hooked up with another tiger, or a lion shifter, and that's who the dad really is. We can't imagine the offspring could result from the union of two shifters who are different species to that degree. Right." He looked at Kyle. "How far along is she?"

"Eight weeks," Kyle said.

"She can have the DNA done with the SNP micro array procedure. If she doesn't want to have it done, then we know she has been with another shifter, closer to her own kind, and doesn't want the truth to be known," Craig said to Kyle. "Okay, Dad, thanks. I'll let him know." Then he ended the call. "Okay, we're not sure *you're* going to be able to get Janice to do this, so the council will send a letter to her address, and she can ignore it or take the test. Have you been in contact with her recently?"

"Yeah, to tell her I was moving to White Bear. I didn't want her to think that I was running away from my responsibilities in the event the twins were really mine, but that I came here because of the new job."

"Wait, does she know that you inherited Dad's money?" Margot asked.

"Yeah. And she knows I have a good paying job and a new home, so she might think that was a good way to get away from

Anchorage and start over if she could sucker me into thinking the babies were mine."

"But she would have to explain to her parents how the father of her babies was a polar bear," Craig said. "And that in truth they have no bear genetics."

"Exactly," Margot said. "I'm glad I don't get myself into binds like that."

Kyle laughed. "Well, I didn't think I would ever get myself into any bind like that either. So, Craig, have you got any sisters?"

"No, I'm afraid not. Just two brothers and two male cousins who are just like my brothers. But we do have female polar bear shifters living here, so you'll have some bears to date."

Kyle smiled. "Okay, that sounds good. So tomorrow is the haunted house then."

"It sure is. We'll meet you there at the time listed in the email I sent to you," Margot said.

"And we'll have lunch afterward at the White Bear Tavern. You can meet my brothers, if they're both there. You've met my parents. Oh, and we're going with a real estate agent before seeing the haunted house to look for a shop location for Margot," Craig said.

"Have you told Mom you're moving here?" Kyle asked Margot.

"Nope. And she would say no if I did. It's my decision. They have their lives. We have ours."

"That's for sure. I'm so glad that we reconnected, despite the circumstances. And I want to be part of your life."

"Oh, me too."

19

"Ohmigod, what do you think about all this with my brother and the twins?" Margot asked Craig as they got into his Bronco and headed back to his place.

"I think there's a damn good chance your brother is off the hook with regard to fathering a couple of babies with a tigress shifter. I'm so glad you'll be able to get to know each other again."

"Me too. At first, I wasn't sure because he'd never tried to get in touch with me. I thought he didn't care anything about me. But now I know it was all my mother's doing."

"Did you recognize him when you first saw him?"

"Only in the face, the same boyish charm he had when he was a kid. But his face was thinner and the rest of him fully grown, so for a moment, I didn't recognize him. I really didn't know how to act toward him, and he was the same way with me. I'm glad we can get through this and be friends and family again."

"Me too, for sure. But right now, this is all that matters to me," he said, parking in the garage, and then escorting her into the house.

They didn't have to tell each other what was next on the agenda. They headed straight for the bedroom, her hand in his. She was so glad she hadn't been stuck with a bear who wasn't good for her and had the chance to find one who was. Everything about her and Craig's relationship had been beautiful. She loved being with him.

In the bedroom, they quickly dispensed with their jackets and boots and socks.

His hands slid up her sweater and he cupped her breasts. Pure need filled her as she felt his hands molding to her breasts. It didn't take long for their pheromones to start working overtime. For their heartbeats to quicken. She felt glorious, responding to him like she had never done with another man. He teased her lips, then pressed for a deeper connection. Her whole body responded, her nether region growing damp with expectation as he continued to kiss her and massage her breasts.

Every part of her was awake and alive for him, his touching and kissing her, stoking the flame racing through her blood. He stroked her lips with his tongue, then he pressed his tongue for entrance and began tangling his tongue with hers. He tantalized her with his soul-searing kisses, and she sucked on his tongue, making him groan with pleasure.

His beautiful dark brown eyes were nearly darkened to midnight, and just as dark as hers were, which made her wonder if she had children with him, would they have the same deep brown color?

Then they were struggling to remove each other's pants, underwear, her sweater and his shirt, and then her bra until they were perfectly naked.

He ran his hand in a deliberate caress over her hip and lower to between her legs, tangling in her short curly hairs for a whimsical moment, then delving into the place that was dewy with anticipation. She sucked in her breath as he poked deep between her folds, wetting his finger, and then he began to stroke her clit.

Then he was stroking with earnest, watching her reactions to his touch, rubbing more lightly, then harder, easing up and pressing forward until her blood was on fire and she felt the climax rising. She couldn't stop the blaze if she wanted to unless he stopped stroking her and then he was in trouble. But he didn't let up, giving her what she needed until she cried out with completion, satisfied, thrilled.

Then she guided him inside her and he began to thrust while she gripped his muscular shoulders and kissed his lips with hungry passion. She wanted more, wanted him deeper and thrust against him, but it wasn't enough. She wrapped her legs around him and gave him leeway to penetrate her more deeply and she groaned with ecstasy.

But then he was maneuvering around her in such an exquisite way, never slipping out of her, working around until he was at her back, and he pulled her leg over his hip so he could stroke between her legs while he thrust. It was an amazing experience, and she couldn't last. She loved it when she came again, and he filled her with his seed in an explosive gush.

And then, they just lay there connected, his hand running over her breast with soft caresses before he finally pulled out and they cuddled together.

"A shower?" she finally asked, not wanting to tell him he would have to sleep on the wet spot if they didn't take one.

He smiled. "Yeah. I never thought of showering as anything but a way to get clean, but with you? It's a whole other wildly stimulating experience."

Which it was when they ended up in the shower and washing each other up in a genuinely sexy way.

～

THE NEXT MORNING, Margot and Craig went for a polar bear run, then had breakfast before they got into his Bronco to see the real estate agent to look at the property Margot was considering. Margot was nervous about it. She was glad they had gone for a polar bear run. It helped to melt away some of the anxiousness she had been feeling, but not all of it.

What if the shop that was closest to Craig's parents' tavern that she was most interested in wasn't what she was really looking for once she saw the inside of it? She loved the way she had fixed her place up in North. But then she thought about the snow leopard Jasper and his brothers and how they renovated places. They could probably make it her dream boutique without any problem. And they might give her a discount on the work too because she was a shifter also. Maybe.

She had to remind herself that the real estate agent had three other places she could look at. Although an alternative was to build a new store. But she liked being in the downtown area where people could walk from shop to shop like she and Steph and then later she and Craig had done. She would most likely get more foot traffic that way also. And when the other businesses were doing special activities, it would help draw the crowds to her place too.

When they arrived at the shop, she liked the big front display windows on either side of the framed glass door. A sloping roof over the front of the shop gave it an alpine look, and ornate corbels held it up, adding to the quaintness. So far, she thought the shop had a lot of potential, at least from the outside.

The real estate lady introduced herself as Paige Stanford and unlocked the door for Margot and Craig. She explained that the former owner had died, and the shop had gone to relatives in Oregon, but they only wanted to sell it.

"Did he die at the store?" Margot asked.

"Oh, no, he was at home when he died. I have the listing for his home also."

"I'm hoping Margot won't be looking for a place of her own," Craig said. "You can stay with me, Margot."

"I'll take you up on it." Margot smiled at him, amused. He sounded as though he thought she might be interested in buying her own place and then seeing other bears. But she was happy to remain with him if he was fine with her staying at his place while getting to know him better, and maybe even living there permanently, if things worked out for them.

She loved the old oak counter and the oak display shelves behind the counter in this shop too.

"He had a store that sold men's clothing, so I figured it would be more like what you could use for your own store without a lot of renovation," Paige said.

Margot agreed with her.

"There's a bathroom back here for guests and another for employees in this back room. It also has a small kitchen to prepare treats or drinks when we're having special events."

"Oh, how nice. I love it. I don't have a kitchen in mine, and I always wish I did so that I could make wassail for the holidays and such. It makes the store smell so inviting." Margot was afraid she sounded too sold on the store and the new owners might not come down on the price.

As if Paige could read Margot's mind, she said, "Don't worry. I'll get you the best deal I can. We shifters stick together. The sister and brother don't want to deal with this and want it sold as quickly as possible. It has been on the market for a year. No one has been interested in it. I'm sure you can get them to come down on the price. I would make an offer of $215, but it would be worth it at $235. The location is great, as Craig's parents can attest to, and you know local shifters will shop here. But if you carry White Bear gifts that are specific to your store also, you'll have the ability to ship all over the world. We have several indigenous peoples of Alaska who create beautiful crafts and can make a certain kind exclusive to your store."

"Oh, I would love that."

"Rob and his partners will also send tour groups your way," Craig said.

She hadn't thought of that added benefit. "Oh, that would be perfect."

"Do you want to look at the other shops for sale?" Paige asked.

"Why has this been on the market for so long?" Margot needed to know if there was something wrong with the building that was the reason for it sitting there and not selling.

"Basically, his son and daughter overpriced it to begin with. Everyone who has come in looking for a shop wants something bigger and for that price, it should have more square footage. Understandably, they want to get as much as they can out of it because they have to split the proceeds once it sells. But they also have to pay the taxes on the property, water, electricity, and maintenance on it until they sell it. You're the first real interested party they've had that could be a good fit."

"And we're good for the money," Craig said.

Margot and Paige smiled at him.

"Okay, then sure, let's look at the other properties," Margot said.

She and Craig followed Paige's car to the second shop after that.

"What do you think about the last one we saw?" Craig asked Margot.

"Oh, I love it. But I realized afterward that I shouldn't have sounded so eager."

"Paige will get you a good deal on it if you want it."

When Margot saw the next shop, it was much larger, a stand-alone store, which meant everyone would have to drive to it and it was much better suited to a business that carried a lot more merchandise than she did. She liked having about three employees—herself and two others who took care of things when she wasn't able to.

Before she got out to look at it, Craig said to her, "I think you have your heart set on the other store."

"Yeah, it looks like my boutique back in North, but even more rustic and prettier. I'm afraid this one is way too big for me."

Craig nodded. "You don't have to worry about it. Paige will get the owners to come down on the price on the other shop. Of course, if you were a shifter trying to sell your property, she would make sure you got the best deal there."

"Wow. I just can't say how much I love being here."

"The feeling's mutual."

Margot and Craig looked at the other properties, but she really had her heart set on the one near Craig's parents' place. "Let's make an offer on this one," she said to Paige as they looked at it again.

To Margot's surprise, Kyle joined them at the shop. "Craig texted me that you would be here, and he believed you really wanted to buy this shop. Am I too late to help you decide on it so you'll relocate to White Bear and be near me?"

Margot gave her brother a big hug. "No. I'm about ready to make an offer." She couldn't believe Craig had contacted her brother to get him to join them and she was so proud of him for doing it and her brother for wanting to help her out.

Craig was smiling, looking glad that what he had done had been the right choice to make.

"I'll tell them they probably won't get a better offer than yours because of the size of the shop," Paige said to Margot.

"And I'll pay cash for the shop," Kyle said. "My gift to you,

Margot, because some of dad's money should have gone to you too."

"Ohmigod, thank you, Kyle," Margot said, giving her brother another heartfelt hug.

Then they made an offer and the brother and sister agreed to sell the shop for the lower price.

"Now that you're moving here, where do you plan to stay?" Kyle asked Margot. "I have plenty of room if you want to live with me until you decide on what to do."

"Thanks. I want to get to know you all over again, but Craig has offered to allow me to stay at his home."

"We'll have you over for meals and you'll have to come to the Halloween family party at the White Bear Tavern," Craig said.

"That sounds like a winning deal. I can grill us fish, chicken, brisket, also at my place," Kyle said.

"We would love that," Margot said.

"I'll send the contract to you to sign," Paige said, ending the call with the brother and sister who owned the shop. "We'll get this all taken care of."

"Thanks so much," Margot said, thrilled. Now she had to tell Steph what was going on. But first she called Melissa about the hypnotherapy sessions. "Hey, I have to call you and tell you thanks so much for your sessions. I've reunited with my brother and I'm moving to White Bear. I remember everything about the car accident, my brother, my father, so I won't need any more sessions."

"Well, if you do, just let me know and I'll get you in for one."

"Thanks, Melissa. We'll see you at the haunted house?"

"Yes, in just a few minutes."

"See you there." Then Margot called Steph. "Well, I have good news and bad. I just bought a shop near Craig's parents' tavern."

"Ohmigod, yes!"

"And I'm moving in with Craig."

"That was a guaranteed move."

"And my brother, Kyle, and I are getting to know each other. You can meet him at the haunted house."

"Yes! What's the bad news?"

"We won't be near each other to do all these fun things."

"Maybe we will be. We'll talk later. I'm so happy for you."

"Thanks! I'm so thrilled."

"Okay, Ames and I will see you in a few minutes," Steph said. Then they ended the call.

"I guess we have two vehicles here," Margot said to her brother.

"Yeah, I'll follow you over, and as soon as the contract is signed, I'll fork over the cash," Kyle said.

"Thanks." Margot would have the money from the sale of her shop and her house in North when they sold, but it could take a while to sell both so she was glad she had the cash to purchase this one and renovate it to suit her style in the meantime.

She and Craig got into his Bronco, and he said, "Are you going to tell your mother that you're leaving North?"

"Uh, yeah, but after our visit to the haunted house. Or maybe after Halloween dinner with your family. I don't know. I don't want to ruin our good time if she throws a fit." She realized how hard it was going to be to return home and move her stuff and get both places ready to sell.

"I can tell you're already worried about moving and—"

"Getting the store and house ready to sell. I don't even want to think of what a job that will be."

"We'll take care of it. All of us. It won't be any trouble at all."

"The only other thing I feel bad about is leaving Steph behind, and the other woman who helps run the shop when I can't be there, Faye? I hate to have to tell her I'm moving. But the benefits of living in White Bear totally outweigh the benefits of living in North, so there's no contest there."

"Good. We'll help you get transitioned and maybe Steph will want to move here too. You never know," Craig said.

"Yeah." But would that mean Steph and Ames would move here? Or was she calling it quits with her boyfriend? If that was the case, she'd have a lot of interest in fellow bachelor polar bears here, Margot was certain.

20

When Craig and Margot arrived at the old hospital building, Margot let out her breath in awe of how dilapidated and spooky the place looked. "Wow, this place is amazing. It doesn't even have to have all the scary stuff inside or outside to look like a haunted building. The building itself looks like it could haunt the daylights out of someone."

Craig smiled and took her hand. "What do you think? Are you game? It's totally up to you."

"Oh, I'm ready, though I might have to take one of the emergency exits out with Steph if it gets too overwhelming. But you and Ames and my brother can finish the house together," Margot said.

Craig laughed. "Okay, there they are. And the others are arriving now."

"Oh, there's my brother. I'm so glad he helped me purchase the shop. I'm really glad he wants to be part of the family."

"I'm glad he does too. Everyone will welcome him into the polar bear community."

Margot and Craig got out of the vehicle.

"Oh, wow," Steph said, giving Margot a hug. "I think I should have seen the outside before I agreed to go inside."

"Too much, huh?" Margot asked. "Well, I'm going, but I might have to escape early. We'll see."

"I'm sticking it out until the end," Ames said.

"I'm going to give it a shot, truly. And if I have to leave, I will," Steph said. "I'm not going to have a heart attack over it if I can't handle it though."

Margot laughed and patted her on the back. "I agree."

"I'll see what happens," Craig said, and Margot thought he planned to leave with her if she decided she'd had enough of being scared.

But he really didn't have to. She didn't want to leave as early as she thought Steph might try to skip out of the haunted building.

Margot's brother joined them, and she gave Kyle a hug, and Craig shook his hand. "Are you ready for this, Kyle?" Craig asked.

"Uh, yeah. I just hope I don't chicken out and take an emergency exit," Kyle said.

"Oh...you always loved scary stuff. I hadn't remembered that before, but the scarier, the better." Margot realized that being around her brother, hearing him talk about things was helping her to recall some of her memories. Good ones. Not all bad. "This is my good friend Steph from North, and her boyfriend Ames."

The others got out of their vehicles and joined them.

Margot hurried to introduce her brother to everyone there. Kyle smiled, looking pleased to be greeted and welcomed by so many shifters. But she wanted to tell him not to mess with the single females here who weren't of his same species! In case he had any idea of doing so. "He's new to town and if anyone needs an investment counselor, Kyle will be working at the White Bear Bank as one starting on Monday."

His face reddened a little when she put him on the spot, and he appeared embarrassed. But then he smiled and said, "Yeah. I will be."

"I can always use some financial advice," Jasper said. "I'll come in and see you sometime. With flipping houses with my brothers, we're often at the bank at some time or another."

"Good deal." Kyle smiled at Margot, looking like he was glad she put in a good word for him now.

"When we lived in North, you never told me you had a brother before," Steph said.

"I didn't remember that I had one," Margot said.

"But we're going to rectify that," Kyle said.

"Wow, well that's another reason you're moving here then," Steph said.

"Absolutely."

"Okay, so I've seen this place before, and it always creeps me out," Fran said, her sisters agreeing.

The lynxes were excited about going into the house. So were the wolves. Even Jasper's brothers showed up, William and Simon, and they were introduced to everyone who didn't know them.

"Hey, are we ready to do this?" Jasper asked, sounding eager as they heard screams coming from inside the building.

"Yeah," Margot said, taking hold of Craig's hand and pulling him toward the building. Kyle followed behind them, Steph and Ames right after that.

Everyone joined in and the snow leopards actually led the way, serving as their protective force, which Margot thought was cute.

When they entered the lobby of the three-story building, big chandeliers covered in dust and spiderwebs hung down from the tall ceilings, and peeling paint and wallpaper on the walls made Margot think of the houses that the snow leopards flipped for a living. She imagined them envisioning how they could turn the place into something of beauty.

A man wearing a lab jacket covered in blood stains gave them a yellow-stained toothy grin, his smile sinister. "I'm Dr. Scott. We're so glad you've come to join us. We have plenty of locals living here with us. You might run across one or two, but don't believe it if any of them tell you they've been experimented on...or that they have been forced to remain here. You can't trust anything they say. We have a happy little family here and you can even stay here with the rest of our family together. Forever. Welcome to our home.

"To ensure that you have the most spooktacular experience, we ask that you refrain from actually hitting our residents. Small groups of you might find yourselves isolated from the rest from time to time. This will give you a more...personal encounter with our friends that way. We will break you off into groups, send you on your way down different paths, but do not worry. You will be able to see every bit of our home that you came here to see. You just might see it in a different order. My assistants will help you get started."

Misty spray filled the lobby, then the scientist disappeared like he had just vanished through the floor. Even though the shifters could see in the dark, it had really turned pitch black and then flashing lights practically blinded Margot. She squeezed Craig's hand hard and had to keep loosening her grip so she wouldn't hurt his hand as screams filled the foyer, coming from guests, she thought. They sounded too real, not like they were produced on a soundtrack.

Something bumped against them from behind, and Steph screamed.

"It's just us," Margot assured her.

Steph was too scared to laugh. She was going to probably find the first exit out of here. Poor Steph, but she was a good sport to even try it since horror was not her thing.

"This way," a woman wearing a hospital gown, robe, and slippers and her head wrapped in stained bandages said to the snow leopards and the foxes in a croaky voice and led them away.

"You will go this way," a man said, looking like a shorter version of Frankenstein, dressed in a suit too small for him as he motioned to a doorway. As soon as Margot, Craig, her brother, Steph, and Ames were in the room, the door shut behind them, but their guide had stayed behind. They were now on their own.

They looked around and realized they were in a morgue and the lights were flashing in there, then the whole place turned dark. Margot saw a zombie-looking character sliding off an autopsy dissection table and coming after them, snarling and growling. It helped that the shifters could see in the dark as it reached for her, and Craig stepped in front of her to protect her. She cherished him for it. She even felt her brother close in on her as if he was going to do something about the zombie if Craig hadn't stepped in as her hero first.

Wouldn't the zombie actors have been surprised if the shifters turned into their wilder animal forms and scared the zombies off? At least these weren't weaponized. They growled and snarled at them in the dark room. But the effect would have been far worse if they could have only seen the zombies when the flashes of light illuminated them and just heard their toe-curling, vicious sounds.

In the meantime, music of an eerie nature played in the background while they could hear screams off in the distance and she wasn't sure if they were from guests or residents. Margot and her friends were trying to make their way to another room off this one as another zombie pulled off his sheet and climbed down off his metal dissection table and stalked slowly toward them.

Thankfully, he moved at a snail's pace toward them, and they ended up leaving the room with Steph trailing behind her, Ames after that. They didn't see the other shifters and wondered what had become of them.

Then suddenly, the door behind them creaked shut with a slam and Steph jumped behind Margot, bumping into her, giving Margot a new heart attack.

She figured then this was what the scientist in the beginning had meant about separating small groups of people from each other to give them more of a frightening experience. When she watched scary movies, she always wanted to tell the actors, "Stay together! Don't go off in different directions!"

It looked like there was no way out of the room as Craig, Margot, Kyle, Steph, and Ames tried to find a way out. The zombies seemed to increase in number exponentially. Two, then four, then eight. They were coming out of the morgue freezer where bodies were put into cold storage.

Cackling laughter reverberated through the rooms, and someone shouted somewhere off in the distance, "Catch her now before she kills anyone!" "No! No! No!" "She escaped, you fools!"

Margot, Craig, her brother, and her friends were being herded away from the door they had entered into, past another table where a zombie tossed aside his sheet and stood up on the table and reached down to grab Margot. She shrieked. Craig laughed and pulled her past the zombie before he could touch her. Steph was practically crouching, and she tried to get past the zombie that was trying to grab for her.

The scary sounds and conversations seemed to bounce off the walls and came from everywhere, making it even spookier. They were rich and cinematic, perfect to add to the haunted ambience. And then in front of Craig, they felt a woosh of cold air and a door creaked open. They quickly moved forward to get away from the zombies in the morgue room and ended up in a funeral parlor with low orange lighting, cobwebs hanging everywhere, and a half dozen, dusty coffins. Two were cut-lid caskets with the upper lid open, two were closed from viewing, and two were fully open.

Again, they only had one path to walk through the rows of caskets and Margot knew at any second, something was going to jump out at her. Craig took the lead again, being his protective self. Nothing happened as he walked down the aisle between the six coffins. She was almost disappointed when everything was still as death. She figured this was a great place where the actors would attempt to spook them.

Then snarling erupted right next to her and she ran into Craig, trying to get him to move faster. But then a zombie popped up out of one of the coffins with a lid fully open in front of Craig, and startled, he jumped back, nearly stepping on Margot.

Margot was surprised that Craig jumped back, but the place was scary, even though they knew it was all for fun. And it wouldn't have been enjoyable unless they were scared witless.

Steph ran into Margot as a growling zombie sat up in an open coffin and grabbed for her.

But then they were chased toward another door, which opened with a resounding creaking noise, making Margot wish she had some oil with her, and she and her friends rushed into another room. The door behind them slammed shut.

They found themselves in the embalming room of the abandoned funeral home. Dim lights showcased the rusty metal cabinets where tools were lying on the shelves likewise rusting. Bottles of questionable brown and gold liquids sat in the window-like sill of a lighted panel. A stained sheet laid across a porcelain table that had raised sides to collect bodily fluids from dripping on the floor, though it appeared the fluids had spilled onto the table and dried there.

The floor was covered in grime and dust, the single, rusting lamp hanging over the table in the same condition, the light bulb flickering on and off like it was having trouble getting enough power to keep it fully lit. Rubber tubing hung inside a rusty metal, deep sink where the fluids would go, some having dried on the floor surrounding the tubing. A dusty old mop sat against the wall in one corner.

It appeared no one was in there, but then they heard footsteps walking back and forth on the other side of the table, like the former embalmer was still here, performing his work on the deceased. The cloth on the table suddenly shot off it and landed on the floor. Steph screeched.

Margot laughed. She couldn't help herself. Steph was scarier than the room. At least this room. Drywall ceilings were coming apart and hanging loose up above, some of the trusses could be seen through the gaps in the drywall and Margot was more afraid of parts of the ceiling falling down on them. The floor was tile, but it was covered with debris.

The door behind them was locked and the door ahead of them was too. It appeared to be just a showroom with a ghost. But then the disembodied footfalls stopped, and a voice said, "Come in and stay a while. Did you bring the cadaver?"

Margot swore the guy just stepped out of the wall. He was wearing a stained, white lab coat, his hair white and wild like Albert Einstein's. He had a large syringe in his hand, and he came toward Margot. Why did they go after her and Steph so much? Probably the actors thought they would get more of a reaction out of the women.

But Craig pulled Margot away from the mad scientist and they hurried to the wall where he had appeared. They found a secret passageway that sounded like the walls were breathing. Margot was glad she wasn't claustrophobic as she felt the walls closing in on them. A small light at the end of the "tunnel" drew them toward a new place. There was room for only one person to move through the hallway at a time, but Craig still had a hold of her hand the whole time.

She wondered if Ames was being as protective of Steph as Craig was of her. Then she realized Steph wasn't following them any longer. Neither was Ames or Kyle either. What had happened to them?

"We lost Steph, Ames, and Kyle," she said to Craig over the spooky elevator music playing all around them.

"Okay, let's turn around and go back for them."

She really didn't want to return to that room, but she didn't want to leave them behind. "It's too difficult to squeeze by each other. I'll go first." Then she hurried back down the hall, but going that way it was total darkness like the end of the hallway had been sealed up, no light at all from the embalming room they had just left.

When she reached the end of the hall, she put her hands on what she thought was the opening, but it was now a wall, or maybe a door, but it looked like a wall. She couldn't find an opening anywhere on it. "There's no opening."

"Then they've separated us from each other."

"All right, onward and upward. Let's keep going. Maybe Steph, Ames, and my brother found another passageway," she said.

"Or Steph found one of the emergency exits."

"She might have, though I thought Ames said he was continuing through the whole building. I'm pretty sure my brother would too."

Craig turned around and kept going forward then and she held his hand as she followed behind. They heard screaming up ahead and Margot was ready to turn around and head back to the embalming room. She didn't like the sound of what they had to face up ahead.

"Are you all right?" Craig asked her.

"Yeah," she whispered back. "I guess they know we're coming."

He chuckled. "I'm sure of it."

When they reached the room, a man wearing a lab coat and stethoscope was poking at a zombie chained to an exam bed with a long stick that sparked with electricity. Or at least it appeared to be. Every time he poked him, the zombie snarled, until he saw Craig and Margot and then he jerked at his chains to get free and come after them.

The doctor turned to look at them, his teeth yellowed and his face peeling off in places. He grinned at them. "Fresh meat to work on."

Then a door opened, and Craig grabbed Margot's hand and hauled her toward their escape.

"Wait, don't go!" the doctor called out and laughed sinisterly.

Craig and Margot laughed.

They finally ended up in a room with several of their shifter friends, including her brother. This had been so much fun.

The scientist who had greeted them in the beginning said, "I hope you enjoyed your little visit and when you go out into the world, you'll tell everyone what a wonderful place this is. A caution, if anyone does say we're not doing right by our guests, we'll track you down through your social media sites and bring you here for an extended visit so we can get it right this time."

Everyone laughed.

Then they were guided out of the haunted house. The consensus from the gathered shifters was that they'd had a blast.

"Thanks so much for inviting me to enjoy the haunted house with everyone," Kyle said.

"Oh, I'm so glad you came with us. This was so much fun. We'll have to do it again next year. We lost you for a while," Margot said.

"I know. I ended up with Ames and Steph. It really was fun."

"And I'll have you know, I stuck it out until the end." Steph sounded so proud of herself.

"I'm proud of you," Margot told her.

"Well, tomorrow night is Halloween, so we have a big family dinner at the White Bear Tavern and then we hand out Halloween candy," Craig said to Kyle. "We look forward to having you spend the time with us if you're game."

"I sure am. And thanks."

But Margot and Craig had other business to take care of now. She gave her brother and then Steph a hug. "See you tomorrow night too."

"For sure," Steph said, then she hugged her back, looking like she was dying to ask what was going on between Margot and Craig, but she didn't.

Which was good because Margot wasn't telling her what was going on until *after* she and Craig mated.

21

"Do you think Steph knows what we are doing next?" Craig asked, suspecting Margot's best friend did.

"Oh, yes. She knows me well enough. Yet, I can't figure out what's going on between her and Ames," Margot said.

"I know. They're a total mystery."

"I'm just glad you and I are on the same page." Margot sounded so happy with the idea they were going to mate next.

When they arrived at the house, Craig knew this was the last time he would be entering it without a mate. He was really thrilled.

They went inside the house, and he swept her up in his arms, making her cry out with glee.

"Wow, you know how to do this right."

"No bended knee."

"No need."

Craig carried her into the bedroom and then set her on the bed. Then he joined her on the bed, and they began pulling off each other's clothes in a hurry as if their lives depended on it.

Craig was so grateful to Rob for his visions—for steering him into looking for polar bears in need that turned out to be

Margot and her friend Steph. To Robyn who had made up the brochure and to Steph who had found it and shared it with Margot, convincing her of celebrating a week in White Bear to enjoy all the Halloween activities. To the White Bear towns-folk for getting on the bandwagon to celebrate Halloween, which had helped to set this whole remarkable journey into motion that led him to meet Margot, the polar bear love of his life.

Then they were naked and kissing each other, rolling around on the bed together, laughing and hugging. She was perfect for him, and he was glad she felt he was the right bear for her. He was so lucky.

"You are so beautiful," he said, kissing her sweet, soft mouth.

"You are too," she said, her hands cupping his face, and tonguing his tongue, dipping and diving, teasing, and caressing. "I'm so lucky you came to rescue us."

"I'm so lucky I came to your rescue. Every day I think of just how lucky I was."

"But being you, the kind of person you are, has nothing to do with luck. That's what made me fall in love with you."

He smiled. No woman had ever made him feel so loved in such a special way.

"You know I got the better deal in this," she said.

"Oh?"

"A home that I love, a new place to live. You."

"The home isn't anything without you here enjoying it with me." And then he began to kiss her again. "You make me the happiest man in White Bear." Then he moved his mouth to her breast and began licking her nipple.

She moaned with delight as she ran her fingers through his hair, caressing his scalp, making him feel on top of the world. Her pheromones beckoned him to finish what he started, while his mingled with hers, telling her he was ready for this too. He was already full to bursting, ready to enter her tight sheath and make her his forever.

She ran her thigh over his hip, encouraging him to join her, but he began caressing her between her legs, finding just the place, the right tempo, the right pressure to make her come. He was enjoying the moments leading up to it, seeing her heated expression, hearing her intake of breath, listening to her rapid heartbeat like his was beating just as rapidly.

She was clinging to his waist like she was ready to come at any second. He loved it. He kept working on her, stroking her like she loved it, until she cried out and she pulled him toward her.

Then she parted her legs further and he began to enter her.

"Hmm, you feel so...good," she whispered.

"So do you, sweetheart. So do you." And he pushed in all the way and began to thrust. Even though they had made love before, it felt different this time. Like they were uniting as one, together, a couple, and he loved her. "I love you."

"I love you right back." She kissed him deeply, her hands cupping his face, claiming him for her own.

And he loved it, loved the feel of her silky hands on his face, the way she kissed him so eagerly, passionately, lovingly. She wrapped her legs around his hips, and moved against him, making him deepen his thrusts. She was every bit of heaven as he kept deepening their connection until the end.

He was so glad he had convinced her to stay with him and then became her mate. He kissed her again, so close to coming and then he came in an explosive way.

"Oh, you are one beautiful bear," she said to him, hugging him close to her body.

"I am so lucky to be with you as a mated bear. What's mine is yours."

"And what's mine is yours. Even my new store."

He laughed. "I will help you get it ready to open and even work in it anytime you need me to. If there's anything you want to change with the house, decorating-wise, feel free to."

"Aww, you're so sweet. I love it like it is. But mostly, I love being here with you."

Then they cuddled together, and he sighed. "My parents and brothers and cousins and their mates will be elated that we became mated bears. But what about your mother and stepdad?"

She smiled. "Kyle will be thrilled and that's all that matters to me. My mother wanted me to stay with a bear who wasn't good for me. She didn't tell me about my brother or take care of him like she should have when he was younger. I hope she's happy for me, but it's not really that important."

"Okay, good. I know it's a little late to think about that, but I really didn't want to discuss it until after we were mated."

She laughed. "I love you."

"Oh, honey, I so love you." He rolled off her and she snuggled next to him. "We were meant for each other. If your mom can't see that, it's too bad. But you have my whole family and your brother to be here for you for anything you need."

"I'm so glad for that. Tomorrow is Halloween. But I guess we can tell everyone in the morning that we've done it," she said.

He smiled. "Yeah. They would be thrilled to hear the news tonight, but I think it can wait until tomorrow."

"Do you think anyone will be surprised?"

"Once you bought the shop here? No."

She smiled. "I guess not."

Bright and early the next morning, Margot woke to find Craig had left the bed and for a second, she thought he might have gone on a seaplane mission, but then she smelled eggs and bacon cooking and she smiled and stretched. She was just going to get up when Craig walked into the room carrying a tray of eggs, bacon, slices of oranges, and pumpkin spice latte.

"Wow. This is so nice. No one has ever done this for me. I was afraid you had to go on a mission. Then I smelled breakfast."

"I wouldn't have left without telling you I had to fly off into the wild blue yonder. So today's Halloween."

"Happy Halloween."

"Happy Halloween. I'll be right back." He left, then returned with a tray to join her. "So after we eat, we can tell everyone the news?"

"Yeah. I can't wait to tell your family and Steph. My parents, not so much. But I have to."

They finished breakfast and cleaned up, then they called Craig's parents first.

"Hey, Mom, Dad, Margot and I are mated bears," Craig said.

"Woohoo, yes!" Genevieve said. "Finally, one of our own sons has done it."

Margot laughed.

"I had to find the right one for me."

"For sure," Ned said. "And she's just perfect for our family. She's a delight. Welcome to the family, Margot."

"Thanks," Margot said. "That's one of the reasons I mated Craig. I gained a whole lovely bear family for my own. You all are the greatest." And she meant it with all her heart.

"Well, we can't wait to celebrate at the Halloween feast tonight with you both. It will make Halloween for us the most memorable ever," Genevieve said.

After congratulating them again, they ended the call and Margot called Kyle next. "I know you know this is where we were going with this."

"You and Craig got hitched. Congratulations and I'm so glad for you both. Have you told Mom yet?" Kyle asked.

"No." Margot laughed a little. "She's last on my list. I didn't tell you yet, but I was supposed to marry a guy in North, but he was seeing another woman and was a no show at the wedding. Mom resented me for it and felt I should have sucked up to him to get him to come back to me."

"No way." Kyle sounded shocked that anyone would do that to his sister.

"Yep. She thought he would make the perfect son-in-law. She didn't get to meet this one beforehand, which works perfectly for me."

"That's for sure. The other guy didn't deserve you."

"I agree. We're celebrating tonight at the Halloween family gathering."

"I'll be there."

Then Craig called his brothers on a conference call. "Hey, brothers, Margot and I are mated."

"Oh, wow, and I didn't have anything to do with it. I'm losing my touch," Ben said.

Andy and Craig laughed. Ben was always saying he was the matchmaker of the gang, but everyone knew he had nothing to do with the mates they had settled on.

"Well, I don't know," Andy said. "Margot, you didn't even give me a chance to shine yet."

She laughed. "Your brother was in rescue mode from the beginning so he was hard to beat."

"Yeah, we knew when he asked Dad to give you and Steph free dinners as part of his rescuing you, that there was more to his being just a super nice guy," Ben said. "And man, here I was trying to serve you the meal and he stole you right out from under me."

She chuckled. "I asked if you would be upset about that."

"Nah, not when he had already captured your interest. Now if I had in the beginning and then he stole you away from me, that would have been a different story," Ben said.

"We were both trying to serve just the tables closest to the door too," Andy said, "watching for when you would arrive."

"Yeah, I was left serving the rest of the tavern's patrons that night because of it," Craig said.

"Until you talked to Dad and got to sit with the ladies and have a meal. Boy, if you hadn't won Dad over," Ben said. "Well, we'll have even more of a reason to celebrate tonight."

"Yeah, and everyone will get to meet Margot's brother, Kyle, too," Craig said.

"We look forward to it," Ben said, since Andy had already met him to return his stolen car to him.

"Okay, well, I have to let my friend know what we were up to," Margot said. Then they ended the call, and she phoned Steph. "Okay, so I told you I had bought a shop in White Bear and—"

"You did it! Yes! I'm so proud of you and I'm sure you'll just love it here."

"And Craig and I mated each other."

"Oh, wow, when you do it, you do it big."

"You had a huge part in getting Craig and me together."

Steph said, "Oh, yeah, between injuring myself with the grizzly and finding the brochure on White Bear, you're right. We'll sure be at the family dinner tonight. Ames didn't bring a costume, but we're all going to be pirates, right?"

"Absolutely." Margot was dying to ask what Steph's current relationship status was, but she didn't want to ask when Ames was around. And she didn't want to upset Steph if things weren't working out for them like they had been for Craig and her.

"Have you told your mom and stepdad yet?" Steph asked.

"Nope. I'm calling them last."

"Okay, well good luck with that, and I'm so happy for you. We'll see you tonight. Congratulations!"

"Thanks." But Margot felt bad that she would be missing her good friend too when Steph returned to North for good. They called Craig's cousins and their mates after that.

"Oh," Rob said, "Alicia and I both had visions that you were getting married."

"Well, *we* didn't," Robyn said. "We're thrilled for you."

Edward and Alicia both agreed.

"We're celebrating with the family at the Halloween dinner," Craig said.

"Perfect timing," Alicia said. "We're so happy for the both of you."

After they talked for a bit, Margot called her mom. "Hey, I've found the perfect mate for me and—"

"Oh?" Her mom didn't sound like she believed it.

"Yeah, we're mated. I hope you like him and can come to the wedding. I'll let you know when it will be when we plan it out."

"What?"

"And I finally reconnected with my brother, Kyle. He bought the store for me so I can open it up in White Bear as soon as I can move my merchandise here."

Silence.

"I've got to go to a big family celebration for our mating in a little bit, so I just wanted to touch base with you and tell you what's going on. I'll talk to you later. Love you. Bye." Margot ended the call.

Craig smiled at her. "Your mother didn't say much."

"I didn't give her the chance, just like she didn't give Kyle the chance to show he wasn't anything like our father. And just like she didn't give me the chance to prove that I could find a much better mate than my ex-fiancé would have been."

"I'm proud of you."

"I am too. I'm sure I'll hear from her later, once she has had time to think about all this."

"Well, it would be nice if she approves of me—" Craig said.

"But if she doesn't, it truly is her loss," Margot said. Steph was right. It was Margot's life and she had to live it the way that was right for her. "Hey, can we go for a polar bear walk, even though it's broad daylight out?"

"Yep. That's why I have all this land out here. Let's go."

They took off their clothes in the living room and he opened the back door, then she shifted and ran out of the house. He walked outside and closed the back door, then shifted and chased after her. When he caught up to her, she rose up on her hind legs and moved her head side to side, telling him she wanted to play. He immediately stood up and began to bite at her in playful fun.

She was thinking how much fun it would be to play with the kids like this too. She hadn't been around kids as a polar bear since she had been a kid.

Later that afternoon, they had lunch at home of apple cider glazed chicken wings, apple slices, and celery sticks. Then they planned to take a nap, but they made love first, then napped. This was so the life. Craig lived so far out that he didn't have trick-or-treaters out here. But it also worked out great for when they wanted to run as bears. She was really looking forward to tonight and really celebrating that they had mated, and she was truly part of the family.

22

Craig hadn't known how he would feel when he was mated to a she-bear, but this truly was great. He really loved being with Margot, day and night. Playing as polar bears was just white icing on the white cake. She always gave 110% and he loved her for it. He might have gone to rescue the ladies, but she was the one who came to his rescue, giving him the kind of life that was so much fuller, much more enjoyable, saving him from a lonely existence. With all his family around him, and the kind of work he did, he always felt he had enough. Until Margot came into his life.

And now they were going to share that celebration of their union with his family tonight, making this the most special Halloween ever. He wished her mother and stepdad would be part of the family too, but he was delighted that she had gotten back with her brother, and it felt to him like they hadn't been apart for any time at all. He was so glad for that because he was so close to his own brothers and his cousins who were just like his own brothers. And he was all in with taking Kyle in as another one of his brothers.

"Hey, Margot, I was thinking for our wedding that we could wear traditional formalwear or—" Craig said.

"We could be pirates of old."

He laughed. "Yeah, just my thought."

"My mother would hate it."

"But everyone in my family would love it."

"You have a much larger family, and my mother, if she even shows up for it, can wear whatever she likes. I already wore the formalwear she wanted me to the first time around and that didn't work out. Besides, Steph will be there too, and she'll love it."

He smiled. "Pirates it is."

"I know it's a change of subject, but I can't help but think about Jasper's missing quadruplet sister."

"Once we learned of it, we did everything we could to try and locate her. But we'll keep trying. We even thought Rob or Alicia might get some clues, but they believe she's not anywhere near White Bear and that's why they can't have any visions of her."

"Oh, I was curious. So what about Rob and Alicia's kids? Do you think they'll have special abilities like both their parents?"

"Uh, yeah. But Rob and Alicia will know more about it when the kids are older and can tell them more about what they've seen. Since the twins are only two years old, it can be kind of hard to understand them and they think that what they see has really happened, when it hasn't. But then again, if you think about, it could be that they just are having dreams or something."

"So nothing they tell them about really comes to pass?"

Craig smiled. "Oh sure. Before they had their birthday party when they were two, they told their parents they had a bubblegum flavored cake. No one had told them that. It had been a secret. So we knew they had the abilities. Now, other things they have seen haven't come true, so we don't know if it's a future event or something that they are just making up as kids do, or they're just confused about a situation."

"But the birthday cake cinches it."

"It does. It's going to be interesting to see what happens in the future. Rob and Alicia will have to tell them the importance of not telling everyone what they see that hasn't happened yet or give themselves away."

"I agree." Margot pulled him in for a hug and kiss. "I could see where it would be fascinating."

He laughed. "Or unnerving if the kids saw something that the adults didn't want them to see."

"True. Are you ready to be a pirate and celebrate with the rest of the pirate family?"

"I sure am. I heard even Kyle went and bought himself a pirate costume for tonight."

"Good. He'll have more fun fitting in that way."

Craig and Margot dressed up in their pirate costumes and drove over to the tavern, excited to go to the family celebration for Halloween. Kids in White Bear were going to all the businesses where the shops had candy set out for trick-or-treaters and the twin boys were handing out the candy at the entrance of the tavern, dressed as little pirates, having a ball.

Craig and Margot walked inside the room reserved for parties that was all set up with a sign that said: *Congratulations, Margot and Craig!*

Wow, Margot hadn't expected that. They all gathered in the party room. Ned had hired shifters to run the tavern while they had dinner and then everyone would help out at the tavern after that.

Steph showed up, all cheerful-like, giving her hugs, and smiling and talking to the rest of the family.

"Where's Ames?" Margot asked her, surprised he didn't come inside with her. Maybe he was having a difficult time finding a place to park his vehicle.

"Oh, he had to leave, business trip, you know. It just sort of came up about an hour before we came here."

"Oh, wow. Not good. And the question of a mating?"

"He didn't bring it up and neither did I. I figure he doesn't want to mate me, and that's fine."

"No, it's not."

"Yeah, it is. Because I'm leaving North and moving down here. While you've been with Craig, I slipped away to have an interview at the Commodore Hotel. I got an assistant manager position! And it starts next week. I'll be moving here."

"What about Ames?" Margot couldn't wrap her head around this turn of events, though she was thrilled they were going to be living in White Bear together.

"Oh, it's over between us. I'll tell him once he returns from his next business trip. I'm going to take a seat between Andy and Ben." Steph smiled brightly. "It's a sign, you know?"

Margot smiled and gave her a hug. "I'm so thrilled for you. Both for getting a job that you've wanted and for moving here. We can plan the wedding together."

"Absolutely."

Rob and Alicia's two-year-old twins were with Edward and Robyn's six-year-old boys in the kids' room. They had a nanny watching them for the celebration and they were having their own special dinner. Their two-month-old babies were sleeping in the banquet room in their carriers near Edward and Robyn.

Then everyone was offering champagne toasts to the new couple, and Steph looked like she was really enjoying the company of both Craig's brothers.

In the middle of the meal and all the conversations, what

they hadn't expected was for Janice's tiger parents to show up at the tavern, looking for Kyle and ready to force him to marry their daughter.

Ned, Craig, Ben, Andy, and their cousins all rose from their seats to speak with the irate tiger shifters.

"We were told Kyle Rider is here. Where is he?" the older tiger asked.

"Here," Kyle said, standing. "I'm afraid Janice hasn't told you the truth of the matter. She has been with a tiger and a lion, and well, me, but as you can see, I couldn't be the father of her twins."

The couple looked flabbergasted when they realized everyone in the party room was a polar bear shifter.

"You're really Kyle?" the man said again.

"Yeah, in the flesh. I dated Janice, and I told her that I inherited some money, and she knew I had a good paying job, so the next thing I knew she was saying I was the father of her twins. I didn't think it was possible, given what we are," Kyle said.

"The Bear Council sent her a note that she had to have a test done to prove the babies are Kyle's which she refuses to do," Ned said.

The man just rubbed his bearded face. "Which tiger and lion had she been with?"

Kyle shrugged. "I don't know their names. But they hung around her a lot. I actually stopped dating her for that reason. I guess she just thought I could support her better than they could. Neither of them had jobs. But it wouldn't have worked out."

Ned walked over to speak to the couple and said, "Listen, it's not your fault in all this and we understand why you would come here looking for the father to make this right, but Kyle couldn't be the father. Since you've come all the way from

Anchorage, we're happy to give you a free dinner on us, if you would like to eat here before you return home," he said.

The dad looked at his wife and she nodded. "Thank you for the generous offer. We're sorry our daughter got you involved in this. We'll deal with her when we get home."

Then Andy escorted them to a nice table where they could have their dinner and soon returned to the family dinner.

"Thank you," Kyle said, "for being so nice to them."

Ned dished up some more roast beef. "That's the way I would like to be treated if one of my sons got himself into a mess like that."

"That wouldn't happen to any of us," Andy said. "I mean, the lying part."

"Right," Ben said, offering Steph more mashed potatoes.

She smiled at Margot as if telling her she was right where she belonged.

Then Andy offered Steph some more carrots. She was having a ball. Margot and Craig might be the center of attention for being a newly mated couple, but Steph was the center of attention where two bachelor bears were concerned.

They all enjoyed their meal and then helped out in serving meals after that, except for Rob and Alicia and Edward and Robyn who took their little ones home.

Steph actually stayed to hand out candy while Andy and Ben were serving meals.

Everyone had told the newly mated couple to go home and enjoy their night together, but they were having fun with the family. Craig was serving food and Margot was helping Steph pass out candy. The tiger couple thanked Ned again and apologized to Kyle before they left for the night.

Even Kyle helped grill hamburgers in the kitchen, which amused Craig and his brothers. But Ned seemed to take Kyle under his wing and wasn't giving him grief like he did the brothers and cousins sometimes when they grilled the meat for customers.

Margot got a call from her mother and Steph glanced at her. "I knew she would call back. Hello, Mother."

"You're really mated?"

"Yes."

"You're really moving to White Bear?"

"To be with my mate, yes. He has three brothers, his parents, and two cousins who are like brothers to him who are both married and have kids, so they have a nice extended family. And I adore them. Plus, Kyle has a job here and I can't wait to do lots of fun things with him. The whole family will too. Steph got a job here so she'll be here also."

Silence.

"So there's no convincing you to change your mind," her mother morosely said.

Margot laughed. "No. We're mated."

"We're not paying for the wedding again."

Kyle overheard the conversation and interjected, "Hi, Mom. I'm paying for my sister's wedding. Don't worry about it." Then he returned to the kitchen to grill more food.

"Your ex-fiancé dumped his girlfriend. He told me what a mistake it had been," her mother said.

"Good for him."

"You won't change your mind?"

"Mom, I love you, but I'm busy passing out candy to trick-or-treaters. I'll talk to you later. Love you. Bye." Margot hung up on her again.

"She doesn't get it, does she?" Steph asked.

"No. Maybe she'll come around, but if she doesn't, it really is her problem, not mine. I'll be right back." Margot couldn't believe that Kyle would offer to pay for her wedding. She went into the kitchen and as soon as her brother plated a couple of steaks, she gave him a hug. "Thank you for offering to pay for the wedding. You don't—"

"I want to. Mom is being Mom. Her way or the highway. You deserve the best. You've got it in Craig. If I ever see your ex-fiancé, I'll deck him for sure. If Mom doesn't like what you're doing with your life when you're happy with it, it's her problem," Kyle said.

"Right. And I'm so glad that the tigers realized their daughter was really lying to them all along and that you didn't have anything to do with getting her pregnant."

"Oh, yeah, me too. I don't think she's going to hear the last of it from her parents."

"I agree. It was a rotten thing for her to do. Well, thanks for offering to pay for the wedding costs."

"Like I said, Dad gave me plenty of money, and if he had been alive, and sober, he would have paid for your wedding himself. So I'm just doing what he would have done for you. When you have kids with Craig, I'll help put aside money for their college education."

"Wow, thanks so much." She gave Kyle another hug. "I'm so glad we're in each other's lives again."

"Yeah, me too, and the family treats me like one of their own. This has been a real treat for me."

Before Margot and Craig left for the night, she gave Steph another hug. "I just can't believe you're going to move down here to be with me."

"This is going to be so much better than living in North. When I told Faye the news—"

"Oh, Steph, I haven't even told her that I would be selling the shop and moving here."

"She wants to buy it."

"What?" Margot couldn't believe Steph had already talked to her about it, but she was thrilled that Faye wasn't upset about it.

"Yep. She adores your shop and always wished she could have one just like it. Now she has the opportunity, and she really wants to buy it from you. Her fiancé said he would put up the money for it. He's so perfect for her."

"Oh, for sure. Nothing like my ex-fiancé who thought I should be a lawyer like my mother and stepdad and bring in more money, even though financially, I was doing fine. I'll give her a good price."

"She knew you would. She said she would buy your merchandise too, if you're agreeable."

"Sure. I'll start over here then. Save us having to move all the merchandise here." Yeah, Margot didn't need the money from the sale of her store to pay for this one, so she would be fine. Plus, Craig would help support her if things weren't going well and she still would sell her own home and have some funds from that when it sold.

"Have you thought of what you want the attire to be for your wedding?" Steph asked.

"We're going for a pirate-themed wedding."

Steph laughed. "Oh, your mother is going to be thrilled. *Not.*"

"She might not even come anyway. But yeah, if she does, I don't expect her to wear what we're wearing. She would probably be too embarrassed. Not to change the subject, but how are things going between you and Craig's brothers?"

Steph smiled brightly. "Time will tell."

"How do you think Ames is going to react when he learns you're moving here?"

Steph shrugged. "He's not interested in any kind of commitment. I am. But not with him any longer. This is the best thing for me. And even if one of the brothers isn't the one for me, there are other bachelor polar bears in town." Kyle stepped in to hand Steph a mug of hot cocoa, smiled, then returned to the kitchen. She winked at Margot. "Even your brother."

Margot laughed.

Craig took hold of Margot's hand. "Ready to call it a night?"

"Oh, yeah." Because it wasn't the end of the night for them. Only the beginning of a lot of beautiful nights with her mate, just like this one.

EPILOGUE

I n honor of the love of the pirate theme Craig and Margot shared during Halloween, they had a pirate theme for their wedding. To Margot's surprise, her mother and stepdad came to the wedding and her stepdad gave her away, both of them wearing pirate costumes like the rest of those attending the wedding like they were pros. They looked so cute. Her mother even reconnected with Kyle and promised they would heal the rift. And her mother loved Craig, agreeing that he was so much better than Margot's ex. A lot had to do with how endearing Craig was toward her mother. Margot adored Craig for it. His whole family treated Margot's mother and stepdad as part of the family, and they loved it.

Margot's brother was one of the bridegrooms along with Craig's brothers and cousins, and he was grateful to be in their lives. Margot's bridesmaids included Steph, Faye, and the fox sisters.

Everyone came to the wedding, from polar bears to foxes, lynxes, wolves, and snow leopards, and even shifters who ran local shops came to the wedding and reception because Margot and Craig had impacted on everyone's lives in such a good way.

Faye was so thrilled to buy Margot's shop in North and Margot was having a ball with her new shop in White Bear that she had called White Bear Dress Boutique. And Steph loved being an assistant manager at the Commodore Hotel in White Bear, while Ames was happily seeing another she-bear in North, leaving the new girlfriend alone as he continued to take his job trips away just like he had done with Steph. Craig was still making his plane trips to rescue people, or deliver supplies to remote areas, but he also helped out at Margot's shop when he wasn't flying missions. She loved him for it—amused as he would make hors d'oeuvres for her customers on special occasions—from cheddar cheese tarts to sweet bacon wrapped chicken bites. And Robyn would promote it all over to draw more customers to Margot's shop.

Amy had come through for both Steph and Margot on the cute skirts she made, and Margot was carrying others like them in her shop now too.

After the wedding, Craig and Margot went to one of the MacMathan's cabins in the wilderness to spend their honeymoon, perfect for playing in the snow as polar bears, fishing and swimming as bears, and loving each other from morning to night.

ACKNOWLEDGMENTS

Thanks so much to Donna Fournier and Darla Taylor for beta reading this book! A special thanks to Laurel Pinkney and Donna Fournier for the ghost stories they shared for our shifters' ghostly tales.

ABOUT THE AUTHOR

Bestselling and award-winning author Terry Spear has written over sixty paranormal romance novels and four medieval Highland historical romances. Her first werewolf romance, *Heart of the Wolf*, was named a 2008 *Publishers Weekly*'s Best Book of the Year, and her subsequent titles have garnered high praise and hit the *USA Today* bestseller list. A retired officer of the U.S. Army Reserves, Terry lives in Spring, Texas, where she is working on her next wolf, jaguar, cougar, and bear shifter romances, continuing with her Highland medieval romances, and having fun with her young adult novels. When she's not writing, she's photographing everything that catches her eye, making teddy bears, and playing with her Havanese puppies and grandchildren. For more information, please visit www.terryspear.com, or follow her on Twitter, @TerrySpear. She is also on Facebook at http://www.facebook.com/terry.spear. And on Wordpress at: Terry Spear's Shifters http://terryspear.wordpress.com/

ALSO BY TERRY SPEAR

Adult Titles

Romantic Suspense: Deadly Fortunes, In the Dead of the Night, Relative Danger, Bound by Danger

***

The Highlanders Series: His Wild Highland Lass (novella), Vexing the Highlander (novella), Winning the Highlander's Heart, The Accidental Highland Hero, Highland Rake, Taming the Wild Highlander, The Highlander, Her Highland Hero, The Viking's Highland Lass, My Highlander

Other historical romances: Lady Caroline & the Egotistical Earl, A Ghost of a Chance at Love

***

Heart of the Wolf Series: Heart of the Wolf, Destiny of the Wolf, To Tempt the Wolf, Legend of the White Wolf, Seduced by the Wolf, Wolf Fever, Heart of the Highland Wolf, Dreaming of the Wolf, A SEAL in Wolf's Clothing, A Howl for a Highlander, A Highland Werewolf Wedding, A SEAL Wolf Christmas, Silence of the Wolf, Hero of a Highland Wolf, A Highland Wolf Christmas; SEAL Wolf Hunting; A Silver Wolf Christmas, SEAL Wolf in Too Deep, Alpha Wolf Need Not Apply, Between a Wolf and a Hard Place, SEAL Wolf Undercover, Dreaming of a White Wolf Christmas, Flight of the White Wolf, All's Fair in Love and Wolf, A Billionaire Wolf for Christmas, SEAL Wolf Surrender, Silver Town Wolf: Home for the Holidays, Night of the Billionaire Wolf, You Had Me at Wolf, Joy to the Wolves, The Wolf Wore Plaid, Jingle Bell Wolf, The Best of Both Wolves, While the Wolf's

Away, Christmas Wolf Surprise, Wolf Takes the Lead, Wolf on the Wild Side, Her Wolf for the Holidays, A Good Wolf is Hard to Find (2024), Mated for Christmas (2024)

SEAL Wolves: To Tempt the Wolf, A SEAL in Wolf's Clothing, A SEAL Wolf Christmas; SEAL Wolf Hunting, A SEAL Wolf in Too Deep, SEAL Wolf Undercover, SEAL Wolf Surrender

Silver Town Wolves: Destiny of the Wolf, Wolf Fever, Dreaming of the Wolf, Silence of the Wolf; A Silver Wolf Christmas, Between a Wolf and a Hard Place, Home for the Holidays, Jingle Bell Wolf

Wolff Family Lodge Wolves: You Had Me at Wolf, Wolf on the Wild Side, A Good Wolf is Hard to Find

Highland Wolves: Heart of the Highland Wolf, A Howl for a Highlander, A Highland Werewolf Wedding, Hero of a Highland Wolf, A Highland Wolf Christmas, The Wolf Wore Plaid, Her Wolf for the Holidays

Billionaire Wolf Series: A Billionaire in Wolf's Clothing, A Billionaire Wolf for Christmas, Night of the Billionaire Wolf, Wolf Takes the Lead

White Wolf Series: Legend of the White Wolf, Dreaming of a White Wolf Christmas, Flight of the White Wolf, While the Wolf's Away, Mated for Christmas

Red Wolf Series: Seduced by the Wolf, Joy to the Wolves, The Best of Both Wolves, Christmas Wolf Surprise

Wolf Novellas: Day of the Wolf, Seal Wolf Pursuit, Wolf to the Rescue, Night of the Wolf, United Shifter Force

***

Heart of the Jaguar Series: Savage Hunger, Jaguar Fever, Jaguar Hunt, Jaguar Pride, A Very Jaguar Christmas, You Had Me at Jaguar, The Witch and the Jaguar, Dawn of the Jaguar

***

Heart of the Cougar Series: Cougar's Mate, Call of the Cougar, Taming the Wild Cougar, Covert Cougar Christmas, a novella, Double Cougar Trouble, Cougar Undercover, Cougar Magic, Cougar Halloween Mischief, Falling for the Cougar, Cougar Christmas Calamity, Catch the Cougar (Halloween Novella), You Had Me at Cougar, Saving the White Cougar, Big Cat Magic

***

White Bear Series: Loving the White Bear, Claiming the White Bear, Bear of a Halloween (coming)

Grizzly Bear Series: Bear in Mind

***

Wolves of Old: Wolf Pack

Vampire romances: Killing the Bloodlust, Deadly Liaisons, Huntress for Hire, Forbidden Love, Deadly Liaisons, Vampire Redemption, Primal Desire

Vampire Novellas: The Siren's Lure, Vampiric Calling, Seducing the Huntress

***

Comedy Romance: Exchanging Grooms, Marriage, Las Vegas Style

***

Science Fiction: Galaxy Warrior

Young Adult Titles

The World of Fae:

The Dark Fae

The Deadly Fae

The Winged Fae

The Ancient Fae

Dragon Fae

Hawk Fae

Phantom Fae

Golden Fae

Falcon Fae

Woodland Fae

Angel Fae

***

The World of Elf:

The Shadow Elf

The Darkland Elf

Warrior Elf

***

Blood Moon Series:

Kiss of the VampireMy Book

Bite of the Vampire

The Vampire Chronicles Series:

The Vampire in My Dreams

Demon Guardian Series:

The Trouble with Demons

Demon Trouble, Too

Demon Hunter

Non-Series for Now:

Ghostly Liaisons

The Beast Within

Courtly Masquerade

Deidre's Secret

The Magic of Inherian:

The Scepter of Salvation

The Mage of Monrovia

Emerald Isle of Mists